PRAISE FOR *SMALL FIRES*

'Rarely will you meet a story as unsettling, nor one as bewitchingly told ... reminiscent of *Midsommar* and *The Wicker Man*. I challenge you to pick it up and, when you do, to put it down' Janice Hallett

'So creepy and unsettling ... dark, twisted and devilishly well written' Jo Callaghan

'Crackles with menace and authenticity. Kept me up late and crept into my dreams' Sarah Hilary

'A deeply unsettling and thought-provoking tale of survival and storytelling, mixing elements of gothic and folk horror with literary suspense. Beautifully woven and eerily atmospheric' Anna Mazzola

'Ronnie Turner has a way of weaving words into a spell – the darkest of spells. Mesmerising, sinister ... this modern folklore gothic will chill you to the bone' Essie Fox

'Absolutely loved the beautifully written *Small Fires* – a twisted, creepy and unsettling gothic tale set in one of the most sinister places I've ever encountered' Roz Watkins

'This is a churning snake pit of a story, one that consistently challenges which characters you trust, and whether hell really is a place on Earth. It's smart, it's stark, and it's painfully addictive. If there's a position that needs filling for the new queen of folk terror then Ronnie Turner's name has to be in the hat' Phillip Drown

'Evil dripping from every page. Brilliant, creepy writing' Suzy Aspley

'A furious female folk horror with a brilliant twist ... terrifyingly dark' Emily Barr

'Clever, dark, and visceral ... a vivid tale that will stay with me for a very long time' Jo Jakeman

'A story that grips you by the throat and slowly unravels. Haunting and lyrical, Turner weaves folklore and myth through the pages like a poisonous ribbon. A book that will linger long after you finish reading' Rachel Greenlaw

PRAISE FOR *SO PRETTY*

'Like Stephen King on crack ... dark, gothic as hell, and genuinely scary' M.W. Craven

'Beautifully written and a real page-turner' C.J. Cooke

'Dark, lyrical and intriguing' Fiona Cummins

'Eerily atmospheric, with brilliant characterisation ... really gets under your skin' *Culturefly*

'Compelling and dark – draws you in from the very first page' Heather Darwent

'Twisted, toxic and deeply dark, this gives off *Needful Things* vibes – and that ending is just *perfect*' Lisa Hall

'This book sucks you in from the first spine-tingling chapter and weaves a dark, twisted and compelling sense of foreboding' Claire Allan

'A disturbing read, both brutal and oddly compelling' Tea Leaves and Reads

'Ronnie Turner has written a cracker of a book, with a startling and melodramatic narrative, its dark and picturesque scenery, and an atmosphere of mystery, fear and dread' The Book Review Café

'This is some seriously dark sh*t!' Melanie's Reads

'This is a story that filled me with dread and disgust. It chilled my bones and shook me to the core. It got under my skin and into my head and left me feeling unclean ... OUTSTANDING' Tracy Fenton

Small Fires

ABOUT THE AUTHOR

Ronnie Turner is the author of the critically acclaimed *So Pretty*. She lives in South-West England with her family and three dogs. She is a Waterstones lead bookseller and in her spare time she enjoys long walks on the coast.

Follow Ronnie on X @Ronnie__Turner, facebook.com/ronnie.turner.9022, and on Instagram @ronnieturner8702.

Small Fires

Ronnie Turner

ORENDA BOOKS

Orenda Books
16 Carson Road
West Dulwich
London SE21 8HU
www.orendabooks.co.uk

First published in the United Kingdom by Orenda Books, 2025
Copyright © Ronnie Turner, 2025

A catalogue record for this book is available from the British Library.

ISBN 978-1-916788-47-3
eISBN 978-1-916788-48-0

Typeset in Garamond by typesetter.org.uk

Printed and bound by Clays Ltd, Elcograf S.p.A

For sales and distribution, please contact *info@orendabooks.co.uk* or visit
www.orendabooks.co.uk.

Contents

'Hell is empty and all the devils are here.'
The Tempest, William Shakespeare

For Bertie

The God-Forgotten

Áine's Well

The Hanging Place

Higher Tor

Lower Tor

Valley of Rocks

The Denes

Pale Bones

The Moloch Inn

The Poor Maidens

Forest of Eyes

HER – Old Town

They say the Devil came here. He fell to the earth long ago and he never left.

There is a silence over this land, the stillness of a muscle before it moves. Somewhere a bird calls a warning to us in its little throat. I see its body and think, I should offer a warning of my own: *We have arrived. Now leave, before we break those wings.*

'This place knows we are here,' my sister says, and I take a breath.

'Why do you say that?' I ask.

'It knows,' she says, and yes, I almost expect the mountain to take a gulp of air, like some great beast come to see us.

Della catches my wrist with her finger. She smiles, says, 'Mind me, Lil.'

I carry memories of *their* deaths. Ghosts living inside a ghost. I think of our old home, our names, changing on tongues as the news spread. Until all anyone could think on were their pale bodies, emptied and hanging, and ours still very much pulsing, alive.

The Witches of Old Town.

We have so many names.

They called us pariahs, and we ran fast. They called down their gods, and we ran faster. They called us a 'condemning', like a murmuration, a moving shadow that palms the sun and takes out the light. And now we have migrated.

To this island with no name.

I count the shadows but I run out of fingers to count them on. The path from the harbour twists down into a valley. There are no animals, or children. The houses are empty. Where are the people?

There is nothing but the mountain. It watches us, throwing down its darkness, so unyielding it makes the light feel like a captive. What things has it seen? What will it say of us to the men and women who will come to this island in the future?

They will not be good stories, this I know. My sister and I do not tell good stories. Mother and Father knew that.

I rub my arms to bring some heat to my skin but all it does is hurt.
I look at my sister. 'Does it make you feel cold, the mountain?'
Della smiles. It does.

I wish I had not asked.

We will find our new home, Lower Tor, later; we do not mind that
it will soon be night. We have always been able to find our way in the
dark.

I follow Della to the Moloch Inn, and as we enter, my spine
shivers, my pulse sings.

We have found the people.

The room stills, heads turning like clock hands, coming slowly to
our bodies. I hear nothing, not even their breaths. I tap my wrist to
check I can still hear at all. We have emptied their lungs. We have
made living shadows.

I look across all their faces, eyes sharp, even the young. Mouths
open, ready to bite our secrets from our fingers. Della tips her chin
at them. We take a table at the back. The Folk speak quietly, voices
low so they can hear our movements.

'We know you,' they say with their eyes. And then, 'Why have you
come here?'

We have come to this island because it is the furthest we could
travel from where we are from.

There is a man pouring ale into two pitchers. A curl of brown hair
falls into the corner of his mouth. He is short – shorter than me. The
men and women around us watch with curiosity, like animals
watching other animals. We were not human, even as children. Or
so our mother said.

A man sits to my right, his nose jutting at an odd angle. He looks
at me so deeply; I think he can see my very bones. I am without a
covering. He can see it all. And despite myself, I think, do my bones
look alright?

Then his eyes move to Della, and my body softens.

'You'll be a favourite,' he says to Della.

'A favourite of whom?'

'Of his.'

'Who is "he"?'

'Our Warden.'

I glance at Della, sweat blooming beneath my ribcage, down my navel. They have fully shifted focus now. They are drawn to the call of her. The blackness of her, the size of her. She keeps spells in her pockets, and she uses them now. She looks like the Folk do: something violent under the skin.

'I don't understand. Are you all mad here? Do you need a policeman to watch you? Who is he?' Della asks.

The man laughs, leans close, pinches my wrist between his fingers and wiggles it. 'If I shake your hand, do you think I'll break it? You are such a small thing, aren't you? Just a bite.'

Some daring voice in my throat wants to say, *If you want to chew something with salt, take my sister.* Instead, I gulp my worry and say, 'Who is your Warden?'

'He'll be along.'

The man sinks back into his seat, smiling. And I turn, looking at every face in this room. They watch Della with something like sweetness before bitterness shows through. They lick their lips, hungering.

Are these people afraid of anything? They will be afraid of us.

They'll see.

The man leans greedily into Della's space. I shrink back. The shadows wrap me like gauze. And I keep going until I am covered.

He says, 'Welcome to our small world. I'm sure you'll enjoy it. And our small world will enjoy you.'

Della nods. She gives what she takes. 'I'm sure we will.'

'You're just in time for the festival.'

'What festival?'

I turn my head slowly, look at the men and the women and the children and their smiles. Dear God. Why do they watch us?

The man says, 'The festival of the Devil.'

HER – Ferryman

We were warned.

Before we crossed over to this island, two days ago, the people on the mainland cautioned us. Perhaps we should have paid better heed to them. It was quiet that day, like the hand of some desolate God had run through the mainland and caught its people between his fingers, took them away. The street was terminal, bare of voices, of music. There was nothing.

There was no regular service to take us across. Every face we looked on was hooded. We asked several fishermen if they could ferry us to the island. Their faces darkened, and their eyes closed, and they tipped their chins up to the rain and muttered a prayer, and we watched and wondered what they were calling down. Something to hurt us? Or to protect them?

Eventually, we found somewhere to order food and to rest. It was cramped, and so dusty, I tried not to breathe. A man sat beside us. He was bent so low, bones poked through his coat.

'We want to cross the water. We want to go to the island,' Della said to him.

'No one will cross the water.'

'We can pay.'

'No one will cross the water.'

'Why?'

'That place takes.'

'What does it take?'

The man looked at us, for the first time. His eyes were wide, afraid. 'What is missing from these streets?'

Della chewed her lip hard enough to draw blood. Anger came off her in steam. She would break this man.

'I ask again, what do you notice missing from these streets?'

I looked out of the window, saw the island, the mountain, grey and strange, a covering of fog like gauze around its middle. As if it was broken. A chill slipped down my fingers and I squeezed half-moons into the meat of my hands.

'It takes our calm.' The man lifted a finger to the window, to the island. 'It is sick. Sick with madness. That mountain is a wound on the world. And it might be rock and moss and earth and air, but it is always watching us.'

'Has it always been this way?' I said quietly.

'Yes. Since I was a boy. Since my father was a boy. And his father too.'

'Have you ever been there yourself?'

'No.'

'What is there?'

The man's bones shivered inside their skin. He was so thin, I could see the blue of his veins. 'The Folk. They do strange things. Sometimes they light fires, and the fires burn all night. And we hear them screaming on the wind. Then we hear them laughing. Like they are hunting each other.'

'Hunting each other?'

He nodded, cupping one hand in the other, like a boy. 'We try not to listen. We try so very hard not to hear.'

'How do you know any of this, if you have never been?' Della asked.

'Because in the past, some of us here did cross the water. And when they came back, they told us stories about the Folk, about the land and what has happened there. It is ill, that land.'

'Do they ever come here? The Folk?'

He shakes his head. 'Sometimes two men come to fetch goods. Always the same two. But otherwise no. The Folk do not cross the water. The young there have never left the island. It is all they know. Such a waste ... for that to be all they know. It is a crime for a baby to be born in that place.'

'What are the men like?'

'They are strange. Like they are mute, like they have never made a noise before. And they look at us as if we are beasts, only interested in a life long enough to kill it.'

'Do they really never speak?' I ask.

'No. They are full of silences.'

'Maybe they can't speak.'

'They can...' he says. 'They can, but not to us.'

'And then they go back?'

'And then they go back.'

I looked into the street, at the grey locals. The ghosts the island had made of them. 'Did you not cross the water to see if they needed help?' I asked. 'You heard noises. But you did not go and check?'

The man opened his palms. 'When I was a boy, my best friend crossed over. Curiosity or an attempt at courage, call it what you will. But he did not come back. A party was sent to look for him. They searched the island, every strange piece of it. They could not find him.' The man closed his palms. 'That night, we heard him screaming.'

The life left my fingers. I tried to move them but I could not.

'What – what happened?'

'We do not know what became of him. I was in my bed when I heard it. And then I screamed too. My mother said it poured out of me like wind.'

I looked at his face, and I thought, *He has gone. He has left his eyes. He's moved into his memories of his friend.*

I turned and said to Della. 'What will they do to us? We must find somewhere else to go.'

My body chilled and I struggled to breathe. I felt as if I'd been drowned.

'Did I hear you correctly: you want to go to the island?'

Another man was watching from the corner. His eyes passed between my sister and me, suspicion plain in them.

'No—'

'Yes. We do.' Della smiled her smile, and it made me sick. She said under her breath, 'Mind me, Lil. *We are crossing.*'

The man nodded solemnly. 'I'll ferry you across. Tonight. Meet me at the harbour once the sun has set.'

'We will.' Della touched me, dug her nails into the soft part of my knee. I winced, pulled away. She grabbed a different piece of me and pinched that instead.

The ferryman watched, horror inside his eyes. 'I know who you are. You're the Pedley women. I know what you've done. And that place deserves to be hurt.' He stood, looked at us as if he wanted to run from us. 'So hurt it.'

HIM – Pariahs

The night is quiet, and then it is not. The women enter the Moloch Inn not as ordinary women do. Not with footfall and breath and words falling from their lips. But with a silence inside their bodies that makes everyone else settle.

Silas would have known the women had entered if he hadn't seen them at all. If it was only their shadows that had come, he would have felt them.

One can always sense an arrival, a bee on skin, a bird in a tree, a body in a room. The women have arrived. Silas sees them, yes, but he feels them inside his chest too, like a second beat.

And these women are something new.

The tall one has long fingers, a thick neck inches wider than his own. A beast among men. Beside her is a smaller woman. She is fair, with blonde curls and slim wrists and worry lines and a hand fixed permanently to her stomach. Is she pregnant? Is she ill?

The beast glances back at her, and the small woman hurries, tripping on her toes to be by the beast's side. Ah. It is no baby. She carries fear inside her body. A drum filled with a cruel music. Why is she frightened of her sister?

Sisters they must be. The likeness is unmistakable. Something about the mouths and the ears and the way their bones move. They have his drinkers leaning forward in their seats; they shift like one muscle, eyes alert, watchful, wanting. The Folk are all wanting here.

The little one wraps her arms around her middle. Her gaze lands on Silas, then it is gone again. Orsan leers across at them. He tells them about the Warden, the festival, and the little one shrinks, and the big one reddens, rises as if the stories are filling her body up.

Silas delivers two pints to their table. 'Welcome,' he says. 'I know you, don't I?'

The small woman's eyes widen. 'You're the Pedley sisters.' Silas taps her foot with his boot, brings her eyes to his. 'Am I right?'

'Yes,' the beast says. 'We are Lily and Della.'

The Folk lean closer. They know these visitors. The women are pariahs, murderesses. Witches, one newspaper called them. Life-thieves. Blood-lovers. Following their parents' deaths, the names for them grew evermore experimental. Silas heard of their gruesome story, even here, where the earth feels as if it ends.

'What brings you to our shores, hm?'

'The quiet.'

'The quiet?'

'How many people live on this island?'

'One hundred and thirty-three.'

Della nods. 'The quiet.'

'We don't have many visitors here.'

'Why?'

Silas considers taking the seat next to Della but he decides not to; she might rip his fingers from his hand. 'We are isolated. It's an hour's journey from the mainland.'

'I see.'

'Aside from yourselves, we have one other visitor. A geologist who came with her family twelve moons ago. But she's leaving soon. She has what she came for.'

'You misunderstand.' Della looks him in the eye, and he takes a step back. 'We are not visitors. We are here to live.'

'You have a property?'

She nods. 'Lower Tor.'

'You're my neighbours. I live at Higher Tor, just along the cliff. You'll get all the quiet you care to have. No one walks there. Even the birds don't fly over it.'

'Why?'

'It has its history, as all places do.' He looks at Lily. She fiddles with a red ribbon, wrapping it tighter and tighter round her thumb until the skin turns deep and blue and strange. 'You'll get a taste of it soon enough.'

Lily looks at him. Finally. 'What is your name?'

'My name is Silas.'

Della then taps Silas's foot with her shoe. She smiles. And it is a sight he doesn't want inside his eyes.

'Tell me about the festival,' she says.

'You don't have long to wait. It's in five days' time. Midday.'

Della rises suddenly, and so the sister rises too. They nod, then they leave, walking without steps. And all eyes watch them go.

HER – A Condemning

This land smells of death. Of something under skin. It's not the reek of an animal taken by the wild, a life rotting away. But I can smell something here and I pinch my nose; Della sucks in a breath so loudly I think a gun has fired.

Perhaps the smell isn't here, really. Perhaps the smell is inside us, our clothes, perhaps we brought it here from our old home, Dyowles House. That place was ruined in the end, and it was our doing.

'Ruined things can be mended,' Mother used to say. But who can mend Mother, now she is dead inside the earth?

Our new home, Lower Tor sits on the cliff, with only two neighbours. A small cottage just a short walk away and a large house further along the cliff. That house is huge, stretched by some irritable god's hands, so it becomes thinner at the top, like a tower or a church. I am surprised it has not tipped into the water, making the earth shake as it comes away.

There is something strange about this land. It is too silent. Where are the children? Where are the walkers? Bird-watchers? I lift my eyes to the sky. Where are the birds?

There is a woman – our new neighbour – tending the cottage's garden. She is the brightest thing I have seen in miles.

'Can you see her? That woman, there?'

Della nods.

'She's watching us.'

'We are watching her.'

Slowly, the woman lifts her hand. She is not smiling. Her hand trembles, and it is not moved by the wind. There is no wind. The island has forgotten to breathe.

'We should say hello,' I say hopefully.

Della pinches me, a mark like a rose reddening my skin, and I nod, take a step back so she can enter our new home so she won't give me any more flowers.

'Leave that woman alone,' she says.

Houses are like bodies. There are always ghosts inside, like illnesses the bodies cannot remove. We left so many ghosts in Dyowles House in Cornwall. We put a cancer inside its walls with the things we did.

Mould blossoms across the walls of Lower Tor, black blooms. Old leaves and dust spill across the floor. The bodies of bees lie across the sills. They have grown a fur. A mould of their own. Every life comes eventually to death.

The bathroom is certainly unfit for use, yet I swallow the bile in my throat, scrape out the bathtub and run the tap until it scalds. Della likes it blistering. When she rises from the heat, her body is so red, she looks like she has fires inside her. Sometimes I visualise throwing water on her, not to put her out but to make her body smoke.

But then her smoke would rot my lungs.

'Is it ready?' she says from downstairs. She does not need to shout. Her voice breaks bricks.

'Yes,' I say.

She arrives, tests the temperature by flicking it against my hand. I wince and she smiles, 'Lily-burning.' The perfect temperature.

I leave her to it, go to the nearest window and look for the woman.

She is still there, kneading the earth. Sweat beads across my scalp and between my breasts as I run down the stairs and out into the fresh world.

The woman rises. I trip over my left foot and fall in the dirt. A glob of it flicks into my nostril, and I cup my hand over my face and dig it out.

'Are ... are you alright? That was quite a fall. Can ... can I get you a tissue?' She pats my shoulder.

Up close, she is older than I realised. Her hair is yellow, grazing her shoulders. She has slim fingers and a beauty spot on the tip of her nose like a button.

'I'm Kit. Katherine. But Kit.'

'I'm Lily. I'm new here.'

'So I gather.' She looks at me with weariness. All women do, especially mothers, because they wonder if their own daughters could hurt them like we hurt ours. They look on their children differently once they have looked on us. We change their eyes, we condemn them to wonder.

'Do you know who I am?'

'I do.'

'He told me you are a newcomer, like I am.'

'Who did?'

I gesture to Higher Tor. 'The man who lives there.'

She nods. 'Silas. The only ordinary one here.'

'What do you mean?'

'If you go to the festival, you'll soon see what I mean.'

'Will you go?'

'No.'

'Why? Is there really a devil – their Warden – who lives here?'

'There are no such things as devils. But that doesn't mean this place is good either. Too many bad things have happened here in the past.' She looks at me keenly, and I feel as if I am being pared back, my insides removed and cold water run through me. 'How old are you?'

'Twenty.'

Her eyes soften. 'Oh, sweetheart. You're too young to know this place.'

'What has happened here?'

'Things you won't want inside your mind. Things which will hurt your eyes.'

HIM – Those across the Water

They call this land The God-Forgotten.

The people across the water, they say the land is so strange, no one dared name it. That no name could hold it, like fingers around something sharp. And isn't there some truth to what they say?

Silas knows what the men and women across the water think, even though he himself has never put his foot on their shores. At night, he sees their lights, and they see his. Strange hands lifted, not in acknowledgment but in warning. They do not come here. Children across the water are told the stories of The God-Forgotten as soon as they are old enough to know what stories are. They tell them that bitterness runs through the land like poison in blood. And if they cross the water, they will get blood on their feet.

'Something bad has always lived that way.'

'What?' Children ask their mothers, 'Who lives over there?'

'The Folk,' their mothers say.

They warn travellers too. And so the travellers do not travel any further.

'Is it not safe?' they ask, heads twitching.

'No. It's never been safe. There are stories. Sometimes we hear things in the night. Strange things.'

'Like what?'

'Singing.'

'Isn't that ... nice?'

They shake their heads, eyes on everything but the land they speak of. Their fingers come to their throats as if they are sore. 'Not this singing.'

'What do the Folk sing about?'

'Bad things.'

'Are you afraid of them?'

Fearful men are afraid even to admit to their fears.

'How can you be afraid of that place?'

'Evil lives in words, inside language. We are afraid because stories are never simply stories.'

'And what do the stories say?'

'That the Devil lives there. A Warden with his Folk. That's what the stories have always said.'

Silas wonders if the people across the water warned the Pedley women. He watches the sisters. They walk through the street, and the Folk follow the freshness of them, the newness of their smells. They are children, palms open for sweet fruits.

Silas knows the Folk. He was born on this land. He has sipped on this poison since he was in his mother's arms. And now his mouth is sore.

The people across the water would have warned the sisters. So why did it not still their feet? Why did they still come?

If they had heard the stories, if they had a god, they would not have come to this godless place.

Silas takes a breath, filling his lungs until they feel as if they will burst their seams. Then he lets it go.

What brought the sisters here? Where nothing but stories grow.

HER – Stories that Bleed

This place breathes.

At least that is what it feels like. If I touch my fingers to the soil, will the soil move? When I take a breath, will it take one with me? Is there something under the earth?

I stand in the street, look at the houses tipping into one another, at the cobbles, their shapes strange and stretched, but try as I might, I cannot bring to mind what they remind me of. I look at the mountain, so far from us all, and yet it feels as if it is close enough to count the bones of me, to take one right out of my body if it wanted.

Yes, I think it would want to. I think it would want all of them.

The Folk move through the street, silent, turning their eyes to Della and me. They are dressed in white, all of them, even the children. If this street is the island's spine, then the Folk are its muscle, moving like a hand before it becomes a fist. They can walk, they can speak, but I have never seen humans look less like humans.

I see a woman who stands in front of the island's only shop. When Della is distracted, I go to her.

'Hello.'

She does not speak. She wears white, but as with all the Folk here, there is some strange violence about this, about the imitation of innocence. Her grey hair is pulled back and her life-worn eyes run over me.

'Hello.'

'What is your name?'

'Stina.'

'I am Lily.'

'I know who you are. Even here, where the world has choked us out of its mouth, we hear news of the mainland. And we know you and your sister. You've come such a long way from where you are from.'

'Cornwall.' I nod. 'Why doesn't this island have a name?'

'The mainlanders have a name for it. The God-Forgotten. But they say if this island had a true name, it would only break it.'

'How can you break a name?'

She shrugs. 'By hurting the meaning of it.'

I point to the mountain. 'There's a fog on its way down to us.'

'It means there is going to be a death.'

'I'm sorry?'

'The Devil – our Warden – is in the fog. It means he will come to us in the village tonight and there will be a death.'

'But ... that's impossible.'

Her sharp eyes come to mine. 'Keep your "impossibles" close. Perhaps they will guard you tonight.'

'You have strange stories here.'

'Why did you follow them across the water then?'

I open my mouth. Close it.

She rubs a scar on her third finger, three lines through the skin. 'This land has more stories than I have the memory to hold.'

I move from foot to foot. 'It feels like I am standing on the back of something, being here.'

'This land makes the shape of a bird. The river runs from its eyes so he looks like he is crying. Our Mourning Bird.'

'And now I live on its back,' I say. 'It's like he's going to shiver and I'll fall straight into the sea.'

She opens her eyes and smiles. 'A funny feeling, isn't it?'

'I don't like it.'

'Then you shouldn't go to the Singing Bridge.'

'The what?'

'A place with so many legends, they've spilled into the water, and now they kill the fish.' The look on her face is one of fear and awe, a ravaged smile that tips my heart into a quick rhythm.

'You speak oddly. In riddles and omens.'

'And yet you can translate our language well enough.'

'What is the story of the bridge?'

'Centuries ago, a farmer worked the land. The land did not give much – it has always been unforgiving – but the man survived on the little he had. Then one day, he found children eating his crop. The more they came, the more he angered. Until one day, he caught them, these five children, and he took them to the bridge. There he cut them, hung them upside down and drowned them, an offering to the Warden for a good reaping.'

Stina is shaking, even to her finger bones. They are frightened of their own history. Of their own stories.

'What happened next?'

'Their mothers found them later. And the wind that day blew through a hole the farmer had made in the bridge's wall. The wind blew and the mothers' mourned. It sounded like the bridge was singing for them.' She tilts her head at me. 'Children do not go to the Singing Bridge anymore.'

'The children ... they all died. They could not be saved?'

'They could not be saved.'

'My God.'

I cast my eyes down. I realise now what the cobbles look like. The shape of them. They have been made to look like bones. We are all standing on bones.

'What about the farmer?'

'He was dealt with.' Her eyes widen, and I can see the whites. 'Our Warden dealt with him as he deals with all of us who misstep.'

'You are frightened...?'

She rubs her scars. 'The children don't go there anymore. The last time they did, they said they could still hear those mothers crying. And that they saw the Devil by the water, come to listen. That place plays bad music.'

'Those poor children.'

The woman takes my wrist, her nails cutting into me. 'We are full of stories here, Miss Pedley. This land is a vein, and if you are curious enough, it will bleed for you. But be sure you want the blood on your pretty, pale hands.'

HIM – Reverence

The Folk make a path for him. They reach, touching just to touch, to know that he is there for them. As he has always been.

'What brought them here, Silas?'

'What will the Warden make of them?'

'They've come for a reason. But why?'

The Folk watch him with a stillness that is almost predatory. They used to look at his father like this when he was a boy, he remembers. They used to make a line outside the door in the mornings, for help, consolation, absolution.

'Now, now,' he says, with a voice he gives himself when the Folk need calming. That's what his father used to say, with his large, calloused hands opening to the sky. 'Now, now.'

'But what have they said? Is it true – what they did?'

'The big one, there is something about her. She's like us. *She's like us*, I'm telling you.'

Silas turns to each of them, faces he has known since he was a boy. 'I do not know why they have come.'

One of them says, 'They are known all over the world, Silas. What if the world follows them here?'

'They have come alone.'

'The Warden will not like the world on his soil. Too many feet. Too much noise.'

Silas sighs. 'Go back to your work. The world is not coming here. They are two girls. Just two girls. That is all.'

'But what if they make the Warden angry?'

'Enough!' Silas points at each individual, then at their door in the street, as if they have forgotten where they live and he must guide them back. 'Go back to your lives and your work. The girls will not bring the world to this place. You are safe.'

'And the Warden...?'

Silas shakes his head. He is weary of all of this. 'You will wake the Warden with all your noise. He does not like to be woken.' Silas points, draws a line from their bodies to their homes. One by one, they follow his finger, giving silence back to the day.

When the last of them has gone, he sees Stina watching him from her shop.

'I've spoken to Lily Pedley. She is frightened of our stories,' she says as Silas joins her.

And we are not? Silas wants to ask.

'What do you think of them?' Silas asks.

'They are curious sisters.'

'They are,' he agrees. 'Why did they come here? All the places, and they chose this one. It's very strange.'

'I'm sure they have a good reason. I'd like to know what it is.'

'I would too,' he says.

They both turn and stare at the mountain. They seem as if they are looking for something; something that has the shape of a man but is not a man.

'Your father was a strong leader,' Stina says suddenly. 'A formidable man. He knew how to calm tempers, to throw water on fires that grew in men's throats. Those are the worst fires, if you ask me. I remember years ago, before you came along, Silas, two Folk fighting over their land. They were furious men, so hard and relentless, I thought they would kill each other.'

Her eyes open wide, wider the more of the story she tells him.

'What happened to the men?' he asks.

'Your father could not calm their tempers. One of them fell on a girl, an elbow to her left eye. She lost her vision in that sad little blue. So do you know what your father did? He burned down their crops.' A pause. 'I remember seeing them wander their burnt acres, pulling roots and husks from the dead soil. I remember their faces. I pitied them.'

'They deserved it.'

'Your father didn't do it to punish them, he did it to preserve them. Those men would have killed each other. Your father saved them.'

He nods. 'I have different memories of my father. He could be cruel. A boy at school once told me he planned to catch the Warden, to trap him. He was young and he wanted to be brave, just like all young boys. But my father overheard. Do you know what he did?'

'What did he do?'

'He grabbed the boy and filled his mouth with cotton wool ... to soak up his bad words. The boy cried and cried. He did not mean the things he said. He just didn't want to be afraid anymore. He didn't want his mother to be afraid anymore.'

'He shouldn't have said those things. He had to be taught a lesson. The boy was lucky the Warden himself didn't hear.'

'My grandfather was the same,' says Silas.

'Wise?'

'Violent.'

'Revered?'

'Ruthless.'

The woman's face has hardened. 'You are their blood. You have the same intelligence. The same analytical eye. That's why we look to you, bring you our concerns and our questions.'

'I know.'

'Your ancestor was the same. Ura, her name. She was so tall, she was rumoured to be able to touch the sky.' She pauses. 'Or break it.'

'How do you break the sky?'

'The same way you break anything else: with your hands.'

'My mother used to tell me about her. She was a strange woman, she said.'

The woman smiles. 'You're a little strange too.'

'In what way?'

'In all ways.'

Silas looks at his hands. Could he break the sky? He bends each of his fingers back, until he can force them no further. He looks at his knuckles, the movement of them. He wonders if they could break something as fathomless as that?

Stina watches him. Then she says, 'Yes, they could.'

HER – Lore

Kit opens the door and gestures for me to come in. She leads me to the kitchen, pours water over her plants. They are dead, dried, and black and curling. But she tries to bring their life back anyway.

Today Kit wears yellows and blues. We have been on this island under a week and she is the brightest thing I've seen here so far. I hear her children's small feet stamping in the room above.

She smiles, and I see some softness where there were only edges. 'Sorry about the noise.'

'How old are they?'

'Three and nine. Laurie and Xander.'

'Can ... can I ask you a question?'

'You can. That's why you have come, after all.'

'What brought you to this island?' I already know something of this answer. She slips into the chair opposite me with a sigh.

'I'm a geologist. After a colleague told me about this place, I came here to study the land. In the beginning, we didn't know there was anything strange here. Then Laurie and Xander came home from playing with the local kids and they would be reciting such strange rhymes.'

'Nursery rhymes?'

'Rhymes about the Warden. My husband and I, we noticed other things. Little things. We told ourselves it was nothing ... Then came the day of the festival. It's a madness that has been here a long time.'

'What do you mean? What is the history of this place?'

She looks at me. 'They say the Devil fell here a long time ago. He lives under the land. They say he poisoned the soil and when the Folk bit into its fruit, they bit into something bad. Devil-Skin, they called it. It sent the Folk mad. Mad and cruel.'

'Are they cruel now?'

'No. They are not dangerous. They are frightened. These days they say they see him dancing with the children. They say they've seen him whispering into the ears of jumpers at Hell's Mouth.'

'Where?'

'It's a cove, close to where Silas lives. It's become a death place. Because the rocks at the bottom are sharp and so many people have gone there to end their lives.' Kit holds her head. 'He has horns. He has red skin, and breath that smells of salt and smoke, and he's as old as the earth itself. Some say he looks just like a man. Any man. Every man.'

'How do they know it's not a woman?'

Kit grins. 'When a woman is rotten, she is a witch. But when a man is rotten, he is the Devil? Isn't that right? Seems unfair, if you ask me.'

I nod. I was called a witch. I have many names. Many faces. I imagine if words caught and they stuck to my body like ink – Huntress, Cunt, Murderess – my skin would look like a letter.

Kit sees me shiver and closes the window. Then she says, 'When the crops perish here, it's because he has drunk the juice from their skin. When a house catches fire, it's because he has blown on the embers.'

'Dear God.'

Kit twists her wedding band round her finger until the finger is sore and puckered. 'Sometime in the 1600s, this island was rumoured to have had a mass poisoning or a collective hallucination. But most of the Folk believe it was the Devil. He put a sickness inside the minds of over a hundred people, and they were lost.'

I watch that ring twist and twist.

'There was the Laughters too. An epidemic. It started with a man on the beach, walking his dog. He came across a dead body. The man, he was a farmer, a sensible man with a family. Law-abiding, rational. Then he started laughing.'

'Laughing?'

She nods once. 'He laughed and the laughter spread. It went from house to house. They couldn't stop. Until one person on the mainland claimed to have heard it in the night. He looked over to the island and he heard them all laughing together in the darkness. In their beds. They sent a policeman over to check, he stayed ten minutes and then he ran. Left the Folk to themselves.'

'What was it? What did this to them?'

'There were witch hunts in the past too. You think Salem was bad? Pendle Hill? But here, they didn't do it in the name of God. They did it because the men of this island were tired of their wives. They called them witches, released them across the cliffs and hunted them for sport. And there is another story of a woman who murdered her whole family, then sat their bodies round the table for dinner. Her husband, their three children. So much history. All of it bad.'

'How did we find this place?' I whisper it to myself, but really I already know the answer.

'I pity anyone who does. For the most part the island has been forgotten. Travellers don't travel here. Deliveries are dropped on the beach and the boats turned. Few people come, no one leaves.'

'How do you know all of this? Where did this religion come from?'

'Where does any religion come from? The lips of a man, I reckon.'

'Has ... has anyone seen anything to justify all these stories?'

She shrugs. 'They claim to. Everyone here has a memory they could tell you.'

'You're scared?'

She nods.

'Of the Devil?'

'No. I don't believe in gods and devils, Miss Pedley.'

HER – Forest of Eyes

'What do you believe, then?'

'I believe that the Folk are deluded. Even the children aren't like children here. They're something else.'

I look out to Lower Tor, see the light from the bathroom spilling out into the dusk. Kit follows my eye.

'You know I've never been afraid of the dark. Not as a girl. It didn't bother me. But the darkness is different here. The light behaves oddly, as if it knows it isn't welcome.'

'I ... I wish I had listened to you. Della and I went to the festival. And now I can't stop seeing everything I saw there. We've been here under a week and I am so weary of this place already.'

I feel that scream I held down rise again. It is a day old, and still it keeps all its violence. For the festival, they had an effigy, realised with twine and hessian and things taken from the land. Its body was drawn with coal and its eyes the red of blood. They brought it through the street to the sound of drums. They danced and they looked afraid as they danced; I had never seen something so animal.

Kit looks at me with sympathy. 'They do it because they are frightened. They want to appease their Warden.'

'That's ... that's...'

'Fear makes people do strange things.' She pats my arm and smiles. 'We leave in a week's time. Come with us?'

I shake my head. 'I can't.'

'I'm sorry about your parents. I never believed that you and your sister were responsible for their deaths.'

'Everyone else does.'

'Don't pay any mind to everyone else, sweetie. You're too young for these troubles.'

'We weren't responsible.' The lie makes the back of my hands itch. I scratch and then I stop when she notices. 'I feel like we have brought madness here. This was supposed to be a safe place, somewhere quiet.'

Kit shakes her head, squeezes my hand.

'Oh, the madness was already here.'

The wind chimes play their music, and I want to pull off my ears.

They hang from every door in the village, thieves of silence. The Folk go where they go, undeterred, moving inside the rhythm because it is a rhythm their bodies have always known. I wonder if their pulse slows when the chimes slow. If the wind stops blowing, will their hearts stop too?

I wet my finger and hold it to the sky. Why do the chimes sing so loud when there is barely any wind?

'I don't like that sound,' I say to my sister. 'There's something wrong with it.'

'Perhaps this place doesn't like the sounds you make.' She smiles, pinching the back of my neck. I wince. 'Is it getting under your skin, Lil?' she asks.

I try to shake her off. 'Please don't.'

'Would you like me to take it out?'

'No.'

'There *is* something very strange about this place,' she says, and licks her lips.

'They are afraid. Of their superstitions. They think something lives inside the land.'

'Who is to say something doesn't?' she asks.

I blow on my hands but I still feel chilled. I have not felt warm since we arrived.

I see Stina across the street and walk across the cobbles to her. She is pale, gaunt and I notice the shadows inside as well as outside her eyes. 'Are you alright?' I ask hesitantly.

She nods. Waves her hand. 'Time of year.'

'What?'

'Time of year. We all shiver when this time comes round.'

They talk in riddles, I think. All of them.

'What happens at this time of year?'

She says simply, 'Harvest.'

I open my mouth and close it. I am about to ask the meaning of her words when she strokes a finger down my neck to my collar bone. 'You have a nice neck,' she says. 'A nice throat. I wish I still had a throat like that.' She grabs a hunk of her own sagging neck and shakes it.

'Why do you have chimes outside your doors? Does it not bother you – that sound all day long?'

'It is music for our Warden. He listens and he knows we play them to please him.'

'It's so loud. I can feel it in my teeth.'

She laughs, peering round me to see Della. 'Your sister...'

'What about her?'

'She's watching you. She looks worried about something.'

I do not know what to say.

'She looks like a beast. I could feed my grandchildren to her when they misbehave.'

'Don't.' I say this with my chest. 'You wouldn't get them back.'

She laughs, but I am not joking.

'Have you found any wandering souls in Lower Tor?' she asks.

'You mean ghosts?' I think ghosts are like bad memories. I don't think they live in houses; they live in bodies, between the fine lines of our bones. Mine is full of them; my sister put them there.

'Yes. At your house and Silas's. The cliff on which you both live is full of wandering souls. All of this land is.'

'It's full of legends, you mean?'

'Is there a difference?' she asks.

'No, perhaps not. What about where we live?'

'Birds don't fly over it. The trees around those parts look like people.'

'I'm sorry?'

Her lip twitches. 'You haven't seen them? The people in the trees.'

I pull my collar up, but it is an excuse to hold my throat because I want to scream. I cannot bear these stories. 'What ... what people?'

'Every forest here has its history. We have three woodlands and no one dares live near any of them.'

'But ... the people?'

'The Forest of Eyes is a strange place. Many years ago, it is said an old witch tried to curse the Warden, and so the Warden took her children and grandchildren, and put them in the trees. They screamed when they were taken so now they scream inside the trees. If you look closely, you can see their faces in the wood.' Stina squeezes my hand, as if she is testing the weight of my body, how much pressure she would have to use to cut me up and serve my meat in the shop.

'How horrible. What happened to the witch?'

'She visited her family every day. She watered their roots. She washed the filth from their faces. She put blankets across their arms, but their arms were branches and the blankets tore.' Stina looks at Della again. Her eyes are drawn to her, again and again. 'In the end, the witch died at the foot of those trees. Her body gave itself to the earth and fed her family. Her family remain.'

I want to tell her stop. I want to take her words and put them back in her mouth even if they break it. This draws back a memory of Della and I as children in Tehidy Forest back home. One I try to forget.

'What a sad thing.'

Stina nods. 'There are worse sadnesses than that.' She gestures to Della. 'Tell me about your sister.'

'Don't you already know our history?'

She nods. 'There is something feral about her. Something sad.'

I look at Della. Children, as strange and worrying as the adults here, gather to her. They dance.

They shouldn't dance round her.

'What do you mean?' I ask.

But I do not receive an answer because my sister is dancing herself now. Her body moves with the song of the chimes, as if it is a song her body has always known too.

HER – THEN – Dryad

'Imagine something for me,' Della says.

'What?' I ask.

'Imagine you could remove every bad feeling you have ever felt. Reach into your chest and hold them inside your hand.'

We walk through the trees of Tehidy, and Della brushes her fingers through the pleats of her skirt; too big for her but she has tied twine around her waist to keep it up. It was Mother's when she was a girl and now Della shivers her hips to make it swing. She looks gaudy. My black trousers and shirt fit this forest better. I look like I am a part of it. Grown from it.

'Would they make my hand sore? All these bad feelings? What would they feel like to hold?'

Della pinches me.

'Ow!'

'I hadn't finished. They would hurt your hands, make the skin sore and scabby.'

'I don't like this.'

'I don't care, Lil.'

I hold myself. 'So – so what am I imagining?'

She smiles. I've never liked that smile.

'You could take those bad feelings and bury them. But those bad feelings would be like a disease. They would spread, rot the earth, kill the trees, kill the birds in the trees. Kill the forest.' She opens her hands. 'Imagine every tree around us now, bending over, leaning their heads to the floor, like old, old men who can't stand up anymore. There is no life left, even the roots are dead.'

'This is ... sad.'

'Now: what would you do? Would you keep all your bad feelings, even if that means they are hurting you, or would you give them away?'

I bite my nail. Della pats my head. She is still so much taller than I am. Is this a game, a trick? I hate it when she tries to trick me. I don't want to give the answer she expects.

'I would kill the forest. I'd kill all the forests.'

'Why would you do that?'

'The trees are just trees.'

She nods. Then she points at our shadows, stretched, looming. Della used to be frightened of shadows, so I would cast them on every wall, make them with my hands and arms. It is the only thing she has ever been afraid of. But then it became a game. As all things become in the end.

'Mine is bigger than yours,' she says. Of course, her shadow is bigger than mine.

'Why did you stop being afraid of them?'

'I grew up.'

'You're fifteen. You're not grown up.'

'Shadows are like bad thoughts. And it's the mind that makes them that you must really be afraid of.' She taps my temple with her finger. 'It's where they come from.'

'Oh.'

'Do you think there are spirits in the trees?' she asks.

'What?'

'Spirits. Dryads. They are beautiful and timid. They are rarely seen. They live inside the woods.'

'Why do they do that?'

'Because they just do, Lil. Why do you live in a house?'

'Are they watching us now, do you think?'

Della nods and runs her fingers along my bare arm, like she is playing an instrument. She likes to play with the red roses she puts in my skin.

'Oh, I expect so,' she says with a grin. 'And you just told them you'd kill their forests.'

'But—'

'You will have made them angry.' She is dancing now, Della, through the trees. 'You told them you would kill their families. Their mothers,' she says, and sticks me with a branch, right into my belly. 'Their daughters,' she says, and sticks me in my left hip. 'Their fathers,' she says. 'Their sons.'

'Stop it!'

'Are you scared, Lil?'

'No.'

'They will want to punish you. They'll tear open one of their trees and they will take your arms and they will put you inside it.'

'Stop it, Della. You're being mean.'

'They will never let you out. Because if they do you might hurt them. You will get older and older. One day you won't be a little girl anymore. Inside that tree, you will be a woman, a wicked, wicked woman. And everyone who comes through your forest you will curse. A girl stuck inside a tree.'

'I'm going to tell Mother!'

'Mum wouldn't come to see you. She would move far away and she would never tell anyone about the daughter she left inside the tree.'

'Please stop...' I cover my ears, tears falling on my cheeks. 'Stop, Della. Please!'

'No one would come to see you. Not Dad. Not me.'

'You would. You would, Della.' I have a soreness in my belly now, a panic in my throat.

She shakes her head, appearing by my side suddenly, fingers digging into my neck, where all the soreness is. There will be so many new roses tomorrow.

'You're right,' she says. 'I would come to see you. I wouldn't be able to stay away, knowing you're here. I'd have to do something about you. Want to know what?'

'Yes.'

'I'd burn your tree.'

HER – Bitter

They said my sister is Devil-Touched.

They said it about Mother too. They said the Devil fucked her and together they had my sister. So, in any case, he touched someone.

The world wondered: did my mother eat something bad when Della was inside her? Did she take a bite out of rotten fruit, and so she made something rotten, expelling it in the body of her baby? Following our parents' deaths, rumours bloated every mouth, words spilled over in newspapers, every mind had turned to the two of us. It is such a poor place for the mind to be.

Della and I watch the Folk move through the street, our arms are full of fruits to take to our new home. I am reminded of what people said of Mother; I look at the apple and see its side soft, bruised and sour. I dig it out. Della smiles at me, lifts it slowly to her mouth and bites. Juice drips down her chin and neck. She does not wipe it away. Her eyes do not leave my face.

'Do you think any of this land is unspoilt?' I ask.

Eventually she says, 'I think this place spoils everyone who comes here.'

I wrap my arms around my belly. Will it spoil me?

Della, who knows my language, as I know hers, pokes me in the belly button, and I feel it in every part of me. 'You're already spoilt. You're hateful.'

The Folk watch us still. No. Not us. Della. Their eyes show their whites for her. Their mouths make curious shapes. They slow when they pass, to feel her close, to take in her presence like a tissue taking up blood.

'Why do they look at you like that?' I ask her.

She rolls the core of the apple in her fingers, pauses, then she swallows that too. 'They tell stories here. That's why they are all mad. Mad on their legends and old tales.'

'But what does that have to do with you?' I ask, and I turn away so she cannot see the worry I have inside me.

'Someone told me that, decades ago, a woman called Ura lived here. She was so tall, when she stood it was like she was part of the sky.'

'What happened to her?'

'She died.'

I look at my sister, the breadth of her shoulders, the height of her hips. When she stands, does she look like she is part of the sky?

'They think you are like her, don't they?'

I hold the fruit tighter, as if their weak skins can keep any harm from mine.

Della smiles, and I can see the red of her gums.

'They are frightened here, of their own stories. And they think you can help them,' I say.

The Folk bend their necks to take her in. I will them to stop. I will their eyes to look at the sky if it is the sky they want.

'They will do anything for me,' she says, picking a seed from her tooth and flicking it into my throat. I wince. 'Troubled people need an idol, and these people have been troubled for so long.'

I will break the fruit, I am holding it all so tight. 'Don't say bad things. That's what Mother used to tell us: "Don't say bad things or you'll bring bad things in."'

'Mother never said a bad thing and bad things came for her,' she says, tapping my chest.

Della takes a plum and presses it against my shoulder, harder, harder until it bursts. My shirt is soiled. I will smell sweet for the rest of the day.

'That hurts.'

'Bad things are coming for you, Lil. I'll dance when they do.'

We shared mother's belly, her pulse, her breath. So how could that body have made such different daughters?

I open my arms, and the sweet things fall. Della smiles, steps through the pulp. We go everywhere barefoot, we have since we were girls. As my sister walks away she leaves prints across the cobbles. And the Folk follow them, this path of ruined fruit.

HIM – Gods and Devils

The women sit in the soil, tilling it with their fingernails. Kit's youngest child waddles up to Lily and makes a space for himself inside her arms. He takes her hand and tucks it under his cheek like a pillow. Silas hears Kit laugh.

Lily has been coming and going from Kit's house with the precision of clockwork. Today, they have settled themselves in the sunshine. He kneels in the heather by Higher Tor, to listen to his neighbours.

'The mountain is watching us.' Lily is looking up. It casts a shadow onto them.

'The mountain does.'

'Does it have a name?'

'The Denes.'

'What does that mean?'

'Doorway.'

'Can you get inside?'

'It's not a doorway for us. It's said that is where the Warden lives. That's his home. He lives between. Above and below. If you don't look at it, sometimes you can make yourself believe it isn't there. It's just a pain behind your eyes then, a thought that niggles like a loose screw.'

'I wish I could bring it down. I don't want it to watch me anymore.'

Kit nods. 'Children go to its feet sometimes, play games. Games I won't tell you about.'

Lily is quiet then. She runs a slow finger down the bridge of the boy's nose. 'You're very sleepy, aren't you, cricket?'

'He likes you.'

'I like him.'

Kit looks over her shoulder. Then, 'You know, some years ago, a woman called Tully lived in your house. She had two children. When they were older, they spoke of leaving her, building a home for themselves, somewhere safe on the island. Tully was paranoid, and when she heard them whispering their plans to each other, she made plans of her own. Do you know what she did?'

Lily shakes her head.

'She crushed pills into their apple juice, and when they were asleep, she laid them out in their beds like dolls. Then she took a mallet and she broke their feet.'

Lily shivers. 'Why did she do that?'

'She didn't want them to leave her behind. She wanted to keep her children with her always.'

'Well, did ... did they get help? What happened?'

'No.' Kit smooths a hand over Lily's. 'They stayed with their mother until she died. They live in the village now. You'll see them eventually. Their bones set funny, so now they can't walk straight. It's like they are being tugged by a fishing line.'

Lily has curled her arms around the boy. She rocks him to and fro, and Kit watches, a mournful expression on her face. 'I should never have brought my family here.'

'My sister and I were warned not to come here.'

Kit's shoulders flutter, and then she sinks low, all the energy filtered away. '*We* had no warning. And we stayed because I had to finish my work. You say the mainlanders warned you. So why did you come? Why on earth did you come, Lily?'

'We followed the stories.'

HER – THEN – Pomegranate

Mother calls for us.

We sit so close, our bellies are pressed together, as if we are trying to become one body. Or as if we always have been. The soft rise of breath from our two mouths sounds like it comes from one. Our legs tangle together and our fingers dig into the flesh of our shared fruit. Two halves, juice making red seams down our wrists; we have zippers.

Mother keeps calling for us, but she is far away so we keep eating. We are greedy, the red seeds dripping onto our chins and chests. We must look like we are bleeding. Or something was.

This forest outside our home is so full of sound. A river runs close by, framed by thick red flowers. Della loves it here, the trees, the earth, the moss, the things under and above, but I love the water, the salt, the sting. The cleansing. Here, in these trees, I feel small. I feel like I might lose myself. I have never felt safe in woodlands. Perhaps that is why Della enjoys them.

'How many seeds do you think are in this fruit?' I ask Della. I lift one onto my finger and hold it to the light. It is not much bigger than the pink bumps on my chests. My nipples. Della's are bigger than mine, round and perfect, but mine will keep growing as the rest of my body grows, and then I will have bigger fruits.

'A hundred.'

I shake my head. 'No. I think there are more than that.'

'Two hundred.'

'Two hundred.'

We say it together. We pretend to be each other sometimes, when there are no other games to play. Then, sometimes, it really is as if we share one mouth. We ask the same questions. We give the same answers.

'Imagine if I put one of these seeds down your throat and it grew in your stomach,' one of us says. 'Imagine if its roots came up through your skin and out through your fingers and you grew so much fruit, I was never hungry again. All my life, my belly would be full. If I ate your fruit, would I be eating you?'

The other one winces, holds our middle. Mother calls out our names. Lily! Della!

We might as well have the same name. I cannot move without my sister moving with me.

Della lifts the fruit, takes a safety pin from her cuff, pierces a seed and licks it up. I do the same, forcing it between the fine gap of my teeth.

'Now we will both grow fruit,' she says. 'Who do you think will taste better?'

I shake my head, and I am about to turn, call out for our mother, but I feel something sharp cut into the back of my hand. Della dips her safety pen into the freckles.

I wince. 'Ow!'

She smiles. She's beginning one of her games.

Blood and juice become a cocktail on my hands. Della dips her pin into my wrist and them my arm, finds all of the little freckles and makes all of the little freckles bleed. Then she drags the point out and across, drawing lines, filling in gaps, bringing in my edges and divining something in me.

I am breathing heavily, all of me stinging. 'Am I still pretty? If I look in the mirror, will the mirror want to look at me?' I ask.

Della shakes her head and my heart hums. 'The mirror will destroy itself.'

'You'll pick up the glass, though, won't you, Del?'

'I'd cut my fingers...'

'Please, Del. Please. You have to pick me up. Then I'll clean your cuts and put plasters on your fingers.'

'No mirror would want to look on you.'

I wipe my nose, pick up the tears and hide them away in my pockets.

'I would grow the most fruit,' I say, eventually, because I do not know what else to say.

'Maybe ... but they'd be poison. And you'd give everyone stomach pains.'

'Well ... well you'd kill them. You'd send all your pickers to the grave!'

She shrugs. 'To the grave they go. Do you know the story about the pomegranate?'

'No,' I say; I hate Della's stories.

'The goddess Persephone was tricked into spending half of her year in the Underworld because she ate a pomegranate given to her by Hades.'

'Why half a year?'

'She ate six seeds so she paid with six months of her life.'

'Because she ate a piece of fruit?'

'It was fruit grown in the Underworld.'

'Oh,' I say.

'Her mother, Demeter, was the goddess of harvest. She made everything grow. She fed plants, crops. She gave life but she could take it away too. When her daughter became trapped, she was so sad, she abandoned her duties and so for six months of the year, nothing grew. Everything died. That's why we have the seasons. Wintertime means somewhere a mother is missing her daughter.'

'So Persephone was stuck, all because she ate some seeds?'

'Yes.'

'I would go. I'd go and live in Hell. If I was Persephone, I'd spend all my months down there. Because I'd never have to come back up and see you. You're mean.'

Della smiles, lifting the fruit to my mouth. 'Eat, then, Lil. Gobble it all up.'

I push her away. 'She ruled the Underworld with Hades. She was a goddess, a queen. People listened to her.'

'So I will live above and you will live below.'

'Yes,' I say, but I only say it because this conversation puts a fear in my belly and I do not want Della to notice.

She digs her hand into the soil. 'Do you want to be on your way now? Shall I dig you a hole?'

There is a soreness in my throat, but I say yes, because I do not want her to see I am afraid. 'Dig me one with big spiral stairs that go all the way down.' Now the soreness is in my chest.

'To the Devil under the earth.'

'To the Devil under the earth.'

Della flicks the soil into my sores. 'Poor Devil. He has no idea what's coming down to him.'

'That's a bad thing to say, Della.' The soreness is everywhere.

'You wouldn't last two minutes.'

'Yes, I would.' I am shaking now. Her stories are inside my body.

'No, you wouldn't.'

'Why?'

'You'd kill the Devil. You'd drown him and watch his body run down his own river.'

'You can't kill the Devil, Della. Like you can't kill God. It's God.'

She pokes her finger into my belly, so hard I think I can feel it hit my spine.

I grit my teeth. 'Does your stomach hurt?'

'My stomach? No. Why?'

'Because it's full of mean things.'

She laughs.

I put a seed in my mouth and crack its shell. Della does the same.

'Nasty, nasty.'

She pokes my stomach again. 'Does that hurt you, Lil?'

'Yes. Stop.'

'That's what it felt like when Mum brought you home and she put you into my hands. It felt like someone was trying to bend something in my body. I've always hated you.'

Mother is screaming now. She worries. About us. For us. We are only fourteen and nine.

Della takes up her pin once more, moving it quickly now, harder, as if she really does have storms in her palm. She pushes and pushes – now it's not just my freckles which hurt. I am weary of this game.

'Girls...'

A branch cracks behind us. Mother has found us. She stands with her hand on her belly.

'Hello Mother, can we help you?'

Her eyes go between us, unsure of where to stay. She isn't sure who has spoken. Back and forth they go. Her mouth opens and closes, open again.

'Mummy?' I say, reaching for her. 'My freckles hurt...'

'It's time for...'

'What's it time for, Mother?'

'Dinner...' she whispers, then she takes a step back, followed by another.

Della takes the pomegranate out of my hand, throws it to the shadows for the shadows to eat the last of it.

Mother does not call for us again.

HER – The Devil on Your Finger

'Why do you all wear white?'

Stina turns her eyes to me, and I think she can see everything, all the parts I want unnoticed. We stand in the street, watch the Folk go about their tasks. They look like ordinary people but for the strangeness of their words and the lightness of their steps, as if at any moment they might need to run, they might wake something living below them.

'We wear white because then we know if we are bleeding. If we are dead, and from where we died. If the Warden has said our time is up. We follow the red.'

'That's strange.'

'We are not strange to ourselves.'

'Have you always been afraid? You must be so weary of it.'

'Generations have lived this way. It's a weariness we are born with. Our mothers gave it to us inside their bellies.'

'And have you always had your Warden?'

She shakes her head, her eyes finding Silas in the street. He is short but toned. He is rolling empty barrels to the pier to be taken to the mainland. She watches him until he has gone. They have a respect for Silas that is old, as old as his family. I wonder what that is like, to be respected, admired, an idol, even if it is only an idol to the Folk.

'No, we have not. The Devil – our Warden – came to this land hundreds of years ago. He dropped from the sky and this is where he fell and made his home. Before he came, the settlers did not believe in anything. They were lost, wandering fools. They were not Folk.'

'So none of you can remember a time when you were free?'

Stina smiles. 'You have sweet thoughts in your head.' Then she taps me on the temple. 'And bitter ones too.'

'Why don't you all leave?'

'He would follow. And we could not leave our land. This land is our history, our story. We are made of each other.'

'What about if one of you did not believe in your Warden?'

Stina's reaction is instant. She takes my hands inside hers and squeezes them to her chest, as if she wants to reach inside and take out her heart. Perhaps then her heart would stop being afraid. 'We all believe in our Warden. We all must believe in our Warden.'

'What happens if you don't?'

She sighs. 'Madness comes.'

And madness isn't already here?

'Who was the first to see your Warden?' I ask, quietly.

Stina takes my hand and leads me inside her shop. Behind the till she has drawings on the wall. Figures made of coal and ink, large and frightening. 'He looks like a man,' I say simply.

'One of his facades, one of his many identities.'

I press my finger to one of the drawings, to a figure with his back to me, his arm raised to touch the moon. None of the drawings show a face.

Stina speaks suddenly and I jump. 'A man saw him standing at Hell's Mouth one night.'

'And you've all been afraid since then?'

'We are all afraid of something.' A pause. 'Are you afraid of anything, Lily Pedley?'

I draw back my hand and see a smudge of black on my finger. The body in the drawing is stretched now, ruined. I have hurt their Devil. And now I have him on my finger.

HER – Stories under the Land

We were born, Della and I, one bitter, one sweet. Mother and Father said that, tucking us into bed at night, one of us struggling, biting, hurting to be freed. The other, calm, grabbing a hand and delicately placing a kiss on its palm, so much bigger than her head.

We grew into pariahs, women who liked to bleed others. We killed our mother and father. We were brought here because a mainlander thought we could hurt something he wanted hurt.

But this place is full of eyes and full of harms. It makes my spine ache.

'Can I ask you something?'

'Of course.' Today Kit and I are once more sat outside her home with her youngest.

'What does it mean – the mark they all have on their finger?'

'Three strikes through their third finger. Three plus three make six. The Devil's number.'

'I spoke with Stina in the village. She told me things about this place. Strange things that ... sit in your head until it feels like it is full of water.'

'There's a woman here who is a self-described doctor. She has all these home remedies, but if anyone is ever very ill, she tells them to take a bite out of bad fruit. She claims that it is Devil-Touched and will cleanse the body.'

'That's ridiculous.'

Kit smiles. 'There are strange communities everywhere around the world but the Folk here are something else. I wonder if it's the isolation. It plays tricks on the mind. I wonder if it's played one too many tricks on them.' She gestures to the flat, grey ocean in the distance. 'Can you see those rocks there? That outcrop is called the Wailing Rocks. Centuries ago, men and women were taken there as punishment for small crimes. It was impossible to swim back – the currents are too strong between the rocks. So they were left there for days, with just enough food to keep them alive. It wasn't starvation or even the weather conditions that got to them in the end, it was the isolation. Can you imagine?'

'That must have been terrible. Did they die there?'

'No. The Folk watched them from the shore for days and days, and when the men and women over there started to behave oddly, to dance and to laugh, to lose their sense, they brought them back.'

'They survived?'

'That's the thing, Lily: some parts of them did and some parts of them didn't. You can have a functional body. It breathes and it keeps on breathing. But the mind is a different thing. So yes, they were brought back, but they were different. Isolation isn't kind.'

I sit with Kit's youngest in my arms again, stroke his small hands, all his softness, and hope he is able to keep it. That nothing will take his softness away from him.

'Do you think this place will always be this way?' I ask.

'Yes. I do. Unless someone changes it.' She sighs. 'The Folk aren't bad people really. They are frightened. And I don't like to see anyone frightened.'

'They are frightened of something they have made up?'

'Isn't that the case for most fears? Fears of the dark, or of ghosts or of heights?'

I nod.

Kit wraps an arm around me. 'Are you alright? Are the stories starting to worry you?'

'I had a dream last night that Della led me to Hell's Mouth. The Devil was down there in the cove and he looked up at me. And then I woke up and I wanted to wash my head out. Does that make sense?'

'There is no Warden – no Devil – here.'

'But—'

'It was your mind, Lily. I've had it too. When I moved here, I was so frightened. They told me that they hear a clock ticking just before the Warden comes. And I heard a clock one time when I was in the garden. But do you know what it was? It was a kid clapping. It didn't even sound like a clock. It was my mind playing tricks.'

I nod.

'I'm not saying I don't think there is something rotten here. There is. But it's something these people have grown themselves. It's the Folk. Nothing else.'

'It's not real.'

'It's not real.'

'Sad.' The young boy reaches a finger to my eye, and holds the tear in his wrinkled palm, watching it slip about. 'Why sad?'

I take the tear away, soak it up with my cuff, drop a daisy into his hand. 'Don't hold the sadness, cricket. Have this instead. This feels much nicer.'

He smiles, running off to pluck more flowers. His fists thickening with petals.

Kit watches him. 'Years ago, a boy died by that tree, there in the distance. He fell and broke his neck. It was an accident. A terrible accident.'

'What was his name?'

'Lornan, I think. You aren't supposed to speak ill of the dead. But this boy ... he was bad. He killed birds, threw rocks into the sky, then, if they were still alive, he drowned them. He was a toxin. When someone dies here, they place their body on a raft and let the river carry it into the sea. Then, when the body washes onto the beach ten days later, they bury it. But do you know what happened when they put this boy's body in the river?'

'No.'

'The river brought it back.'

'I ... I don't understand.'

'The river changed its course. Like it did not want that boy's body in its water. It threw him up against the bank and tried to deliver him back to his mother.'

'But that's impossible.'

She takes my hand. 'That's what I'm trying to tell you. This place has impossible stories. But that is all they are. Stories. Don't forget yourself, Lily.'

'Okay. Okay.'

The boy comes to me, opens my hands and fills them with flowers.

There are so many of them. They fall through my fingers, dripping onto the ground. Bright and smelling as sweet and as fresh as the world after rain. How has he managed to gather so many?

'There,' he says. 'Sadness gone.'

HIM — THEN — Nettle

Della reminds him of his sister. They have different faces but there is a whisper of something familiar. Silas recognises the smell of it. Of a mind burning. Hers was always burning. She was born on fire, Gaia. As if she could sense that a boy was who Father dreamed of, not a girl, She bore the distress of being an unwanted child, and it made her angry.

She told Silas if she had been born like any other baby, soft and weak, she would have been abandoned. A girl was no good to Father. But when he picked her up, she wrapped her gums round his finger and bit him hard enough to bring a scream to a full-grown man's mouth. It stayed his hand. He liked her venom.

As she grew so did her bite.

Gaia turns Silas round in circles. It is a game she likes to play with him. She is ten, and he is four, his legs still carrying their baby thickness. He thumps onto the floor but he does not cry. Not much can move him; he surprises his mother with how little he cries. His cheeks are always dry.

Except when he plays games with his sister.

She brings him to the foot of the mountain, to where they bury the dead. They hide behind headstones, jump from plot to plot. She tells him, beneath the earth are the bodies of everyone who has ever lived on their island. She tells him that one day his body will be here too.

'I'll bury you, myself,' she says, running a finger down his arm, as if she is already sizing him up for death.

'I don't want to die.'

'You have to.'

'But I don't want to. Father of mine would be sad.'

Gaia smiles, but he has never seen something that looks less like a smile. 'Father of ours is stupid.'

'Can we go home now?'

'No. We haven't finished dancing.' She twists his wrists in her hands, forcing his body to move. Her fingers leave red marks, welts, the harder they go. Still, he does not cry. He smiles.

Gaia runs to the edge of the cemetery. She takes her shirt off and wraps it round her hands to protect the skin. Then she tears nettles from the earth, returns to her brother.

'Open your hands,' she says.

He does so.

She lays the nettles in his small palms, then she squeezes them into fists. She squeezes so tight, green juice drips between his fingers.

He fidgets, tries to pull away from her. 'Stings!'

His hands swell, doubling in size until it looks like he is wearing gloves. But still he does not cry.

'Why are your cheeks so dry?'

He shakes his head. 'Hurts!' he wails. 'Hurts!'

Gaia throws his body away from her, then she drags it back, as if she has forgotten something. 'I hate you,' she says into his ear.

And then the boy cries.

HER – Haunting of Men

'Before we crossed the water,' I say, 'A man on the mainland told us a story about a boy who had gone missing here. His parents searched this land but they could not find him. Then, that night, they heard their boy's screams. What happened to the boy?'

Kit shakes her head, holding her youngest in her arms. He makes a rumble in his throat and wriggles. I open my hands and Kit passes his chubby body to me. 'The mainlanders are frightened of the Folk. They always have been.'

'What happened to the boy, Kit?' I am holding her son so tightly, I worry he will bruise.

'From what I know, the boy took a boat and came ashore here. On his way home he was knocked overboard, and he screamed and screamed. He could not swim. Who sails when they cannot swim?'

'So ... they let him drown?'

'There was nothing they could do. If they had gone out there, they would have risked their own lives. They were frightened.'

I nod, look in the distance at Higher Tor. 'What do you know of the man who lives there?'

I pat the boy's back, feel his cotton-soft skin and his dainty pink fingernails, marvel at his youth. We were all like this in the beginning. A fresh human without trouble in our mind. Born innocent, then the innocence leaves us.

'Oh, you mean Silas?'

I look for a light in the window, for the suggestion of a man inside its walls. But it looks dead. It looks like a dead bird that has fallen to the earth, feet pointing to the sky.

'He had a sister once, I think,' Kit says. 'But no one talks about her. And now there is just him. He's decent Folk, Silas. The only one here who is ... ordinary.' A line has furrowed into her brow. 'He's a quiet man but he is kind. When I first came here, he helped me adjust. He was always showing up at my door to help me with the gardening or putting the washing out. I think he wanted a friend.'

'If he is sane, why doesn't he leave?'

She shrugs. 'This is his home. He has probably never even seen the mainland. Few have.'

'His house is strange.' I gesture across the distance to the tall, tall spire of his home. 'One strong wind could tip it into the sea.'

'Higher Tor...'

She watches her son settle in my arms, his cheek pressed against my chest. A line of dribble slips between my breasts, and I wince. Kit does not see. Her face is troubled, turned to the house.

'That place is a haunting.'

'You mean it's haunted?'

'No. It's a haunting,' she says. 'Look at it. It's haunting us now.'

HER – THEN – Knocking in the Earth

Father watches us in a way other fathers do not watch their daughters.

Della and I tangle our legs in the sea, make a knot of bone and salt. We push each other under the surface, hold each other down. Other girls do it too. I see them, smiles sticking on their lips. But their fathers do not watch them like ours watches us.

'Dad's looking at us,' I say.

'Dad's always looking at us.'

'He's worried.'

'He's always worried.'

Della picks seaweed from her hair. 'Do you know the local legend about the giant, Cormoran?'

'No,' I say. 'And I don't want to.'

She pulls a sad face. 'But you'd like it, Lil.'

'I never like your stories. That's why you always tell me them.'

We plant our feet in the sand and look at St Michael's Mount rising in the distance. It is frightening and beautiful. We climbed to the top years ago; Mother separated us because Della told me she was going to push me off the edge.

'Fine.' Della smiles. 'I'll tell you about the Knockers then.'

'The what?'

'Some say they are the ghosts of dead miners. Others say they are something worse. They live underground, and back in the olden days, they would guide the men to the seams of tin running through the land. But then the workers stopped giving them offerings. The Knockers grew tired of the men's arrogance so they started knocking on the walls, leading the men to danger. They knocked out the supports and laughed when there were landfalls.'

'Maybe the men shouldn't have whistled so loudly.'

Della grins. 'Maybe they shouldn't have been down there in the first place.' She nudges my foot with hers. 'These days, the Knockers have gone quiet, but sometimes children still hear them. They hear them from their windows at night, knocking under the earth. Have you never wondered why children go missing?'

'They fall into the sea.'

'No. They are taken.' Della reaches down and wraps her fingers round my ankle. 'They follow the knocking. Out of their homes, across the moors to the abandoned mines. And then they are pulled under the earth.' She tugs my ankle and I claw my way back to the surface.

'Some say the Knockers eat the children. Others say the children are still down there. They are so lonely, they start knocking themselves. They bring other children down to the mines. More and more.'

'They won't get me.'

'Won't they?'

'If I hear knocking, I'll put my fingers in my ears.'

Della laughs. 'Lil, they won't need to come for you. I'll take you down to them. They can have you. Then I'll be free. You'll knock, knock from under the earth, trying to get my attention, but do you know what I'll do?' She snaps her teeth at me. 'I'll close the window.'

The sea is too deep. The water too cold. I turn, wave at Father, but Della snatches my hand back. Father is still watching though. He does not like her games.

'He won't come.'

Della wraps her legs round mine. The waves beat at my head. I look back at Father. He is on his knees.

Della wraps her fingers through my hair and holds me down, under the water. I scream and she lets me up.

Father is walking.

Della fastens her legs around mine, and I cannot escape. I can only scream.

Now, Father is running.

HIM – Suspicion of Women

Silas brings up an old online article. There is a photograph of the Pedley women standing outside their childhood home. Their parents' faces are bright, warm, and brown as a nut, like Lily's. They have Lily's blonde hair, freckles across their chins.

And then there is Della.

The article does not offer any new information, so he moves on, finds a podcast from two men, Michael and Rupesh, who are friends with an appetite for true crime.

'Alright, loyal listeners, we have an interesting one for you today. A mystery, if you will, of the most frightening nature. The case of Lily and Della Pedley. Two sisters from Cornwall, England, who murdered their mother and father.'

'Mikey, let's give 'em some backstory before we grab them by the balls, huh? Only polite.' The sound of a handclap, then two palms rubbed together. 'Okay. So! Lily and Della were the daughters of Oliver and Sarah Pedley. They lived at the edge of a forest, not far from the old fishing town of Penzance. They were good gals, polite. But there was more to them than meets the eye. They had bite, these gals. Teeth! They had a darkness under the surface. I can almost hear the horny psycho-lovers out there wanking off to this.'

'Rupe, mouth!'

'Ahhh. Right, right. Sorry, folks. Carried away. So the gals were raised on the edge of a forest. Our source – a key witness if you will – tells us that they would play in the woodlands; games they made up, games that would send them home with bruises on their backs and cuts on their hands. And sometimes they would stay out all night. These gals were not afraid of the dark. These gals were not afraid of monsters. Because *they* were the monsters.'

'As Rupesh says, there was always something worrisome abou—'

'Fuck me in the mouth, did you just say "worrisome"? Talk like yo'self, Mikey. No one is impressed.'

'Language!'

A sigh. 'Right. Carry on.'

'The girls' behaviours was ... worrisome from early on. Our witness says they had an evil that didn't belong in two little Cornish girls. That their parents were frightened of them.'

'Yep. These gals were the Devil's whores. As time passed, it only got fucking worse. No one knows what triggered it, like. Why they did what they did. But one morning they strung their folks up downstairs.'

'Just barbaric.'

'Mm-hm. Little angels, these gals were not. But you know what the worst thing is? It was the way in which they were found.'

'Tell them how they were found, Rupe.'

'So a neighbour goes round to their house, right, and she finds the big one, Della, scraping last night's shit from their plates. Washing the dishes like nothing happened. Like her parents weren't hanging in the next room going cold, like. The little one was found sat under them, hanging on her mum's feet. Nasty lil' bitch.'

'Why weren't they convicted?'

'Well, they couldn't prove it, could they? There were no signs of asphyxiation, like. Nothing in the autopsy. No signs of a struggle. It looked like they committed suicide, right.'

'So what happened then, Rupe?'

'The gals were taken into custody on suspicion of murder. But the evidence wasn't strong enough, so in the end they had to let them go. The press picked up this case and ran with it. It's juicy, fucking mental. Two sisters, like. Their story crossed oceans, you know. The Yanks drank this shit up. And who can blame them, this is the *good* shit.'

'Do you remember how people started taking sides? Team Della, Team Lily?'

'That's right, man. Some fuckers thought it was Della who killed them, that Lily was just some stupid bitch who was afraid to stop her. That divided people like an election. Fuck me! That shit got aggressive. People put banners in their gardens. Posters. It was on television. It was everywhere. Families split down the middle. It became like a religion. Wars are fought over less.'

'And what's the general consensus now, Rupe?'

'That they were a team, that they did it together.'

'Why though? Do you think their parents were monsters? Were the girls abused? Were they fighting back? Did they even kill them? What if it was a double suicide?'

'They denied it all. But if I killed my fucking mother – and honestly, no plans to – I'd deny it too.'

'So no one really knows the truth.'

'Speaking of my mother ... bet she knows. Bitch knows fucking everything. She could always find my old porn. Once I hid weed in my gym shorts, you know – thought the smell would mask it. Thought I was clever. Nah. She stuck her snout in the air and hunted it down. A dog looking for crack, that's my ma. Maybe I should call her.' A laugh. 'She'll sniff the truth outta this case. She'll take on this big cunt, Della.'

'Rupe?'

'Huh?'

'You've lost your way here, a little...'

'Ah! Sorry, my lovely fuckers. Carried away.'

'What do you think happened, Rupe?'

'I think it was Della who did it. They find her washing the dishes? The fucking dishes – while her parents are hanging from their necks and her little sister is crying in the next room. That's inhuman, that's cold. Animal. She's an animal. Ya can see she's something evil, just by looking at her, like.'

'She is quite frightening to look at. I remember seeing her face in the papers when it all happened. I'd not read the headlines yet, so I didn't know anything about the case. But I saw her face, Rupe and, I felt ... afraid.'

'What made you afraid though, Mikey, exactly?'

'She's got this look. As if she could slaughter a village. That she wants to. She makes me feel sick.'

'Hm.'

'And as for Lily – honestly, I don't know. Perhaps they really were in it together. Perhaps they are both broken. Perhaps it was revenge, and they were fiddled with as children.'

'Not gonna lie though, Lily is one fine fucker.'

'Rupe!'

'Come on! You saying you don't think the same, like? She's got the looks of an angel, blondie, blue eyes. Small as a fucking mouse. Gorgeous. I'd fuck that. Wouldn't say no. Not sure any man would, murderess or no. A proper *femme fatale*.'

'Why do you have to make it weird?'

'It's not weird. I'm just saying I reckon she'd be a wild one in the sack.'

'Are you quite finished?'

'Okay, Yes, I'm done.'

'Good.'

'Sorry.'

'You sure you're done?'

'Yep.'

'Thank you.'

'Honestly though, I'd let her fucking kill me if she'd let me shag her first. Deceased. RIP Rupe.'

'For the love of God.'

HER – Folktales

'Can I ask what it is troubling you?'

Kit and I stand on the headland. From a distance, it must look like we are about to open our arms and fly. If only they could fly us to somewhere else. The wind is fingers through our hair, twisting it into strange shapes. A shadow on the horizon. Everything is shadows on this island. I feel as if I live with them inside my eyes. Like a swell of cataract, moving across my sight.

'When we came here, I was pregnant,' Kit says. 'Four months along. We were hoping for another boy. We wanted the trilogy, you know?' A laugh, small, then quickly buried. 'We were going to name him Patrick. We didn't tell anyone here. Even my boys didn't know. But somehow when I lost Patrick, the Folk here knew. I woke up one morning, heard this rattling outside. When I opened the door, I found a crib, it was small. Like a child's plaything.'

'Isn't that nice?'

Kit looks at me. 'There was a baby inside it. A baby made of wood.'

'Oh.'

'It looked so strange, almost real, like they killed it and carved it a home. It had round cheeks and fists held to its chin. It was terrifying and beautiful. And it was made from an old oak tree. A tree the Folk once tried to burn down. But it would not burn. Or so the stories say.'

'So they cut it down instead?'

'Yes. And they made a baby from its cursed wood.'

'Were your boys afraid?'

She nods. 'We all were. I don't think they meant harm, but that whole ordeal unnerved me. My boys have had to cope with their own troubles as well.'

'What do you mean?'

Kit smiles but it is a bruised smile. 'This was long before the baby. Long before that. My eldest came home one day from playing with the local kids. He had this mark on his throat. I thought it was a little sunburn or he'd caught himself when he zipped his jacket.' She shakes her head. 'Imagine a four-year-old trying to explain that the children he played with had put a rope round his neck and pretended to hang him.'

'My God.'

'I don't think he realised what it all meant. I don't think they would have really gone through with it. They are just kids. But he had the marks on his throat.'

'But ... why? Why?'

'Have you been to the Hanging Place?'

'No.'

'It's a forest not far from here. A long, long time ago the Folk strung up men and woman by their feet. They hung from the branches like human ornaments. And then they cut them and let them bleed into the soil. It was something they did to honour the Devil. The kids were re-enacting it.'

'Does this place have any *good* stories?'

'I don't think it does. Fortunately, it has been mostly forgotten by the world.'

'What will you do when you leave? Will you tell anyone about this place?'

'No. I'll never tell anyone. No one should know.'

'But—'

'If I tell anyone, they'll be curious. They'll want to know if the stories are true. They'll want to see for themselves.'

'I don't understand.'

'If I keep my mouth shut, then this place can stay forgotten.'

'And your boys?'

'They want to leave. They want to forget themselves. I should never have brought them here, Lily.'

'I wish you were staying. I know that is selfish.'

Kit wraps an arm round my shoulders. 'You'll be okay. Get to know Silas. The Folk listen to him, respect him; he has some influence here. He has sense. He'll look after you.'

'Has he looked after you?'

'Yes. He's helped us keep our minds. He'll help you keep yours.'

HIM – Deity

He watches the sisters. The Witches of Old Town.

They move through the street. The Folk watch them too. The sisters stop, and the Folk stop. It is a parade of silent bodies. A wind blows from the mountain, comes to him, and he can smell their hot curiosity.

The sisters continue, and the Folk too, smooth as blood in water. Lily turns on her heel and screams, 'Stop it. Just stop! Leave us alone.'

'Be quiet, Lil.' Della's voice is gravel, and Silas wants to clean out his ears.

'No. Stop it!' Lily tears away from her sister, shaking her head. 'Stop following us...'

'Mind me, Lil...'

'I will *not* mind you.'

Fury wakes in Della's eyes, and Silas takes a step back, even though he's ten feet away. Lily shrinks, brings her arms into a cross above her face. But it does not help her. Della grabs Lily by the shoulders, her great hands beginning to shake.

A coldness drives down the street. Silas feels it in his fingers. The Folk take a breath, hold it, their mouths opening. They watch as sister shakes her sister. Lily's head wobbles on her thin neck, until he thinks it will come off her body.

She's going to kill her, he thinks.

She shakes and shakes and shakes. He cannot even see Lily's face now. Her lovely blonde head swings. Suddenly, he is running. He throws himself into Della's body and tears her giant hands from Lily.

Lily scrambles away, tears and snot making shiny paths over her face. Della stands in the street panting. Her hands are red.

The Folk take in a breath, all of them. The drag of air between their teeth makes him jump, then they move. They do not move to Lily, as he expects. They go to Della, already reaching. Countless hands claim a space on her body, her chest, her cheek, her throat, as if she is a deity. As if she is someone who will save them.

Then they begin to sing.

HER – The Bitterness of Memory

Silas gently pulls me into his arms. I can still feel my body being shaken, my heart banging like a bullet inside a glass. It if beats any harder, it might break its shape. I go with Silas, take some comfort from the rough calluses on his hands. He looks over his shoulder. I don't. I know, soon, she will follow. As she always does.

'Are you alright?'

I nod. I see him in motion. Nothing – not this floor, nor my hands, nor his body – is still. Everything shivers. 'Yes – yes. I'm okay.'

'Has she done that before?'

'She was angry.'

'That wasn't what I asked.'

'Yes. She's done it before.'

'Will you do something for me?'

I look at him. 'What?'

He lies on the ground, crossing his ankles, threading his fingers through the soft grass. 'Lie down.'

'I don't understand.'

'Join me. Please.'

I do as I am asked.

'Now close your eyes. Keep them closed for five minutes. We don't need to speak.'

I take a breath and will the world into stillness.

'What if I want to speak?' I say.

I do not look but I think I have made him smile.

'Then you can speak.'

'Can you tell me what we are doing?'

'You'll see.'

A pause.

'Do you have a watch? I don't know how long it has been.'

'It's not even been a minute.'

'Oh.'

'She shouldn't do that to you, you know.'

'I know.'

'I thought she was going to break your neck.'

'I thought that too.'

'Does it hurt?' he asks, and I feel two fingers press themselves to my neck, before quickly vanishing. 'Sorry,' he mutters.

'Yes, it hurts. I'm trying not to be sick.'

'This will help with that. You'll see.'

'Thank you. For helping me.' I want to open my eyes but I don't. 'Why did you? You don't know me.' I consider. 'You know *of* me, perhaps.'

'Because no one else would have.'

'You seem ... ordinary.'

'So do you, witch.' I grimace, and he sighs. 'Sorry. I don't get out much.'

I smile, despite myself. 'That's okay. When did you last leave this island?'

'You mean ever?'

'Yes.'

'Then never.'

'What? You've never been anywhere else?'

'No. I am the last in a long line of Mairs – my family. This place is all we have ever known.'

'Do you want to leave?'

'Sometimes. But I worry if I go somewhere new, I will feel like a child again. Learning the world. And I don't ever want to be a child again.' There is a shadow in his voice, and I bite my lip.

'I want to be a girl again.'

'Did you do it?'

The question rips into me. 'Is that what this is about? You want to know what happened to my parents.'

'No. I wanted to help. Now, open your eyes.'

I do. The world has stilled.

'Has it helped?'

'Yes ... How did you know?'

'I had something similar. Found that lying flat on the earth helps ground you. Takes the sickness away.'

I rise to my feet. He remains where he is. He does not open his eyes.

'Thank you.'

'You're welcome.'

I turn and begin walking home. My neck hurts, and when I turn back to look for him, I must turn my whole body. He is still lying there, alone. A man on a hill, watching the sky as if it might hurt him.

HIM – THEN – A Woman, Burning

The sky is the colour of bone. Pale, infected. Clouds gather to them, as if he and his sister have cast ropes round their bellies. Silas notices now how quiet the evening sky is. There are no birds. No life above, or below, except for him and his sister.

They stand on the headland, looking down into the cove. The evening sun splashes their hands with warmth. He wishes he felt it.

'There's a devil who walks down there,' Gaia says. 'I know him.'

'Who is he? Will I meet him?'

'Come. I want you to do something for me.'

She guides him to a rocky outcrop, moss and lichen a fur across its peaks. The shape of it is like a man on his hands and knees who has crawled so many miles he has tired and turned to stone. Silas runs his hands across the mass, finding a hollow in the middle of the man's back.

Gaia takes his hands in hers. The grip is not gentle, and before she has even touched him, he is trying to draw away. His body knows to do this now, to retract before the hurt comes.

'You love me, don't you, Silas?'

'Yes, Gaia.'

'You want to please me, don't you, Silas?'

'Yes, Gaia.'

She takes a knife from her pocket. It is the size of her middle finger, with a blade that looks worryingly like bone.

'I don't trust you, Silas. I don't think you mean it. Not really. Words are easy to say.'

'I love you, Gaia. You're my big sister.'

She nods, passing the knife into his fingers, still soft and thick from his childhood.

'I want you to show me how much you love me. Cut your hand and fill this hollow. Right to the top.'

'But...'

'It's not deep. It won't hurt.'

A noise comes through his lips, and he hates how frightened he sounds. Her smile is the kindest he has ever seen, and he doesn't trust it.

But he wants it.

Silas cuts a keyhole into his palm, and blood runs into the bowl. Gaia watches, then she throws out her arms, trying to collect the last sunlight. It slips through her hair and makes her look like she is a flame. She is a gypsy, dancing; a witch, casting; a woman, burning. She is beautiful, and Silas cannot keep his eyes from her. His heart thumps, a small drum in his chest. He wants to be like his sister when he is grown. He wants to dance on the top of their small world and not worry about the bottom.

Silas looks at his hand, pale now. The blood clots and so he forces himself to open the wound. Halfway to the top. How is it not full?

'Gaia…?'

'Keep going.'

'Gaia?'

'Not long now, Silas.'

Coldness curls between his shoulders. Tears, fat and shining, tip onto his chin. 'I don't want to do this anymore.'

'You have to do this, for me.'

His lip is wobbling, and he pinches it between his fingers. He doesn't want her to see him like this. He doesn't want her to think him weak. 'Please…'

'Silas!' She stops, hands in the air, as if she is a bird about to fly. If anyone human could make it to the sky, she could. 'You must do this. If you don't, I will know you don't really love me.'

He wipes his cheeks. When he tries to look for his sister, he sees only darkness. He has shadows inside his eyes.

'I… I don't feel well.'

'Keep going…'

'Something is wrong.'

'Keep going…'

The hollow is not full. He touches his fingers to the lip of it, its shape, then he pushes them to the bottom. He feels a crack. The cove below them. This hollow, this bent stone man, is directly above it.

'I… I…'

Silas looks at his sister, and he knows then. He wishes he did not.

There is a hole, it runs down through the earth into the cave. A whole body of blood could not fill this hollow. Certainly not his. Gaia is smiling. He knew he could not trust her smile. It was an armed one.

Silas tucks his bleeding hand under his armpit and watches the last of himself drain away. The sun is running off the edge of the sea now. Then the darkness will come. Gaia has not noticed him. She closes her eyes and spins in circles.

He will not let his sister bleed him. He has always loved his sister so powerfully, he once thought they shared a heart, all their hurts. He thought they shared a mind, a pair of lungs, and that when he laughed, it came from her lips; when their mother brushed her hair, he felt those fingertips in his.

'Come here.' She has her eyes on him now. There is such fury in her face, he can feel it.

'No.'

His sister cut three lines into the heels of her feet when she was twelve. It is the sign they use for the Warden. When Gaia walked barefoot, she left this mark in the ground for all eyes to see. Did she bleed, did she hurt on each step? Does she still hurt now on the steps she takes towards him?

'Mother and Father won't want you to hit me.' His legs shake, and he wobbles back, back, away.

'I don't care. Boy or no, I am more powerful than you.'

'Please.'

'Come to me, scab.'

'I ... I'll tell Father. You know what he'll do.'

She stops, her smile drip-dripping down her face. Father is the only one she has ever feared. Silas wields their father's name like a blade, but his mother's name is a blunt one. These knives are all he has. 'He'll give you the back of his hand.'

'I don't care. Father can do as he likes.'

She wraps her arms around his body. He knows these arms, the circles they make. They are loose at first so you think they are kind, but then they close like belts, and your body weakens.

Gaia squeezes until he cries. He can feel the pieces inside his body *moving. He will not grow, he thinks, in some small place in his mind. His body will stop trying; it will leave its efforts there. She brings him into her belly, and he thinks,* Is this the best I will be? I will be a boy-shaped man.

But I want to be big.

The air claps out of his lungs. She breathes in, takes it all. His air is hers now. He screams and she laughs and he screams. This mad song fills the night. She could not bleed him so she will bleed him another way. He wonders if this is why the birds have gone. He wonders if the stars will shiver in their sky, if even the moon will turn its face from them.

HIM – Warnings in the River

A bell rings, and Silas sees Della enter the village shop. He does not often see one sister without the other. They move with stitches in their wrists, a binding, so they are always together. But today, Lily is nowhere.

Silas follows Della, moving quietly into the shop. Stina is talking to Della. They do not see him.

'You're the Pedley girl. The elder sister.'

'Yes.'

'Della?'

'How do you know us?'

'We have newspapers delivered regularly. We have signal. We are not cut off from the world, we are just apart from it. Silas looks after us. We heard about that man who abducted a mother and son, kept them in an old curiosity shop. Berry and Vincent, was it? We heard about the little girls who went missing from the market town in Penzance. Poor little missing girls. Then we heard about two sisters who killed their parents, in an old house by an old forest. We know what happens in the world. We know all about *you*.'

'Do you have many travellers come here?'

'Some. But never local people from the mainland. They stay far away. They do not like our stories.'

'Is there no God here?'

'No god would come.'

'Yet you have his Devil?'

Stina shakes her head, as if Della has misunderstood her. 'There are many devils walking through the world, girl. Why do you assume ours belongs to the Bible?'

Silence.

'Most of us have never even held a Bible. We know what we know. We believe what we believe. What do you believe?'

Della shows her teeth. 'I have no apostle.'

'Hm, I see that. You are your own god, aren't you, girl?'

Della twitches, and there is something so animal about the movement of it, Silas wants to wash out his eyes.

'Are you all inbred then?' Della says eventually.

Stina laughs, a throaty cackle that Silas has not heard before. 'No, girl. We are not.'

'Are you simple?'

'No. We are not.'

'You go about like you are simple. Like you are in a trance.'

'We live with fear in our feet. It does funny things to your walk. Understand?'

'How are there so many of you? Men who travel to this place fuck your women?'

'Men are men. They'll fuck anything.'

Della smiles.

Stina smiles too.

'You speak oddly.'

'You understand us well enough though.'

A pause, heavy and thick. Silas holds his breath, hides behind the tins and glass jars. Stina moves around the counter, studies Della closely.

'You're not like your sister, are you? One salt, one sugar. One bitter, one sweet. Which are you?'

'You know which sister I am.' Della towers over Stina, her head grazing the ceiling. Her face is expressionless but her hands are in fists.

'You interest me, Della Pedley.'

'How so?'

'You're like us.'

'How am I?'

Stina's eyes are intent. She licks her lips, takes a breath, then lets it out. 'There's something feral about you. I can feel it.' Stina strokes Della's hand. 'I can feel it.'

'Don't touch me.'

Stina cups Della's face. 'You have so much emotion in you. You're a river.'

Della jumps at that word, and he wonders why.

'Yes ... yes. I wonder if I hold you upside down, will it all just fall out of you. I'd have to get the mop and clean you up. But my floors wouldn't dry, not really. And you'd stay there, moulding my shop.' Stina nods. 'Such emotion. Such a river.'

'Let go of me.' Silas sees fury in Della's face, but Stina sees it as something else.

'Ahh.' She pauses, sniffs, taps her nose. 'I smell sadness ... and ... fear. What are you frightened of, girl? Is it us? ... No, no.' She shakes her head. 'This is old. Like dead things. You've been near dead things. Of course you have. You came with this fear.'

'I am not afraid. I don't believe in your Warden.'

'No ... no, you don't. But like us, you're afraid of something.' She laughs. 'Girl as big as you, powerful, you could touch the sky. But that don't help with terrors on the ground, does it?'

'You're mad.'

'I'm no madder than you are. Is it your parents? Hmmm, no, I don't think it is.' She shakes her head. 'Something else. Poor girl. Poor beast.'

Della pushes Stina back. 'Enough!'

'You're like us. We're the same.' Stina taps Della's hand. 'That's why the children come to you in the street, that's why Folk follow you. Because we recognise you. You're us.'

'I have no Warden.'

'Devils come in all skins, girl.'

HER – Mind Medicine

'Are you alright?' Kit asks.

I nod. 'I'm fine.'

'It's just you look ... troubled. Like you have something heavy on your soul.'

I smile, and it feels like it might crack my face. My whole body might shiver into slivers. 'I've been having bad dreams since coming to this island. That's all.'

'Oh.'

She has her youngest strapped to her back. His head wobbles on her shoulder. I touch my little finger to his nose. He sleeps deeply. I think even this cry I am holding in my mouth wouldn't stir him.

I force myself to pick up my feet as we climb the hill. The land spreads out, wild, an untamed thing. Sometimes it feels as if this land is alive, and I am a tick, living off its back. This incline we climb, this is its ribs. Those trees to the south, those are its feathers. Where will all of us go, if this body, this monstrous bird, ever decided to rise?

'I think ... I think this place is getting to me. I suppose you heard about what happened in the village the other day?' I ask.

'Did she hurt you?'

'No. Not really.'

'Why did she do that? I've spoken with Della and she ... she isn't what I expected. She doesn't seem much of a monster. Why would she do that to you?'

'Because she has always hated me.'

Kit bites her lip. 'You should leave her then, Lily. Come with me. I leave in two days' time. Get on the boat with us.'

'I can't.'

'Why?' She takes my hands in hers, forcing us to stop. 'There won't be another boat, Lily. We had to beg our friend to come and get us. No one else will come.'

'I ... I just can't, Kit.' I do not tell her why. If I told Kit everything, she'd shake so hard her hands would fall from her body.

'Fine. Fine. But just know that if you ever need to leave this place, I'll come back, okay. You have my number. Ring me, day or night.'

'Thank you.'

We continue walking.

'What did the Folk do – in the street, when it happened?'

'Silas pulled me out of the way. Then they all went to her, laid their hands on her body like ... like they were worshipping her. It was strange. It's like they think she is something ... primordial.'

'Like is drawn to like. Do you know what my mother used to say to me when I was young?'

'What?'

'She'd put my arms through a fine dress, brush my hair back and tell me to look my best. "Cast a pretty net, Kit, and you will catch pretty things." The Folk are casting a bad net. And they are catching bad things. Or they think they are.'

'Hm.' I recall their faces, the sounds that chanted from their lips. 'I think you are right.' I wonder if the Folk think Della can save them.

I touch my neck, recalling those fine, slippery threads of hair. 'The other night, we went to the inn and I saw a photograph on the wall. It was a photograph of everyone on the island. The entire community. But ... there were faces crossed out.' I look at her. 'What does that mean, Kit?'

She looks at me, and I look away, because there is something I don't want to see, something I know I won't want to hear. The question sits between us, and I wish I could gather it up and burst it with my fingers.

'They are marking their dead.'

'What for?'

'The Folk say that the Devil comes to the village once every year to thin his herd. He takes three people. Man, woman, child, it doesn't matter. Every year, three people will die. They call it Harvest.'

I gasp. 'No. No, that's...'

She smiles sadly. 'Lily, it's not real. It's a delusion. People die. It would be stranger if they didn't. Statistically, it's nothing out of the ordinary. Think about this: accidents, human error, illness, old age.

Three people is a good average for a community living like this one. The most frightening thing about it all is the power of this delusion. They believe it.'

'It's ... it's every year? So when is the next Harvest?'

Kit dips her head. 'It's now. That's why they are all so worried.'

'Oh...'

'Listen to me.' She grips my hand. Her eyes burn, and I blink to help the heat. 'Listen good and clear. This place is ill.' Her fingers dig deeper. 'There is no illness like the illness of the mind. They think they have a devil. I think they have groomed themselves into a delusion. Don't forget yourself, Lily. Remind yourself what is real and what is not. Remind yourself of this like you are taking medicine.'

'I will. I will.'

'Lily, please don't forget to take your medicine.'

HIM – Departing Suns

Kit gathers her children inside her arms. They do not cry, they have no sad words, they are not pale moons. They are suns, calm suns, who smile like this is not a departure. They stand together on the dock, overflowing bags and suitcases spilling around them. Silas watches from afar. He gives them their space. He does not intrude. He will miss Kit, her bluntness, her humour. When she first arrived on the island, he went to her home every day, helping her weed and cultivate her garden. He hated how his palms grew calloused and sweat coated his neck, but he did it for her company, to be close to her. He loved to be close to her.

Lily stands with Della. Anywhere Lily goes, Della goes too, as if they are stitched together with a fine thread no one can see. But he can. He can see it. He recalls overhearing Della and Stina in the shop, and wonders what it all means.

The Folk have not come.

A boat crosses the water, and they all watch its approach. Kit helps her family onto the boat, a smile on her lips. Silas does not think he has ever seen her smile. It's a nice one.

Lily waves, and Kit waves back. She mouths something, and Silas squints to see what it is. Lily nods. She has her hands wrapped round her stomach. Her legs shake through the thin fabric of her trousers. What are they saying to each other?

Della is wondering the same. Her eyes toss back and forth. She could kill a man with those eyes. She reminds him of Gaia. And his organs hurt.

Then Kit looks at him, and he tips his head. Once their belongings are stowed on the boat, they pull away from the land. The family is smiling now, all of them. They are laughing over a joke the eldest son has made. Their faces are bright, the shadows have split.

Silas looks at Lily. But the shadows are still here with her.

He realises then what Kit said to her:

'Medicine.'

HER – The Bleeding Tree

I watched Kit load her children onto the boat. Della stayed with me, her fingernail grazing the back of my hand, a thorn, a reminder to mind her.

The Folk think they know her, after less than a month, but only I know the truth of her. We could tear a wound in the world. A bite the size of our mouth. We murdered our parents, hung them from their necks. Then we fled from one edge of the land to another. But it was only ever one of us who really did all of this.

Mother used to dip her finger in milk and hold it to my nose. I'd tip my head back and licked the drop from her finger. Wolf, she called me. Little Wolf.

She had no name for Della. What name could she give?

Medicine, I think, as we enter the inn. How can I keep my medicine down when my body wants to throw out every breath I breathe on this land?

The Folk once more fall silent, just as they did when we arrived on this island. I recognise most of them now. I know most of their names even though they prefer to speak to my sister than me.

All their eyes spin. I could get an infection from their eyes. But, of course, it's not me they are looking at.

Della smiles. 'Hello,' she says. 'Hello.'

Silas appears from behind the bar. 'Can I get you some drinks?'

Della nods. 'Two vodkas. No ice.' She takes my wrist and puts me in a chair. A man shuffles closer to her, begins talking in her ear. While she is distracted, I cross the room and sit with three children, two girls and a boy, who have been abandoned in a corner. I cross my legs, smile at them.

'Hi. My name is Lily. What's yours, crickets?'

They do not answer.

The girls are dressed in white. The boys too.

'What are your names?'

They look at me. Then look away.

'That's Mira, Pallas. And that's Iona, the little one.' Silas crouches beside me, slipping a glass tumbler into my fingers. 'Don't be rude. Lily spoke to you.'

Their heads snap to me, and there is such fear in their unblemished faces, I gasp.

'Erm ... that's okay. They're just shy.'

Silas shrugs.

I swallow the lump of bile in my throat, touch a finger to Iona's red curls. 'I like your hair. It's beautiful. I wish I had hair this colour. Like fire.' I stroke the shell of her head. She is so young and unspoilt.

Suddenly the girl, Iona, grabs my hand and wraps her mouth round my little finger. She bites, and I wince, try to shake her head from my hand, but she does not let go.

Silas takes her body in his arms and whispers in her ear, 'Devil's on your back.'

She releases instantly, her body going limp. He delivers her to her mother and father, waves his hands at the two other children to make them scarper. Then he sits beside me, legs crossed, wipes the spit from my finger with a rag tied to his waist.

'Thank you.'

'That's alright. She shouldn't have bitten you.'

'What did you say to her? What does it mean?'

'It's just a trick.'

'I don't understand.'

'It means if she's naughty, the Devil will take her for Harvest.'

'Why would you say something to frighten her? It's cruel.'

'I had to get her off you. And I got her just in time. Look.' There are marks on my finger. 'Any longer and she would have cut that vein.' He rubs the blood back into the empty space. 'It's a trick. That's all.'

I nod.

The last of today's sun rinses through the room, catching on the walls. There are flecks of red, and I think it is paint. But I realise they are beads. The light fractures across them, sending strange marks onto the Folk's pale faces; they look like they are bleeding from their eyes.

I gasp.

'What ... what are they?'

Silas looks at me. 'We put them there for our dead.'

'To ... to remember them?'

'Yes.'

'But why?'

'Why does anyone want to remember their lost ones?'

I nod. 'Are they made of glass?'

'A little.'

There are so many. Small as teardrops you would not want to touch. I look at my hands, my arms. I look at Silas's face. At Della's. At the children. We are all crying. Mourning.

But the dead do not belong to me. I do not want to cry for them. I wipe my face, as if to rid myself of the marks.

'What do you mean, a little?'

Silas dips his head. 'When someone here dies, we take a drop of their blood and put it inside glass. These beads are how we remember them.'

'You ... you...'

He looks up at the ceiling. 'These are just a few from my family. The rest, we hang on the Bleeding Tree. It's in the square. The tree is full, holding every person who has passed on. They are all together. There are families. There are stories up there.'

'It's a history?'

He nods. 'You think it's strange? But isn't this kinder than taking a body and burning it? Putting it into a jar and polishing it when you remember it's sitting there, on your mantle?'

'But ... but it's strange.'

He shakes his head. 'No one is forgotten. Every day the evening sun brings them back.'

A shiver runs down my spine. 'I don't ... I don't like this ... I don't like this.'

'Lily, calm.'

I stumble my way through the room. The Folk have gathered, eyes up, their hands out, as if they are catching rainfall but really they are touching their dead's light. As I break into the fresh air, I see Della lift her own hands, catching stories, catching losses that are not hers to catch.

They hold death in their hands.

I gasp at the evening air, close my eyes, but I cannot stop seeing those red-splashed faces.

Silas comes up behind me. 'Are you alright?'

'Show me the tree?' I need to see it.

He takes my hand with a softness that makes me jump. We follow the path through the village to the quiet square. Its branches are so full, I wonder how it still stands, how it has not dropped its head to the earth like a wearied man. The sun filters through its branches, and for a moment I am blinded. Red light strikes gashes in the land, in the houses, in our bodies. If this is a history, I do not want to know it. I turn from the Bleeding Tree.

'What is wrong with you people?' Tears are running down my cheeks. I touch them, frightened for a moment they really will be red.

'It is just our way.'

I hug my body tighter. 'This place is madness.'

HIM – THEN – Tithing

Silas slips from his covers and out onto the landing. He holds his ear to the door of his sister's bedroom. He hears only silence. He brings his hands together. The sudden clap makes him jump.

His ears aren't broken then.

He takes the stairs slowly, thinks of the books he has hidden beneath each step. They are not allowed 'shore books' his father says.

'They will rot your mind, boy. They will bruise it. And no son of mine will be ruined like that.'

But the boatmen who goes to the mainland once a month for supplies bring him some back, contraband hidden beneath their great coats. His father does not know. Nor his sister. One night he lifted the wooden steps and wrapped them in old T-shirts. Two steps down lie his adventure books, two steps below that are his mysteries. Sometimes, when he is alone in the house, he lifts up the steps and runs his fingers along their covers. He speaks to them. And they listen. They are wrapped like small people. Like bodies. His people.

Now though, he is quiet, holding his breath deep inside his belly. He follows the silence out of the door and then he sees them.

The lights. A path of candles, tapering through the street and into the distance. The flames are burning dancers, arms thrown out to touch the dark. They are beautiful, beautiful and doomed. No fire can live if it has nothing to burn.

A wind plays with the flames. It plays with his pyjamas, and he shivers.

'Stop it,' he says, and sighs when he realises he is talking to the wind. His heart drums and he can feel it through his whole body. Then it gets louder and he thinks, Can the Folk hear my drum? Can the Warden in his home in the earth?

He keeps walking, following the light. He realises then that the drums are real. They fill the night, fill his veins, and he wraps his arms round his middle and wrings himself out.

He can see men and women gathered around a fire. All the women *have babies in their arms. He sees his father, a tall grim figure standing apart from the rest. There is another man. He knows him. He works in the grocery store. Silas has given him his pocket money, and the man has given him oranges and hard-boiled sweets.*

He isn't holding sweet things now though. He holds a knife. It flashes in the fire. He flicks his wrist, and the women gather in a line, a procession of mothers.

Silas knows what this is. It's the Tithing.

HIM – THEN – Wet Fingers

He has never seen it before; he wishes he wasn't seeing it now. The mothers carry their babies to harm, and the men nod, like they have lost the muscle in their necks so their heads slip back and forth.

Silas brings his third finger to his eye and looks at the pale, stiff scars on the meat. Babies have their tithing at six months old. Everyone has the mark. He scratches his; he tried to wipe it off, he tried to wash it off. One time he even tried to pick it off. But you cannot remove a scar without leaving a scar, and now his is thicker than it was before.

The man with the knife takes a fistful of soil and rinses it over the baby's forehead. He takes the small baby's third finger and presses the tip of the knife into it. The baby's eyes widen and it screams. The man taps the blood into the earth. Three drops of red for the Devil.

He goes through the line until there is a soft, dark spot at his feet where the soil is wet. Mothers pinch their babies' fingers. Their babies will be safe now.

The Folk are always so frightened.

It makes him turn and walk back the way he came, along the path of lights, which was not made for him but for all the fearful mothers to follow.

When he returns home, he smells burning. He checks his body, worried he caught one of the candles on his way. But his body is fine. The smoke meets him at the bottom of the staircase, and that's when he sees them. The wooden steps have been ripped away and all his books are gone. Empty places.

'Oh!'

His legs loosen and he grabs the rail to pull himself up. Words come to his lips then dribble away.

His books! His books! His books!

He can hear the crackle. He can hear the voices too, his favourite voices from the stories, crying in the burn. There are tears on his cheeks, inside his mouth. He did not cry for the babies. He wanted to but he stopped himself. But he cries for his books.

His head throbs and he wishes he had never left his bed. If he had not left his bed, she wouldn't be punishing him now.

She doesn't like it when he wanders.

He whimpers, holds a hand to his mouth. He does not want to see. He does not want to see. But he must. As he rounds the corner, he waves away the smoke and sees his sister with ink on her fingers, crouching, feeding the fire. Her smile reaching, reaching. Right into his body and opening his bones.

She laughs. 'They were cold under the floor, Silas.'

His books are in the bath and they are burning.

HIM – Feral Women

Silas's mind hums with the memories of his childhood and the tithing. He plays another podcast to distract himself:

'So! Guys and Gals, we are BACK. And we want to say a big fucking thank-you for subscribing. You make it all worthwhile. We love that you love listening to us. Makes the narcissists in us smile like creepy little kids. Anyway-just-wanted-to-say-I-love-you-all-and I'd-fuck-the-fucking-lot-of-you.'

'Alright, alright, Rupe. That's quite enough of that. This week, we will be dedicating an episode to each of the sisters. We'll be exploring their pasts in more detail and illuminating some previously unknown facts about the case.'

'"Illuminating"? Seriously, man?'

'Be quiet.'

'What this guy is trying to "illuminate" to you is this: we are going to be focusing on Lily in this episode.'

'That's right. So I subscribe to the theory that Lily is only responsible for one of the murders.'

'Huh? You ... you subscribe ...? Huh?'

'I think she killed her father. I don't think she killed her mother.'

'How's that then? "Illuminate" us, why don't ya?'

'If you remember, there was a report that claimed the authorities found Lily hugging her mother's body. That they had to tear her away. That she cried and cried but she didn't touch her father or show any grief or remorse to him. What if the plan was always to kill the father? What if he abused them?'

'Ah. Young, pretty girls – or one of them was. So Daddy Pedley fiddles with his little gems, and the youngest snaps and fucks him up.'

'It's a possibility. Perhaps she wanted to escape. Wanted to save them all from him.'

'But what about Mama Pedley?'

'I think that's where Della comes in. She kills the mother – because she wants Lily to herself. She wants to possess her. And with both parents out the way, she has control.'

'So this is a chain of events, then? Lily kills Daddy because she wants freedom. Della kills Mummy because she wants control?'

'Yes.'

'Nah. I'm not buying it, mate. They both did it together. How could Lily lift those bodies up by herself? Della, fucking monster, that she is, could do it, no problem. They made it look like a double suicide.'

'I really believe Della is the culprit here. If you look at photographs, watch clips of the sisters, you'll see. They are always pulling away from each other. Always trying to put space between themselves. We have a victim and a villain.'

'So if Lily is a victim, is she in danger?'

'I believe so.'

'Where did they go? The sisters? Should someone be looking for the poor bitch?'

'They vanished. Or seemed to. No one quite knows. There are rumours that they are still in Cornwall, hiding away.'

'Hm.'

'Wherever they are, I hope Lily is alright.'

A pause.

Rupesh speaks, and his voice has lost its buoyancy. 'So ... so you think maybe one day we'll hear about a body turning up somewhere? Think maybe it will look like Lily Pedley?'

'I do. Yes. I think so. I've been saying for some time now that there is more to this case than everyone thinks. It's been glorified; it's been shined like a penny and it's caught the attention of the public. Two sisters murdering their parents. Yeah, wow, shocking.'

'But...'

'There's more to it. I think Lily is a victim too. But perhaps she doesn't even know it yet.'

'All monsters come out in the end, right, dude?'

'That's right. It's only a matter of time until the monsters inside Della come out.'

'Plural?'

'There's more than one monster inside that woman.'

Silas sees the sisters in the distance. There is something strange about their movements. Lily's body jolts, her head swinging back and forth, checking for Della. Her blonde hair snaps through the air. She trips, drags herself up and away. Away. To the Hanging Place.

Silas realises then, Lily is running.

HER – The Hanging Place

The bodies are gone, but the ropes remain.

They hang from the trees as if they still feel the weight of bodies. They are countless, curling, twitching. But they hold only ghosts now. A wind drives through this forest, the ropes sway, and the ghosts swing.

I can feel them all around me, almost see the men and women and children who were hanged here. This land has been hurt; the Folk dripped their hurts into the earth, and the earth is soft and bruised. A skim of it sits on me, on my chest, and makes it hard to breathe.

It is silent. I lift my eyes but the trees have taken the sky. There is just their darkness. I could not see any birds even if they were here. This piece of land has been left. Abandoned. And yet, as I run among the ropes, I think a reaper must still walk here, or a devil. Something lingers that is not just a memory.

The silence is shot through with the sound of footsteps. They sound more like dropped bullets. I run faster, head throbbing. I twist and glance over my shoulder. She is coming.

'I'm sorry!' I scream. 'I'm sorry.'

Her legs eat up the ground, her face is red. She wears a skirt, but her strong strides have split the sides.

'Della!'

Her name tears off into one long scream, and a fraction of my mind is surprised my body has such volume. It has always been so quiet. I did not know these lungs could make trouble. I imagine I have woken the ghosts. And I imagine, if there were birds, they would ride the wind into safer spaces.

I feel two hands snap round my shoulders. We fall onto the soil, and her body drives the breath from mine.

Tears drip from my chin. 'I'm sorry...'

'I told you to mind me, Lil.'

'I am tired of minding you.'

'Mother and Father are turning in their graves. Can you feel it, Lil? Can you feel them turn?'

'Please, Della. You're hurting me.'

'You're hurting yourself.'

'Stop it.'

'Mother is crying. Can you hear her? Inside the soil, she's crying. And they can hear you. Both of us.' She taps my chest, my heart. 'They can hear us wherever we go.'

I throw out my arms. 'Let go of me. Let go!'

She pinches my nose, takes fistfuls of soil and forces it between my lips. I cough and push it out with my tongue, but her hands keep filling, taking and filling, until my mouth is so full I cannot close it. My chest burns. There are knives inside me, and I am bleeding out breaths.

I feel pieces of soft soil inch down my gullet, and I choke. I do not want to die under these trees. I do not want these old swinging ropes in my eyes. I do not want to die under Della. A noise burbles from my chest, and I lash a hand against her face. A speck of blood drips into her eyebrow. But my hands are like those of a child, and that is all the damage they can do.

'Say you're sorry for upsetting me, Lil. Say you're sorry,' she says, and even the lonely trees shiver.

I drop my hands and close my eyes. I do not know what is worse: that I cannot breathe or that I cannot see the sky.

'Say you're sorry, Lil.'

I shake my head, and my body convulses. These arms move with a movement that does not belong to me. My legs kick at the ground, my back arches.

And I think, My ghost will make a ghost of her. I will never let her rest.

'Lily?'

I hear a voice, and open my eyes. Then, I feel Della's body lifted from mine, and I breathe through my nose, give the soil back to the earth. Silas stands with his arms around Della's body.

She grabs a hunk of my hair, whispers into my ear, 'I wish you were tied up in these trees.'

Then she turns and she walks away.

HIM – Gaia

'Are you alright?' Silas asks.

Lily puts a finger in her mouth and hooks out a glob of soil. Her eye are red, bloodshot. Two veins have burst, and it looks like bombs have gone off inside her eyes. She is panting.

He puts a hand on her belly. 'Breathe deep, through here. It will help.'

She does as he asks, keeping those red eyes on him. He breathes with her, deeply, as he did as a boy, as he learnt his sister's small violences.

'That's it. That's it. Keep going.'

'H-h-how?'

'I saw you. From my window. I saw you running.'

She takes a swell of his shirt in her hand. 'Tha-thank you.'

'Are you alright? I ... I thought she was going to kill you.'

'So did I.'

He crosses his legs, sits beside her, a hand resting on her shoulder. 'I heard what you both said. About Della minding you. Is it an older-sister-type thing?'

She nods, her head lowering, as if a poison is leaving her body. It will not harm the earth; the earth has never been clear.

'I told her I would not mind her. I was angry. It upset her. You can only bite your tongue so long before you bite through.'

He nods. 'I know. What was it like, growing up with her?'

'We were girls. We played games, we danced and told stories. When I was young, Mother would find red marks on our skin. She thought it was eczema. Then she thought we were scratching ourselves. But we were pinching each other. We called it "Growing flowers". Red petals all over our legs and arms.'

'Does she do it now?'

'We love our flowers.'

'I'm sorry.' Their skin is covered in filth. 'I had a sister too. A long time ago.'

'What was her name?'

'Gaia.'

She looks at him. 'Was your sister like mine?'

'Yes.'

'Where is Gaia now?'

'Gone.'

'Gone where?'

'She left.' He runs a hand across the land like a mechanic with a broken thing, but this thing wants to be broken. 'She left many years ago.'

'I'm sorry, cricket.'

They are silent then, breathing. The wood watches them as if it has enjoyed all that it has seen.

'What happened here, Silas?' Lily is staring about them with wide eyes. 'It's like when you wake up after a nightmare and you feel ill with it.'

He reaches out and tugs the nearest rope. It does not come down. They have been hanging here longer than he has been alive. 'A long time ago, Folk wanted to honour the Warden, so they gathered everyone they deemed a burden to the community and they hanged them. It's rumoured that they set fire to the ground, so when their souls left their bodies the smoke took them away, like a wind, to the mainland.'

She takes the hem of her shirt and rubs it along her teeth. 'We were warned. On the mainland.'

'Why didn't it change your mind?'

'I don't believe in your Warden,' she says, and takes a gulp of air. He does not entirely believe her. 'When we were girls, our mother and father separated us. Ripped us apart. Father took one, Mother took the other. Father drove for miles and miles, came to this part of the country. Heard the stories of the God-Forgotten, the strange lore of this island. And years later, here we are. We followed the stories. That's why we came.'

'You followed them a long way from home.'

'Why don't you take these ropes down?'

'If I did that, they would think I am opposing the Warden. And they would not care for it. It would be heresy.'

She nods. 'They would cast out one of their own? They would ... ostracize you?'

'Yes. It's not very different from the way a sister would upset her sister.'

She shrinks away from him as if he has cut her.

'Or a sister would upset her brother.'

She loosens, comes back into him.

'How did you cross the water? No one from the mainland would have brought you.'

'One man did.' She sighs. 'You know who we are. Where we have come from. Well, this man did too. And he brought us over here to hurt all of you.'

'You haven't hurt us yet.'

'We will. It's only a matter of time.'

'*You* won't.'

'What did she do to you?' she asks him suddenly. 'Your sister?'

'She wounded me every way you can think of.'

'That's why you knew what to do – to lie down to ground myself?'

He nods. 'One time she shook me so hard, I bit the edge of my tongue clean off.' He pokes it through his lips, and Lily winces. 'Another time, she gave me such a headache, it lasted for a week.'

'Why did your parents not stop her?'

'They didn't know. She was smart. She was smarter than them.'

She drags her knees up to her chin. She is twenty and looks ten. He is thirty-four and feels eighty-four. Her chin dips. Her shoulders sags. And he realises she is tired.

'You can sleep ... if you want? I'll um, stay. I'll wait by you. I won't let her near you. You can rest.' He feels awkward, clumsy. 'I don't mind.'

She studies him, looking for malice, he thinks. Then she lies back, closes her eyes. 'Thank you, Silas.'

He rests his head against a root in the ground, folding his hands across his stomach. He does not intend to but he closes his eyes, and soon he is sleeping, listening to the ropes above them swing and the ghosts move.

HIM — THEN — The Cruelty of Language

She takes Silas to the water.

Gaia undoes his laces, removes his socks, and he thinks, *This looks a lot like care, like kindness. But this will hurt. He can feel it in the soles of his feet. But he does not know how to stop it.*

'I want you to go into the water,' she says.

He looks at her. Has she forgotten? 'But ... but I can't swim.'

'I know.'

The tide licks at the shore, trying to reach him, closer and closer, as if there is something under it. A storm hums in the air, gathering clouds and casting out its shadows. There are so many shadows, it might as well be night.

'You've got your head so full of stories, but stories will make you unwell.' She pinches the skin on his forehead, and he winces. Then her fingers go all the way around his head and under his ears, as if she is trying to find a way to get in. 'Zip, zip,' she says.

'I like my stories. Why will they make me unwell?' His stories don't have her inside them.

'Would you like me to tell you a true story?'

He shakes his head, and she smiles. He does not trust that smile.

'Once there lived a boy who read stories all day long.'

'Like me?'

'Exactly like you. This boy had hundreds of books – old books, new books. Books about knights and thieves and princess and witches. About fairy tales with no fairies and cold desserts and waterless oceans. He coveted them. His books were stacked so high, he felt he could climb them and keep climbing all the way to the moon. His mother and father worried for him.

'"You need to sleep," they said to him. "You need to rest. You are pale and thin. You are ill. Get rid of some of your books. You do not need them all."

'This made the boy angry. He wanted to read every book that had ever been written. He wanted to know every story ever told. But he couldn't read fast enough. So do you know what he did next?'

Her face looms above him. She is still tickling the back of his head. Please don't let her find a way in, he thinks.

'What – what did he do?' Silas asks, tongue thick and clumsy in his mouth.

She smiles. 'He ate his stories.'

'He...?'

'He tore the pages from his books and he swallowed them. All those words sat in his stomach and made it sore. He cried and cried, rubbing his poor belly ... but he did not stop. His parents tried to take his books away from him but he found more. And the more he ate, the more his stomach hurt.'

'Did he sick the words up?'

She shakes her head. 'No. The words found another way of coming out.' She runs a finger across his neck. 'They came out of his skin.'

'What?' Silas says, but he really wants her to stop now. He does not like this boy, he does not want to know more.

'Words ran down his back and between his toes and got lost in his hair. All those things from his stories stuck inside his skin. He tried to wash them away. He scrubbed so hard, he cried. But the words would not go.'

'Then what happened? Did he stop eating?'

'No. He was a greedy boy, a strange boy. He could not stop. His father was ashamed of him and cast him out. So the boy walked into the sea, thinking the salt would clear him. But the boy was wrong. His body was full of words, and they were so heavy, they pulled him down, down to the bottom.'

'He drowned?'

'No,' she says. 'He's still there.'

Silas shivers, makes his hands into claws and tucks them under his arms. 'He's at the bottom of the sea?'

'He lives there. And he can't have any books, so he reads his own skin. Over and over again. The same words. They must make him mad after so long a time. He shouldn't have been greedy.'

'But stories aren't ... bad?'

'Aren't they?' She taps his skull. 'They made the boy mad, then they made him lonely.'

'That's sad.'

'He's so lonely, Silas. I hear him crying sometimes, you know.' She lifts his arms out of his coat. 'He calls for his mother. Even his father. He wants a friend. But he has been down there so long, he doesn't know they have all gone.'

Silas holds himself, stamping his feet. 'It's cold, Gaia.'

'I know. I know.'

'Can I have my coat back?'

'No.' She removes his shirt. 'This boy has been alone for so many years. I don't want to hear him crying anymore. He needs a friend.'

'I can't be his friend. I can't swim.'

'You don't want him to be lonely, Silas, do you?'

'N-no.' Tears are coming into his eyes. His heart is louder than the waves. 'No. No!' he shouts. 'You're just trying to upset me. You're being mean. You're just being mean! Stop it!'

She strokes his hair again, zip zip. Where are his seams?

'Silas, you're being selfish. Do you want to be like that boy? Do you want words, lots of frightening words, on your skin? You can't get them off, you know. No matter how hard you rub.'

'No...'

'So go and see the boy. You'll find the way – can't you hear him calling to you?' She turns him round and points into the water. Silas licks the salt from his lip. He is panting and he can't quieten the sob coming up his throat.

'I can't swim. I can't swim.'

'Don't let the boy be lonely.'

'Please ... I don't want to.'

She walks him forward. She's found it, she's found his opening. The noise in his mouth breaks into the air. Birds lift up and leave them. Even the storm halts its movement, calms its voice to better hear his begging.

'Silas, do as you're told. You must do as you're told.'

'But I'll drown. I'll die, Gaia...'

'You won't. You'll live with the boy at the bottom of the sea. And you'll tell each other stories.'

'I don't want any more stories. I don't like them anymore...'

'You'll tell him of fairy tales with no fairies—'

'No!'

'You'll tell him of knights and thieves and cold deserts and waterless oceans—'

'NO. PLEASE! I don't want to go into the water. I don't want to.'

'You'll stay down there with him so I don't have to look at you. Perhaps I'll find some words of yours washed up on the beach. Perhaps I'll stand on the edge and wave at you sometimes.' She smiles, and he wants to be sick. 'But probably I won't.'

Her hands drive him on. He claws at her, but she is so much bigger than him. He screams but her voice is loudest. He tells her he will never pick up another story. He begs, but begging has never helped with Gaia.

She pushes him forward into the water. Rocks pierce his skin. He cries, he does not think he will stop. He will drown the boy all over again. He will make another ocean.

'Go on. He's waiting for you, Silas.'

And so Silas goes, picking up his feet and making himself not mind the cuts. He looks at his pale skin. Is that a word there, inside his wrist? Is that one under his fingernail? He lifts his eyes and follows a voice he cannot hear.

He goes to meet the boy at the bottom of the sea.

'Gaia weaponised stories.'

Silas has not looked away from the river for a long time now. He is so still, he is like the earth. I wonder if he moves, will the ground move with him?

'After she told me all of this,' he says, 'I went down to the water. I could live my life with the boy. We would both be boys forever. And that would be that. But my father found us and he ripped me out of harm's way.'

Silas takes a breath.

I wrap an arm around his shoulder, bring some warmth to his cold.

'How did your sister react?'

'She was furious. She set fire to a grave. I don't remember who the grave belonged to. I think it was my great-great grandfather's. His name was Silas too. Perhaps that's why she chose it.'

His eyes are those of a boy again. He watches the river move, unblinking, wide. I could rap on his head with my knuckles and I don't think it would bring him back.

'I'm sorry that all happened to you.'

'I have not touched the water since. This is part of the reason I have never left.' He smiles suddenly, and his eyes come to me. 'I was going to cross though. I was going to do it. Really. The morning after you came. But I met you and I wanted to know you ... so I delayed.'

'Will you still go?'

He sighs. 'Perhaps.'

'She had a strange nature, your sister.'

I squeeze his hand. I think something inside him sees something inside me and understands it. This feral language is one we both speak.

'Why does her name ring a bell? Gaia – what does it mean?'

'It means Earth. In Greek Mythology, she was the first immortal. She has power over the land and the sea. She lives in the soil, in the mountains, in everything that grows. She is where everything began.'

'Strong name.'

'It wasn't strong enough for my sister.' He laughs. 'The biggest name a girl could have, and she broke it.'

'Was that fairy tale real? Inside a book somewhere? Or did she make it up to frighten you.'

'It's real. It's a local legend. That boy supposedly lived decades ago, and he was spoilt and greedy. The children here stand on the cliff and sing, tell him the story of himself. And he listens. It's a tale many of the Folk tell their children when they are young. A cautionary tale. But my sister didn't use it to caution me, to guard me against bad things. She wanted to drown me with it.'

'You were lucky your father was close by at the time.'

'If my sister was the earth, then my father was the sky. He was the only one who could control her. Or try to, anyway. Mother never stood a chance.'

'She reminds me of Della.'

Silas looks at me. 'Somehow ... I think your sister is worse.'

I try to cover my surprise. 'How so?'

Silas frowns, opens his mouth then closes it. 'With Gaia, you could read her face. You knew what she was thinking. It was always obvious, even if it upset your stomach to see it. And it really upset mine. But with Della ... it's not so clear. There's a lot that goes on behind that face of hers, and I don't think that any of it's good. But what is most worrying is that I can't tell what any of it is.'

'You're right. None of it is good.'

'Was she always like that?'

'Yes. And when we were children, she would tell me stories too. Such bad stories, I used to think they would sit in the bottom of my mind and start to rot like leaves. I'd shake my head and listen for the rustle.'

'What happened in the stories?'

A wind picks up the ribbon in my hand. Silas catches it with quicker reflexes than I have ever seen. He ties it gently back round my wrist.

'Thank you.'

'You're welcome.' He smiles at me. 'What happened in the stories?'

I smile, nudge him with my elbow. 'I cleared out those leaves a long time ago, cricket.' I tap my temple. 'They were getting heavy.'

'I understand.' He pauses. 'Can I ask you something?'

'Of course.'

'The world thinks it knows you. You and Della killed your mother and father. You're pariahs, witches, murderers. You have lots of names, lots of faces. But what's the truth, Lily? What really happened to your parents?'

HIM – Damned Tales

'Have you spent much time with the Pedley women?'

'Yes,' Silas responds. 'Have you?'

Stina shrugs. 'Not much. They interest me though. Especially the big one. She is like us, I think.'

'Like us?'

'Yes.' Stina does not elaborate.

They stand inside her shop. She sits behind the counter, drawing Della Pedley with fires inside her palms, and Lily Pedley with the ears of a wolf. The coal smudges and makes the girls look frightening. Well, one of them anyway.

'What do you know about them?' she asks.

'Their story is different from the one we have heard. It wasn't a suicide. It was something else.'

'What have they told you?'

'The truth.'

'Really? The truth about what happened?'

Silas nods, solemnly.

Stina holds her head in her hands, mouth hanging open. 'What's the truth of them? Tell me.'

'Poison,' he whispers. 'Poison, Stina. Fed to their parents over time. It built up in their system and killed them in their beds. Then they were strung up so everyone would think they had committed suicide.'

Stina's eyes widen. 'But how ... how?'

'There are poisons which are nearly undetectable, like arsenic. You have to check the heart to know it's there.' Silas pauses. 'They were killed slowly, over the course of a year. And the pathologists didn't think to check their hearts. He was too busy with their necks.'

Stina touches her throat. 'Murderers. So that's why they aren't in a cell right now, then?'

'Yes.'

'Clever girls. Frightening girls.'

'Hm.'

'They did it together?'

'No. No, one of them is innocent. I'm sure you already know which one. Innocent and afraid. She's been afraid her entire life.'

'Why didn't their parents get far away from them? Why didn't they escape beforehand?'

'They were their parents, which means none of this was simple. Perhaps they loved them still, somewhere very deep inside.'

Stina is silent, then she says quietly, 'Do you think some part of Sarah and Oliver Pedley knew that their daughter was death counting down? Do you think they had some sense of what was to come when she was born?' Stina's face is glass, cold and emptied. 'Do you think they knew they raised a reaper?'

'I don't know.'

'Hmm. They've brought quite a story to our shore,' Stina says.

'Do you believe it?'

'Yes and no. And you?'

'Yes. I do,' Silas says; then: 'This must stay between us.'

'Why?'

'If the world discovers the girls are here, the world will follow them.'

'I see.'

'This stays between us.'

'Yes, Silas. You know best.' Stina nods. 'You always do.'

HIM – Bone Music

Silas opens the door for her, and she timidly takes a step then quickly takes it back. 'My ... um ... my feet are dirty.'

'I don't mind dirty feet.'

'Oh ... are you sure? They are really dirty. Mud.'

Her eyes fix onto a loose thread in Silas's shirt. There they remain. Her cheeks are flushed and her hands still cup her stomach, as if there is thread loose in her body. Perhaps that is why she stares at his shirt; she wants the thread to stop her body coming undone. She can have his thread. He does not mind.

He leads her into the kitchen and offers her a seat.

She does not smile. She simply nods. 'Your house looks like a church. Like it's been stretched.'

'It does. But you won't find any churches here.' He fetches the biscuit tin and presses it into her hands. 'Help yourself. There are some nice ones in there.'

'Thank you. Do you ... do you have a tissue?' She takes one from his hand and presses it to the soles of her feet.

'Why do you and your sister walk everywhere barefoot?'

'I don't know.'

'You don't know? Doesn't it hurt?'

'It's just something we have always done.'

Silas nods. Then he says, 'The Folk tell stories about you. And especially about Della.'

'What stories?'

'That you were called to us. That your sister heard the calling.'

'Have you ever seen your Warden?'

'No.'

'Have you ever heard him?'

'No.'

She sighs. 'This place is madness.'

He takes the biscuit tin and picks out one of the nice ones. 'We are all madness.'

'Are *you* madness as well?'

'I'm the giver of madness.'

She smiles, and he settles into his chair.

'Can I ask you a question?' he says.

'Alright.' Her eyes go to that piece of thread.

'What happened to Della's hand? It looks crooked. The way her wrist sits at an angle.'

'When we were girls, we played games. And sometimes those games upset us.'

'You're not talking about chess then?' Silas tries to bring a smile but one is not forthcoming.

'No. I'm not talking about chess.'

'Then what?'

'Games we played with our bones.'

HIM – Fragile Gods

'The games always hurt in the end.

'At first Mother and Father did not know we played them. We didn't keep ourselves entertained with boards and wooden pieces but with our own bodies: who could drink the most water; who could keep the sickness down for the longest after turning in circles; who could throw themselves against a wall without breaking something.'

'Strange games,' Silas says.

'I prayed sometimes for it to end but nothing helped me. So I stopped praying. Even gods are afraid of my sister.'

'We live in a world of gods and devils, but they are not much use to us,' Silas says.

'We broke her wrist.'

'She broke it herself.'

Lily nods. 'We broke it together.'

Silas gestures to her fingers. 'Is that why you hold your stomach? You have all those dead prayers at the bottom of you.'

She nods. 'They give me stomach ache.'

Silence rests between them. Silas is reminded of Gaia, of her infinite, impossible cruelties.

As if she knows his thoughts, Lily asks, 'What was your sister like?'

'Mother and father of mine wanted a boy but she was born a girl. It made her angry. She had to have somewhere to put all that anger, so she put it into me.'

'I'm sorry, cricket,' she says. 'For your loss.'

'Hm?'

'For the loss of yourself.'

'I'm sorry for yours.' He points to her belly, which she is still holding.

Lily slumps across the table. 'My dreams hurt sometimes. Do yours?'

'Always.'

'What do you dream about?'

'That Gaia will come back. And you?'

'I dream about Mother and Father. My mother was beautiful, you know. She had such a delicate neck, and I remember seeing her dot perfume there with her little finger. Violence didn't suit that neck. I dream about her. She blames me for what happened.'

'It's not your fault.'

'I killed her. I killed them both. It's my fault.'

'A child isn't responsible for saving her parents, Lily.'

Lily sighs. 'When our mother gave us dolls, she was always so disgusted because her daughter would fill the sink and hold their heads under, wiggling their fingers so it looked like they were struggling. They died in so many ways of so many different things. I think now it was practice. That these deaths were always going to become the deaths of our parents. Dad used to say, "My beautiful daughter, small and perfect and sweet, but she has a beast in her eyes. As she grows, so does the beast."'

Lily brings her eyes to him, then she rises to leave.

'Do you really not think your sister will come back?'

Silas shakes his head. 'No. Not to me.'

'What made her go?'

'I don't know.'

'Whatever it was, can it take Della too?'

HER – Skin Drum

Girls have come to the God-Forgotten.

Hand in hand, they come along the pier. This place is cruel in daylight, but it is worst in the gloaming, when darkness sticks to the edges of the land. Now it holds its breath. The land watches. And we watch too.

The Folk have come now to see the newcomers, standing in a line like a strike through the earth. Their eyes are unblinking. I want to run down to the girls, push them into the water. *Leave, leave*, I would say, *do not take up lives here. Be mindful of the stories, be mindful of the men and women who look at you now like gathered fruits. Fear has turned them.*

The Folk begin to sing. The men first, the deep growl of their chests like unspent thunder. Then the women and children lift their hands to the air, beat them together. This is no applause, this is no welcoming. This is a chant, a lament, a skin drum, a calling-down of the Devil to meet maidens.

'Who are they? Why have they come here?' I ask Silas.

He stands by my side, his eyes heavy and low. 'I don't know.'

There are three of them, young, with wide eyes. Still sweet and smelling like their mothers. They must be in their twenties, with mud on their legs and smiles on their lips. They do not know this place. They have not heard the stories. If they had, they wouldn't be smiling.

'Travellers come here sometimes. They are curious. They want to see the land, to speak to the community. They want to explore.' He pauses. 'The men here are always pleased when the travellers are women.'

Folk watch the travellers and there is something concerning there. They have spent too long in fear and isolation. They are undone by the newness of the girls.

The song is mournful, slow, tipping into the world the way rain tips across skin, drowning. It is wordless, yet it is tears and bitter winds. It moves between bodies, cresting, and lilting, it throws out its slow arms and makes slow hurts.

'What does the song mean?' I ask.

'It means sad things.' Silas looks at me, deep enough that I can feel his eyes go through mine to the back of my head. 'Are you sure you want to know?'

'I want to know,' Della says, her eyes taking in the girls. 'Tell me.'

He takes my hand. And I am grateful. 'Hundreds of years ago, men would go to the mainland looking for girls, brides. These girls would give the island children, fresh blood. New generations. And when the men came back, they would sing. It's a hunting song. A gathering song.'

'That's horrifying.'

'Is it so different to the cruelty of any man wanting a new girl, a replacement for an old wife?'

I open my mouth. Close it.

The Folk move, gathering to the girls, who are then guided across the shore, along the cliff path, and we all look up at them, their bodies above. They stand at the edge of the earth like young fires, fresh wounds.

Then I hear the girls' voices rise, half laughing, half humming, because they like the attention. The clumsy, lightness of their innocence burning. Do they not know they lament themselves? *You are singing your own hunting song*, I want to say. *Don't you know, this place will upset you? The stories have hurt the Folk, they have hurt me.*

There is a girl who is smaller than the others, younger perhaps. She is moving her lips but she is not singing.

'They shouldn't have come here,' I say.

I am talking to Silas but he does not answer.

HER – Alchemy

The girls do not know what it is they have found here.

Two have travelled from a small town in America, the name of which I do not know how to say. They are full of smiles, a freshness to the Folk – like fruit. But fruit is made to be devoured. The men look on the girls as all men look on young things, to cut into them and waste their sweetness.

The girls have not heard the stories. They know nothing of the Devil.

They are in the street now, children dancing round their legs. Della's eyes go from me to them, drawing a thread like a spider's silk.

'I wonder what their names are,' I say.

A low hum starts in the back of Della's throat; that's where she keeps her chaos. A tuneless song. I know this song well.

'They look so unburdened … so fresh.' I do not feel fresh anymore. I have not for some time.

I walk closer, tap one of the girls on the shoulder, hook my arm through hers and guide her away from the Folk. I will take her away from this, I will help her.

'Listen to me. Listen. This place … it's not what you think it is.'

'I'm sorry?'

'You've not heard the stories, but this land is full of madness.'

Her face twitches. 'I don't know what you mean. It seems totally cool here. The Folk are so welcoming. I think we're going to stay a little longer. We like it. We only came here by process of elimination really. We thought this island would be quieter than Skye or Scilly. But it's beautiful.'

'Haven't you noticed anything odd about the Folk?'

'No … I mean, they all dress the same, which is a bit weird but…'

'Look at them!' I say, with a sharpness to my voice that makes her jump. 'Look at them looking at your friends. Can you see how they touch them? It's like they are petting them. Isolation has knotted them up. They might mean you no harm but that does not mean they are like the rest of us.'

'They're just being friendly.'

Della is watching me from across the street.

'Did you know they used to hunt each other here?'

'What?'

'They used to hunt each other. For fun. For sport. They think something lives under the land. This place has so many stories. It's full of ghosts. The Folk are frightened of their past. Of their own home. You should take your friends and leave. You came on your own boat, didn't you?'

'Well, yes but—'

'Take it back.'

She shakes her head, her chin thrusting out. 'No. No. We like it here.'

'You must.'

'Why are *you* here? Why don't *you* leave, if it's so bad?'

I look for words but I have none. 'I have my own ghost. And she won't let me leave her.'

HIM – Trouble in the Throat

The girls are troubled.

Silas follows them with his eyes, notes the curled shape of their spines. Their faces bare. They move through the street, silently, as if their bodies have run out of words.

He sees one of the girls, Olive, by herself. 'Hello,' he says. 'How are you? I don't see much of you at the inn anymore.'

'Oh,' she says. 'Oh. Fine. Fine.'

'What about the others?'

'They're fine too.'

'You've been here three weeks now. How long did you mean to stay?' he asks.

She looks at him vacantly. 'We have already stayed longer than we meant to.'

'Why?'

She shivers. 'Curiosity.'

'Is something bothering you?'

Olive shakes her head, then nods. 'It's nothing anyone has done ... It's just this place. It gets under your skin, you know. Well, I suppose you can't know. You've always lived here.'

'What troubles you?'

'It's the land, the stories. They...' She pauses. 'They've gotten into my head. And I can't get them out. It's like they are inside me now, and if I leave, I'll be tearing out a lung. You know?'

'I understand. We have strange tales. We cannot help it. But you can leave. You are not stuck here.'

Olive nods. 'I can. I can.'

Her eyes wander. Silas follows her gaze to Orsan. He is stroking a girl's back. Silas realises it is the girl with the curly hair, the one Olive came with, Moss. He cannot place her age. She has the innocence of a child but she looks older.

'I don't like him.'

'Who? Orsan? Not many of us do.'

Olive shivers. 'I don't like the way he's touching Moss. It's not right.'

Silas sees it too. Orsan pinches Moss's lobe, strokes the bones of her ear. She pulls away, and he pulls her back.

'He's always had a temper. He's always been trouble, even when we were boys.'

Olive wraps her arms round her body. 'I wish he would leave her alone. He's been following her round a lot. She can't shake him.'

Silas has noticed this too.

'Have you met the sisters?' he asks. 'They live at Lower Tor.'

'Yes,' Olive says. 'One of them is very sweet. One of them is ... I don't know. She looks like a monster. She's so ugly ... And she's always saying weird things.'

'Like what?'

'Warnings.'

'What sort of warnings?'

'To be careful. Of stories, of nice faces. Makes no sense.'

'This place has been different since they came.'

'Oh. Do they like it here?'

'One of them does.'

Olive pauses. 'I think this place feels like a hand round my throat. I'm sorry, I know it's your home. But I feel like every day the fingers get tighter and tighter. And soon I won't be able to breathe at all.'

'Are you really breathing now?'

'No. I don't think I am.' She looks at her shoes, as if willing them to move her away from this place. 'Do you understand that feeling?' Her eyes are on him then, wide, beseeching.

'Yes,' he says. 'I am familiar with that feeling.'

HER – Artillery

'Do you think you can ever really know someone?' I ask.

We are by the river. The water bites my legs it is so cold; wolves in the water. I do not pull away, there is some part of me that likes their bite.

Silas picks at the scar on his finger, the one they all have. Only, his is bigger than the rest. I wonder why. A knife slipping? A heavy-handed cutter? He is silent, then he is full of words:

'I don't think you can ever know anyone,' he says, throwing his scab to the river. 'We all wear faces.'

'What do you mean?'

'I remember my father telling me a story about a god. A cautionary tale. I was a boy, so I didn't fully understand it, but it was about pretending to be someone you are not.'

'What was the god's name?'

'He didn't have one. He belonged to no mythology, no religion, so I wondered if he was something my father made up.'

'Oh.'

'He was unkind, as all gods seem to be – arrogant and merciless. Yet he could change his face to deceive those around him. To trick women into his bed, to torment ordinary men, to bend the world to his will.' Silas pauses, then wonders aloud: 'If identity is like a weapon, how many identities can you fit into your artillery?'

'Perhaps we never run out of room,' I say.

Perhaps we are full of guns, I do not say. I have so very many faces. Pariah, I am called, witch. Murderer. I imagine I am empty of heart, of vein, of nerve, of human movement, and when someone comes to undress me, they pull back a door, and inside my ribs is a weapon room.

Silas nods. 'That didn't help the god. He changed his face so many times, in the end, when he looked in a river, he could not recognise himself. He had one blue eye, one brown, mismatched lips. A man made up of a hundred men. It frightened me at the time. I was a boy.

I spent all night looking at myself in the mirror, making sure I was still myself. I remember tugging my front tooth, just to make sure.'

'That's sad. Why did your father tell you that story?' I ask. 'Was he teaching you to be honest?'

Silas laughs. 'No. No, he was teaching me to be clever. To be smarter than a god. Identity is a powerful thing.'

'I know it is.'

Silas looks at me. 'Do you want to know what happened to the god?'

'What happened to the god?'

'All of his identities frightened him. He had a girl's voice in his mouth. The hands of an old man. So many kinds of people in his body. He travelled for a long while, and every mirror he came across, he looked in and saw these faces. So he moved on. Looking, always looking, for a mirror that told him the truth. But the truth was gone. And no mirror would give him back to himself.'

'I pity him.'

'The further he travelled, the wearier he became. And then one day, he stopped at a river and cried. The river burst its banks with all the tears. He was in ruins. He was broken ... and so weary he drowned himself.' Silas pauses. 'Eventually a farmer found him. But do you want to know something sad? The farmer did not see a many-faced monster. He saw a young man with two of the same blue eyes, matching lips. One man, one identity.'

'So ... it was all in his mind?'

'Yes.'

'None of it was real?'

'It was real to him. So it was real enough.'

I sigh. 'Poor god.' Then, 'Did anyone ever know him – as himself?'

Silas smiles. There is something inside his smile and I do not know what it is.

'No. The women he tricked into his bed and raped knew him differently to the men who fought with him in wars, on councils. If they told you a story of his life, it would be about countless characters.'

'There is something sad about being unknown.'

'My father said he should have been smarter. That he shouldn't have lost himself to his games. He could have won them all.'

'Games can be hard to stop playing.'

Silas nods. 'To answer your question: no, I don't think you can ever know someone. We are all wearing faces to get through the world. We are all pretending, slipping on new identities.'

'So who are you?' I ask.

'Oh, I'm a devil.'

I laugh, splash him. He laughs too.

'And who are you?' he asks.

'I'm a wolf. My name – Pedley – in Anglo-French translates to "Wolf-Foot".'

'And what about your sister? I suppose she is a wolf too, then?'

'She's a strange thing, my sister. Not many people can put their finger on who she is.'

Silas touches the marks on his finger. 'You can though?'

'Yes,' I say. 'We used to play a game when we were young. We'd pretend to be other people, just like every young girl in the world, I guess. Then we pretended to be each other.'

'In what way?'

'We were like your god. We took each other's faces. We stole each other's voices right from each other's throats.'

'Who won?'

I smile sadly. 'Who do you think?'

Silas nods. 'You can make people do anything if you wear the right face. Make them believe anything.'

I laugh, because isn't that the truth?

'Are we all gods then? Are we all on our way to the river?'

'No. The smart ones keep their feet dry.' Silas winks, pulls my legs from the river and dries them with his sleeves. 'There. You're dry now.' He pauses. 'What is it with you and rivers?'

I shrug. 'Memories.'

'Does your sister come here too?'

'No,' I say. 'She's scared of rivers.'

'Why?'

'Memories.'

'I overheard a conversation between her and Stina. Stina mentioned that word and your sister jumped. Like she'd been shot.'

I wrap my hands round my stomach. 'Like I said, memories.'

'Of what?'

I breathe. 'Dead things in water.'

HER – Devil-Marked

Time passes, and now the girls are like the Folk: dressed in white, with that strangeness of their eyes, even the words from their lips. Two months have gone by and they have new tongues, and new minds to match.

They are not travellers anymore. They have settled. They are Folk.

But there is something torn in them, something giving more and more each day. They have lost their smiles, or had them taken. Their feet do not dance. They are quieter. Innocence dripping out of them. They know now, I think. They have this land's stories in their heads; the rot of this land is on their fingers.

They do not look like girls anymore. They will never look like girls again.

I have rarely caught sight of my sister since their arrival; she is gone all day, going between them like a bad wind, whispering in their ears. And the sight of her curling herself around them puts a sickness in my belly.

I do not know who they should be more frightened of. This community, its history. Or my sister.

I see Della now with one of them, in the distance, walking the cliff. The girl is the eldest of the crop, with long brown hair to her waist and rings on every finger. She is the most beautiful of them all. And she seems to be Della's favourite.

She and my sister gather flowers in their pockets, talking quietly so I cannot hear what they say. But Della's mouth is heavy with words. I can see them tumbling out as the girl's face loses its colour. And yet my sister puts a gentle hand on her back and strokes it, as if she is comforting her.

'What is she saying?' Silas asks beside me.

Whatever it is, she shouldn't be saying it.

'I don't know.' I look at her pockets, full with colour. 'Della can always find the sharpest flowers.'

'Look at the girl's face. I saw her earlier – she was alright. Now she looks like she's dying from the inside out.'

'My sister,' I say simply.

He shakes his head. 'What is she telling her?'

'This is what happens. It's easy to find someone's weaknesses. You just have to press until they give.'

'The girl is about to give.'

'What's her name?'

'I think it's Verity.'

'Can you take Verity back to the village?' I ask Silas.

He nods. 'Alright. Will I see you tomorrow?'

'Yes.'

'Shall I meet you at my house?'

'No. Let's go to the river again.'

He frowns, then shrugs and walks off.

I see him wrap a gentle arm around the girl, guide her away. Della remains where she is, stood with more stillness than the earth. Her eyes come to me then.

'What are you doing?' I ask.

'Don't forget to mind me, Lil.'

Silas is still within earshot, and he turns, looks at us both.

'What game are you playing with her?' I demand. 'You with all your bad words. You're full of them.'

'My words? You're right. I am full of words.' A cruel smile twists her mouth. 'Things about the Red Room and about fires burning.' She strokes my cheek, and a shiver runs all the way to my fingers.

'You know, you have always been full of bad things. Stories you told me as a girl to frighten me. And now, you are doing the same with her. Isn't that right?'

'Lily?' Silas shouts.

I wave him away. 'Take Verity away.'

He does as I ask. Then I mind my sister. 'Don't talk to her. Don't even look at her. I'll protect her from you, Della.'

She rests a hand on my shoulder, and I am reminded of the difference between us. I am small enough to be lost in the rain. And Della, she is a moon passing across the sun.

'I'll do as I like,' Della spits into my ear.

HIM – The Howling

The storm has come to the women as if they've cast out their arms and gathered it to their bodies. They stand at the headland, over Hell's Mouth, and the clouds are dark like blood when it dries. Thunder makes the land shiver. Silas really does live on the back of a bird and it is shaking rain from its feathers.

Silas does not like the rain.

It reminds him of his sister, and the night she took his hand and led him to the Howling, a cabin at the bottom of the mountain where they used to take birthing mothers in the old times so the men did not have to hear their screams. He was seven, and he had forgiven her for burning his books, as he forgave her for everything, but he still mourned them in a way he had never mourned his grandparents' deaths. His books were his people.

'You'll like the Howling,' Gaia told him, with a too-wide smile that made his stomach cold. 'It's deep in the trees. Only a few of us even know exactly where it is. Rumour is you can still hear women screaming. A lot of mothers died giving the island children.'

'Why are we going there?'

'Because I want to see if you howl.'

'But ... why?'

She did not answer, only took his arm and walked him along a path to the cabin at the bottom of the mountain. Then she fastened twine round his wrist and left him tied to a hoop in the wall. The cabin was small, with holes in the roof and no lights. The night gathered its arms around him, and he listened to the sounds. He tried to bite through the twine and cut his tongue. He told himself he was safe, but then doubt curled up his throat and he screamed.

When he wasn't screaming, he listened to the rain. It ran through the holes in the roof and dripped onto his shoulder, and for a moment, he thought it was the spit of some animal come to chew him up.

His sister left him all night. When the morning came, his voice no longer worked as it should. He'd broken his throat with all his howling.

Silas does not like the rain.

But these women do not mind the storm. It is the Pedley sisters. He wants to tell Lily to come away from Hell's Mouth. He wants to drag her back – from the edge and from her sister too, which is somehow the same thing. But then he realises the second woman is too tall to be Lily.

It is one of the travellers. Verity.

Della places a hand on her back, as if she is guiding her, moving her forward. Della's eyes are wide, concerned and her mouth moves so quickly he cannot see the words.

What is she saying?

Della gestures to the fall below their feet, the rocks which split the air, or is it the mainland in the distance with its warm lights?

The girl holds her stomach as if she is trying to hold together the shape of herself. Her pale cheeks wrinkle, and her fingers cut into her palms. 'NO!' she screams. 'NO! I don't want to do this!'

Della leans close so their bodies are flush. Her lips move above the girl's ear. He imagines even the clouds pull themselves closer to hear these words. What is she saying?

'You must,' Della says. 'You must.'

The girl shakes her head, then somewhere between one breath and the next breath, she opens her arms, and Silas thinks she looks like a bird, a strange, delicate bird the world has not seen before. She steps and she steps and she steps off the earth. For a moment, he thinks this storm she has gathered in her sadness will save her, it will fly her across the water to the lights.

But it does not.

She flies down into the sea.

HER – Death Procession

The Folk lift her body from the rocks and take her away. The blood has spread out from her – a red shadow. Only, when she moves it remains where it is, a tattoo on the earth. The Folk who carry her wear strange faces, exposed, raw. I have not seen them like this before. They are too quiet, too reserved.

I follow the cliff path away and knock on Silas's door. 'Have you heard?'

His eyes are gummed with sleep, a sickly sheen coating his skin. 'I saw it.'

'What?'

'I saw what happened.'

'Do backpackers always kill themselves?' There are nettles in my voice, and he catches the barbs.

'She was pregnant, the girl. She didn't want it. The rumour is that the child was Orsan's. He ... he raped her. She was afraid and lost. But it was because of your sister she killed herself. She whispered into her ear before she jumped. Della did this.'

I open my mouth, and close it.

'I saw them on the cliff together. I thought it was you and Della, then I realised it was Verity. I watched as your sister told her to jump, Lily. I watched it happen.'

The procession of bodies pass the window. Their heads are lowered. The girl has been covered over with a sheet, but I can still see the shape of her, the delicate curl of her nose, the bumps of her knuckles. I realise that the Folk are not sad. They are afraid.

I follow them past Kit's house, past my own house, to the village. My hands shiver so violently I look like I have wild animals inside my pockets. Silas is watching me, confused, curious. Every man and woman stands outside their door to watch the body pass. I look along their faces, then I stop.

I see Della. Her arm is hooked round the shoulder of one of the other newcomers. The young girl with curly hair, who I noticed the night they arrived. Anger bends my body into a new shape. I curl my fingers, then I run to my sister and I rip the traveller from her side.

'Come with me. Come,' I say to the girl.

The girl does not resist. Della takes a step, eyes like bullets and their smoking guns. But I am saying, 'Leave her be. Leave her be.'

'What is your name?'

The girl and I sit with our feet in the river, turning rocks with our toes as the fragile sun tries to burn our necks. I lost Silas in the procession, and Della has not followed us here. My mind still has not settled since then. The shivers are back in my fingers. So I take out the red ribbon and twist it round them tight to make them still.

The girl is small. Her shoulders punch through her shirt. I count all the bones of her I can see, and think, I shouldn't be able to see these parts of her. How old is she? She looks older but she seems so innocent, like a child.

Her voice when it wobbles through her mouth is light and sweet. 'My name is Moss. Moss Gulliver.'

'I'm Lily.'

'I know who you are.'

'Yes, I suppose you must.' The ribbon hurts me, but I keep pulling it.

'You did a bad thing. You killed your daddy,' she says, tucking her hands under her armpits. I wonder how old she is to speak like this.

'What was it like?' she asks. 'Killing your daddy?'

Has she forgotten about Mother?

Silence swells between us. Then the soft, breathless sound of her crying. I squeeze her little fingers, hope I do not break them.

'Do you miss your family?'

She shakes her head.

'I can help you get back to the mainland.'

'I don't want to go home.'

'Don't you know the stories about this place?'

'Yes. The other girls, they're American. They've never heard of this place. But I lived on the mainland. I know everything this place has done. I still asked if I could come with them.'

She pulls her legs to her chest, tucks her chin in the V of her knees. Her sad eyes watch the river.

I shake my head, confused. 'Why ... why would you ask to come? Do you know what this place is? What the Folk are? Do you know what you've come to?'

She nods. 'We learn about the God-Forgotten when we are little.'

Look at yourself, I think, you are still little.

'Stories about the people here who have a strange god. Stories from years ago. My grandmother woke in the night and listened to them laughing. Sounded like madness, she said.'

'A friend told me about that – the Laughters, she called the epidemic.'

'This place is damaged, and it damages anyone who comes to it, Grandma said.'

'So why did you come to it?'

She fidgets. 'It was the only place I could think of. Dad is scared of this place. He always has been, even as a kid.'

'You came so you wouldn't have to see your dad again?'

She nods.

'Why didn't you want to see him?'

She lifts her waistband away from her hip, and I see buds of old colours. Fingers of green and yellow. 'Dad is always angry.'

'Oh.'

I look at the thin frame under her shirt. The short curls; she has cut them herself.

Her nose runs and she rubs it away with her sleeve. 'Life got mean around primary.'

'Was it life or was it your dad?'

'Aren't they the same thing?'

'Was it when you started getting pretty?'

'I don't like pretty.'

'Pretty doesn't have to hurt.'

'Pretty hurts girls. It always has done.'

I nod. Because, she isn't completely wrong.

'That's why you came here, Moss?'

She takes a big gulp of air. How does she fit all of that inside her?

'What has ... your dad done? Has he touched you...?'

She nods. 'Daddies shouldn't touch their daughters like that.'

I wrap an arm round her shoulders, and she jumps, so I quickly remove it.

'No,' she says. 'Can ... can you do that again?'

I bring her fragile body into mine. 'I'm sorry.'

'He won't come here. He's scared. He won't come here.'

'Where is your mother?'

'She's gone. She died having me.'

I look along her little body, wonder where her father has touched, what places he has been. Then I consider the places inside those bones, the hurts that are unseen but nevertheless felt. Skin can be washed, but there is nothing that can be done for that.

'What's it like, killing your dad?' Moss asks.

'Is that what you think about?'

'I fall asleep thinking about it. It calms me down.'

'You wouldn't feel calm if you did it.'

She nods. 'I know.'

'Was there really nowhere else you could have gone? Did it have to be here?' I ask.

'My dad has only ever been scared of one thing: this place. He won't even go to the beach because he says it feels like it's watching him.'

'So this place feels safe?'

'Hm.'

'Just because this place isn't the danger you are used to, doesn't mean it is better.'

'I know that.' She sighs.

'The Folk think there is a devil here. They are mad but I think they are afraid too.'

'I don't mind that the Folk are mad.'

'I'm sorry about Verity. Had you become friends?'

'No. They brought me across with them, but we didn't really talk. They wanted to see the islands in the UK. But they only came by accident really. Thought it would be quieter here.'

'They seem like nice girls.'

'They're pretty.'

'Yes. I suppose they are.'

Moss looks at me. 'Now one of them is dead.'

HIM – No Girls

As soon as Silas sees Lily the next day, he knows something troubles her.

She walks with a lilt, her left arm stitched to her body, her chest rising and falling too quickly to be calm. Her face is full of shadows. He doesn't think he has ever seen it without them. Shadows to her are like freckles.

'What's happened?' he asks.

'Do you have any gauze?'

'Erm ... I think so.' He guides her into his kitchen, drags a first-aid kit from under the sink and throws out its contents.

'You helped Moss, didn't you? Where did you take her yesterday?'

'The river. I needed to get her away from Della.'

Silas leans close to her, gently peels back her sleeve. He tries to swallow and finds he can't. Among the old, pale scars are two words scratched fresh into her skin:

NO GIRLS.

'She did it last night,' Lily says. 'She was furious with me for taking Moss away from her. I screamed. I couldn't help myself. I'm surprised I didn't wake you.'

'Oh my...' Silas looks at the lines. 'Why has she written this?'

'It's a warning. A threat.'

'About what?'

'She doesn't want me near the girls because she knows I'll protect them.'

'But why?'

'Because *she* wants them. She has her reasons. She always does. This is another game, Silas.'

'What are you going to do?'

'I'm going to make sure Moss stays away from her. Protect her.'

'But she'll keep hurting you?'

She runs her fingers along the old, raised lumps of skin. 'She's going to do that anyway, cricket.'

HIM – Death in the Water

The next traveller dies in the water. She swims and swims, cutting a tear into the ocean with her young body like she has sealskin. Silas stands on the shore with the Folk, who watch her with a hole in their throats: no sounds come from them, no name given to the wind, no callings for her to return. But what is remiss in words, is present in their red, smoke-raw eyes.

Fear.

He imagines he can hear the sounds of her body slowly coming to its death. The lungs begging down breaths, the slowing of muscle and the water's persistent fingers bringing it under. Of course, he can see none of this really. The girl is too far away now.

Silas looks at the man next to him: Orsan. 'Get the boat.'

He does as Silas asks.

But the girl is gone by the time the boat reaches her. She died trying to leave this land. Silas saw her hands lift into the air before she vanished, like she was opening them for some god. But no god reached for her.

Her body is lifted out by the women of this island. They look at the swell of her naked belly and shake their heads in sympathy and pity. She was pregnant? Like the other girl?

'Is the Warden punishing us?' Orsan asks him, his fat hands pawing at Silas's chest.

Silas looks at him with fury. Did he force himself on her?

'She was pregnant. Her baby died too.'

Orsan spits, 'I don't care about that!'

'Was the baby yours, Orsan? Speak the truth, now.'

The man's lip curls. 'Yes. But you are not listening to me. The Warden—'

'That was your child. *That was your child.*' Silas rubs his temples. 'You are the worst of us. The very worst of us. Do you know that? You've always been a beast, even when we were boys.'

'She was no one. She was just a traveller, Silas,' Orsan says, a high whiny pitch to his voice.

'Be silent!'

'But the Warden. Is he angry with us? The girls ... they are killing themselves.'

Silas holds his tongue when it comes to their Devil. He must.

'Why is this happening? Why are these girls killing themselves? Not because they were pregnant. Not because of that.'

'You forced yourself on them, didn't you?'

Orsan opens his mouth, closes it.

'You are an ill man. A very ill man.'

'But ... but they didn't do this because of that. Not both of them.'

Silas shakes his head. No, there is more to this, he knows. He has seen it.

Eventually he says, 'This place is too much for them. We have too many stories under the land. Maybe it is the stories that are the poison.'

'I do not understand. We have Tithed. It is like he is angry with us, Silas. And now he is putting a rot in the girls.'

'I do not have the answers, Orsan.'

'That's two girls now. What is making them do this?'

'I do not have answers, Orsan.'

'What do we do?'

Silas shakes his head. His throat is sore for words. So he says the only thing he can think of to settle Orsan: 'Ask for forgiveness.'

Silas turns and leaves the Folk to bury the body. He does not wish to see it. He does not tell them that it isn't their Warden who takes the girls.

It's something else living on the land.

Silas saw the drowned girl yesterday, sitting on the shore, her arms knotted round her knees. She was troubled. Then he saw Della whisper a restless song in her mind. And this morning, the girl slipped from her bed and slipped into the water. The Folk had removed the boat because of the storm. She could not sail back so she decided to swim in her desperation.

Silas wonders why Della is unravelling the girls. Lily mentioned the games Della made up as a girl. Is this one of them? Is it sport to her?

Silas sees her then, as if his mind has conjured her to him. She walks like a beast, always on the edges of her feet. And he wonders, what mad wind brought this woman here?

Their Warden will not help them with this beast.

HER – The Dangers of Beauty

'I wish I hadn't come here,' Moss says.

'But you wanted to come,' I respond.

Moss hooks a tooth under a scab on the back of her thumb and gently rips it away. I press a tissue to the sore. And she jumps, hides her hand from me, tucking her knees tight to her chest.

'I just wanted to get away from Dad. But this place is worse than all the stories. The girls I came with are dead.' Moss watches the river. 'I thought I would be safe here. But I don't feel safe. There's a man here who keeps looking at me funny. Not like the rest. The rest of the Folk are fine … He looks at me like Dad used to look at me. I know that look.'

'Moss, how old are you?'

She wipes her nose. 'I'm twelve.'

'What?'

'I'm twelve but I'm tall so I look older. Dad didn't like that. He wanted me to be little for the rest of my life. It made him angry. He started getting mean when I started needing bigger clothes. He took me to buy new shoes and later he hit me in the eye so hard I couldn't see out of it. I shone my torch into it to see if it still worked.'

'Why did he want to stop you growing?'

'I don't know.' She wraps her arms round her head. 'I would have stopped if I could.' Her voice is rising. 'I would have. Honest.' Her slim chest moves in gusts, and I want to put my hand on it and make it slow. 'I cut my hair with the scissors at school. He didn't like it when I painted my nails either. He was so cross he made me sit on his knee while he picked all of it off with his front teeth.'

'Moss…'

She unravels her arms and leans in to me. 'I couldn't have stayed but I shouldn't have come here either.'

'The girls shouldn't have taken you away from your home, even if you did ask them to.'

'I told them I was older. They believed me.' She stretches out her arms, shows me how high she can reach, and I think, *You are trying to show me you are grown but you are like a child stretching her back when she is measured against the wall.*

'Do you think there might be a Warden under the land?' she asks after a moment. 'Stories have to come from somewhere, don't they?'

'Don't think on it, Moss. There is no devil. Not really. It's all just a strangeness they have in their heads.'

She looks at me. 'But who put it there?'

'It's going to be alright, cricket,' I say.

I wait and I listen to the grief her body has confined, and I wait for her to breathe like she is breathing again and not like she is emptying her bones. I pat her back, and then it is as if I have burst something – all the air rattles out of her mouth.

'Can I stay with you?'

'I'm sorry, you can't.' I think of Della; her whisperings. 'But you could stay in Kit's house. It's just been left there. I won't be far.'

She nods, sucks her bottom lip. 'They say there is a devil here. But my daddy lives over the water. So there is a devil there too. What am I supposed to do if they are every place I can go?'

HIM – Omens

A restlessness runs through the Folk like a blood they all share. Their eyes skip from one another, never quite landing. Their bodies move, but they have lost all their softness so when they walk, they walk like they are made of sticks and twine; so stiff, how can they be living?

'Silas.'

He turns and sees Orsan. Again. 'What is it?'

'I was just talking to Stina – she thinks the Warden is punishing us. Do you think so too? She thinks a change is coming. Something that will devastate this land. Something terrible.' He rubs his neck. 'The girls ... the girls ... This has never happened before. Why did they kill themselves?'

'I do not have the answers, as I've already said.'

'What do you think it is?'

'I do not know.'

'It is like the Laughters?'

'You think it's an epidemic? You think it's something that's spreading?'

And it is in its way. Della is everywhere.

'What else can it be?' Orsan's eyes are red and swollen. 'They are killing themselves. What can we do?'

'I do not know.'

'Is he angry with us, Silas? Are these his actions?'

'No, Orsan.'

'Have you seen the little one? The one with the curly hair?'

'Her name is Moss.' Silas hears Lily's voice when he says that name. 'No, I haven't seen her. I don't know where she is.'

'She asked to come here. Did you know?'

'What?'

'She begged them to bring her. She knocked on the door of the inn they were staying at and she told them she wanted to see the island. But now she is the only one left.'

Silas sighs. 'These are strange times.'

'I'm worried. I'm worried for us.'
Silas thinks of Della, and he thinks, I am worried for us too.

HER – Smoking Skin

I dream there are roots inside my veins. And they grow and grow and split my skin, so when I rise from my bed, I look no longer look like a woman.

I am in my old home again, in my old room. Mother is downstairs – I can hear her singing. How can she be so calm when my body is separating? Coming undone at all its fragile seams.

A noise rips from my throat. My body is louder than the wind; it could frighten birds from their skies and shadows from their corners. I take all the quiet out of the house.

The roots are growing, curling, and they are black. Why are they black? Where is the green, the newness? I pick at a knot of wood above my knuckle and cry when I cannot break it off. Are they black because my body is trying to grow something out of me?

'Help me!'

The door opens, and I see Della and I beg her to help me. She brushes her fingers along the strange roots that I have grown from my veins.

'What's happening to me?'

'Your body does not want to be your body anymore. It's growing into something else.'

Tears run along my chin, catch on a small growth in my jaw. 'IT HURTS.'

'Lots of things hurt. You know that, Lily.'

Della taps her fingers along my arms, my legs. She cuts her palm on me, wipes it away.

'Make it stop,' I say.

'I can't make it stop.'

'Get a knife. Get a knife. We'll cut them away.'

She shakes her head. 'You can't cut them away. They'll only grow again.'

My body will keep stretching, changing and one day I will pull down these walls, my roots will be branches, and I will be my own forest. Perhaps one day people will come to my trees and hang their victims from my arms. Bodies will swing from my wrists, fires will be lit at my feet. People will use my fingers for all their burnings and then I will live inside the smoke. I will sit in their lungs and I will grow inside their bodies. One day they will have roots in their veins.

They will hurt like I am hurting.

Della rises and leaves me. Mother does not come. Father does not come. The house has emptied. But I scream for them anyway.

A root grows through the top of my spine. I throw my hand back and touch it with my fingers. It is sharp. Like a match.

I rise then, and every inch of me weeps. I dig a matchbox from my drawers, swipe up a flame and then I hold it to the root in my spine.

My body begins to smoke.

HER – Mythos

'Do you think the stars feel sorry for us?'

Moss lifts her eyes and cups her chin in her hands. She lies on her stomach, grumbling when a rock digs into her side. We have lingered by the river. And though it is now dark, I cannot bring myself to leave.

'What do you mean?' I ask. Her questions still surprise me. Unexpected and nonsensical and innocent. I wonder at what age we lose our questions. Is it when we stop growing? When we fill our skins and our bodies finish changing? Does our curiosity fall from our heads and become part of the earth? Does the earth ever give it back?

'Well...' she says, and she makes a knot of her legs. 'I wonder if they live up there, those stars, and they are lonely. If they watch us and they feel sorry for us. Because we are so angry and sad and afraid all the time.'

'They are fire. Lots and lots of fire. They burn and that's all they do. Nothing else, Moss.'

'But what if they do see us? How can you know they don't?'

I rub the space between her shoulder blades. She is bony, and I want to feed her up. 'They aren't real like you or me.' I sigh. 'But they do have their stories.'

She turns, and even in the dark, I can see the widening of her eyes and that curiosity still living determinedly inside her mind.

'Do you know the story of the Pleiades?' I ask.

'The what?'

I carve a shape above our heads. 'Follow my finger. Those stars there. Can you see them? They are called the Pleiades. They were sisters and they lived thousands of years ago, or so the myth says. Their father was a god called Atlas, and one day he stole something he shouldn't have. So he was punished and tasked with holding up the sky for all of eternity. He bore the weight of it on his shoulders, night and day.'

Moss's mouth is open, lifting at the corner. 'Did he ever drop it?' she asks.

I smile. 'No, he didn't drop it. Although, I imagine it would be quite hard to drop.'

'I probably would have dropped it.'

I put my hand over her lips. 'This isn't his story.'

She licks my fingers, and I wipe them on the grass.

'Ugh!'

She laughs, rolling onto her side and holding her belly. 'Ha! Won't do that again, will you?'

'No. I certainly won't. Now, do you want to hear this story or not?'

She quietens, pulls her knees up to her chest. 'Yes. I do. Tell me.'

I poke her in the ribs. 'As I was saying, Atlas had seven daughters. They were beautiful. Doted on by their father. By most Olympians. But because they were beautiful, they caught the eye of Orion. He was a great hunter, violent and unyielding. A giant among men. A son of the god Poseidon. Orion saw the sisters and pursued them. But they did not care for him or his desires.'

Moss curls her hands round her neck. It looks like she is strangling herself. I pull apart her fingers. 'Did he ... hurt them?' she asks.

'No. He didn't get what he wanted, Moss. This isn't his story either,' I say. 'Atlas was tormented, bound by his duty but unable to help his daughters. Zeus, taking pity on him, transformed the sisters into white doves then opened his palms and lifted them into the sky. They were given a safe place. Now, they are a constellation. They are stars known as the Pleiades. And explorers use their lights to guide themselves to their own safe places.'

Moss looks at the sky. 'But ... there are only six stars?'

'One of the sisters, Merope, fell in love with a mortal. And so she came down from the sky to be with him.'

Moss bites her lip, bringing it to blood. Silence sits between us, then finally she speaks:

'Did anyone ask them if they wanted to be stars?' she says. 'Did anyone ask them first?'

'I think they just wanted to be safe.'

'But shouldn't they have been safe as women? Did they have to be moved to the sky just so they wouldn't be hurt?'

'Yes, they should have.'

'Do you think they are watching us now?'

'If you believe the story, then yes. Perhaps they are.'

She nods firmly. 'I believe the story.'

'What do you think they see?' I ask, and smile.

'I think they see us sitting by this river, on this strange island that has no name and has never deserved one. And I think they wonder if we might need to be stars too.'

Her eyes are heavy, sadness flushes her body. I see its drip.

'But they are safe now. And they make others safe too.'

She nods. '...But ... but isn't Orion up there too?'

'Well, yes...'

'He followed them, didn't he? So they aren't really safe, are they?'

I squeeze her shoulder. 'They are. He is a constellation too. Stars cannot harm stars.'

She comes to me, curls into the gap between my arm and chest. 'How do you know this story?'

'It isn't mine, cricket,' I say. 'It's Della's.'

Lily looks at me, eyes wide. 'She used to tell you stories ... Isn't that, erm, nice?'

'Yes, she used to tell me stories. I hated them. And so she never stopped telling them.' I do not say that Della always found a way to make the stories hurt. Or that they came from her lips and sat under my skin, and stayed there, no matter how much I rubbed at them.

'What other things did she tell you?'

'You don't need those things in your head. They won't do you any good.'

'Why not?'

'Because you can't get them out. Della puts things there you can never get rid of.'

'Why?'

I bring Moss closer so she can feel my heart and she will know to stop asking me questions. 'Because she can. The story of the Pleiades is perhaps the oldest story ever told, and she found a way to frighten me with it as a girl.'

'Why did it frighten you?'

'Because she told me that good people go to the sky when they die: children look at their mothers when they look up; fathers look at their children when they look down. We are always looking at each other, the same way the sky looks at the earth. After we are gone, that is all we can hope for.'

'That's ... so nice.'

'Yes. It is. But she also told me that bad people go into the earth, and the space is so close down there, they cannot turn over.'

'Oh. So like heaven and hell.'

'If you like.'

Moss tips her head. 'Did your sister say you would go into the earth? Is that what frightened you?'

I smile, and by the look on Moss's face, it is not one she likes.

'No, Della told me when I died, I would go into the sky. But no one would look for me. Not she, nor our mother, nor our father. They would cover their eyes. And so I would live up there, looking down at the earth, and it would be bare for me.'

'That's sad.'

'I would be no star. I would be a black hole. I would consume, take in everything around me. I would be forgotten.'

Moss shivers inside my arms. 'I'd remember you.'

'Thank you.'

'When Della dies, I wonder if she will go into the earth?' Moss says.

I shake my head, say between my teeth, 'Della will find a way back up.'

HIM – Warden

'You don't believe in your Warden, do you?'

Lily asks this so quietly, Silas thinks he has imagined it, then her eyes come to his and he shakes his head.

'No, I don't.'

Her eyes are red, and there is a darkness around them he wishes he could brush away. Her spine droops so she hangs over her own legs like a question mark. The river hums, and Silas wonders why she always asks to come here.

'Do the Folk know you aren't like them?'

'No, they don't. They can't know.'

'Why?'

'Do you need to ask?'

'Why are you not like them?'

'I've never believed in the Devil. There are just ordinary Folk on this island with a bad history, and that is enough.'

'Why do you stay?'

'Because it's all I know. Just as you stay with Della because it's all you know.'

'If I tried to leave Della, she would follow me. She would hunt me,' Lily says; then: 'The Folk are scared, aren't they? About what has happened to the girls?'

'They think it is punishment for something.'

'You live on mad land.'

'We made it mad ourselves,' he says, and thinks, the Folk do not know that Della is the reason the girls are dead.

'Will you *ever* leave this place?' Her lips are pale, but he does not think it is just because of his story. Some weariness moves under her skin.

Silas thinks of crossing the water, and he is reminded of his sister, the legend she told him, how it put fear in his feet. 'I don't think so,' he says, eventually. 'I don't know how to be anywhere else. I belong to this land.'

'You don't have to.'

Silas smiles. 'I do ... Something is worrying you, Lily. What is it?'

'I've had nothing but bad dreams since I came here.'

'You still aren't sleeping well?'

'No. And when I do sleep, I do not rest.'

'You dream?'

'All the time. Last night I died, and everyone I knew let me.'

'It was just a bad dream.'

'I know.'

'I dream that I will always be this. That I will never have a family of my own.'

'You will.'

'How ... how can a family find me if I am here?'

She nods solemnly. 'You'll find them.'

Silas smiles and squeezes her hand. 'Orsan is looking for Moss, you know? The Folk mean no harm, but him ... He won't stop. I know you are hiding her in Kit's old house.'

'They can't have her.' The space around her eyes hardens. 'You won't tell him where she is, will you?'

'No.'

'She came here to get away from her father. He was hurting her, Silas. And that man Orsan, he just wants to fuck her. Child or not.'

'Don't let her go near the village and she'll be alright. Does ... does Della know where she is?'

Lily nods. 'She can't have her either.'

Silas thinks if he were to touch Lily now, his fingers would sting. There is such a burn in her eyes, he can feel it inside his skin.

HER – Wire in the Body

'There's a gap in the clouds there, and it's like a crack in the world.'

Moss's face is full of wonderment, and I want to dip a brush in the colour of it. 'If I could get myself high enough,' she says, 'I could leave this world.'

'Do you really want that?'

She looks at the ribbon I have wrapped round my palm. With fingers that feel like feathers, she takes it and smooths it. 'Why do you have this?'

'It's a memory. One of my best memories.'

She nods. 'One of my best memories is when I thought my daddy had died. He didn't come home one night, and I turned on all the lights in our house and I danced.'

'Why did he not come back?'

'He got drunk. Slept in a ditch. I wished he'd stayed in the ditch.'

We sit by the river, and I remove my socks, then hers too, and I lift her feet into the shallows.

'He came back the next day. That's when I started to think what it would be like to hurt him back.' Her eyes are deep waters, sad waters, and I wonder how she fits that ocean inside her. 'What it would be like to kill him.'

'You're twelve – you can't mean that?'

'I have hands. Any hands can kill someone.'

'But ... but you'd have to live with it. You'd have to cope with that guilt.'

She wraps her arms around her knees. 'What if there was no guilt? I might be like Daddy.'

'Is that what you want for your life, Moss? Because your life isn't just your daddy.'

She gulps a breath, and I wonder if it is the first time she has ever been asked this. Her eyes skim the river, and she lifts the ribbon to her nose. 'This ribbon smells of shampoo and strawberry sweets. It smells like a little girl.'

I think, *You say that like you are not a girl yourself.* And then I think, *But your father took all the girl out of you.*

'What do you want, Moss?'

She pats her middle. 'I feel like I've got wire inside my belly. I don't want the wire in my belly anymore.'

For the first time I notice her fingernails, and I swallow.

She catches my eye. 'Daddy liked to sit me on his lap at night while he watched the football. When he got bored, he'd pull my fingernails back so I would wriggle in his lap. I'd try to keep still.' She cries, and her face wrinkles, curling into sad shapes. 'I did try. I know why he wanted me to wriggle on top of him. I'm not stupid.'

'Moss...'

'My hands always hurt. Even in the day.'

'Did you tell anyone?'

'I tried to, but they didn't believe me.'

'Do your hands hurt now?'

'No.' She holds them to her lips and blows on her nails as if they are painted. 'They stopped growing after a while. Like they'd given up.'

'No one noticed? No one reported him? Your teachers? Other parents?'

'No. They thought I did it to myself for attention. Daddy liked to rub his chin along my shoulders, and his whiskers hurt. Made my skin red so it looked like sunburn. They didn't notice that either. People don't notice much.'

'Hm.'

'One night I filled my back pockets with the sharpest rocks I could find, so when he put me on his lap, I cut him. He screamed and threw me off. I laughed. I couldn't help it.'

'What did he do?'

'He hit me in the belly. I was sick.' She shakes her head. 'It was okay. It was just food that came up. Shame it didn't take the wire out though.'

'I'm sorry, cricket.'

She turns to me. 'I still have the wire now. And it has those barbs on. The type that keep animals in their pens. It hurts when I move.'

'That wire won't be there forever.'

I take the ribbon from her fingers and use it to wipe the tears from her cheek, like a mother with her child. She is and she isn't a child. She does not speak like a girl, she does not move like a girl. And yet she is. She is a girl who has too much life inside her.

'That man Orsan is looking for you in the village. The rest of them think you might have drowned like the other girl.'

She nods. 'I thought I would be safe here.'

'I don't think anyone has ever been safe here. The Folk aren't safe themselves.'

'What do you mean?'

I think of Silas, hidden, pretending to align himself with them. 'They are all so afraid. Where's the safety in that?'

'It looks safe from a distance,' Moss says. 'I used to watch this island at night ... all its lights. And I used to imagine those lights were for me. So I came here, and now those lights are like fires. There are fires all over this place.'

'You're a fire. You made yourself one. That's no bad thing. You burned your father's fingers.'

She says, 'I used to think my hands wouldn't know how to kill him. They wouldn't know what to do. But they would. That's why I came here. I know I sound bad. I know that. And I don't want to be.'

'You aren't bad.'

'I should have gone somewhere else. Because now I feel stuck.'

I pat her knee. Orsan has splintered the boat to stop her leaving and the Folk will not move against him; they will not help us.

So I say, 'You're stuck with me.'

She smiles, leans in to me. Her head fits into the shape of my chest.

'Will we be alright, Lily?'

'We'll be alright, Moss.'

She wraps her long arms around my body, tucking her cheek into my stomach; she hugs like a child. I hope she cannot feel my sharp edges.

HER – Burial

The sound of her scream moves across the moors. It throws back the wind and drives its way through stone and glass. I am rising from my bed with the shape of one breath in my body, running through darkness out into the tangle of gorse.

The lights are on in Kit's house. I meet Silas at the front door. We push our way inside, taking the stairs two at a time, and together we chase the screams down the hall into her bedroom.

The sight lifts the skin from my bones.

I see Moss with a knife.

And a body on the floor.

Moss stands over him, tears making pale tracks down her cheeks.

She is still screaming. It jumps from her mouth, endless, and so high, I want to take my ears off.

Silas stares at the body in shock. We stand there for what seems like an eternity but can only be minutes before we move as one muscle. He goes to the body, and I go to Moss. I bring her into my chest and cover her mouth with my hand.

'Shhhh. It's alright. It's alright. I'm here.'

'It's Orsan,' Silas says, his fingers pressed to the man's neck. 'He's gone. He's gone, Lily.'

I turn Moss's head and rock her into something quiet. 'Shh. Please. Someone might hear. You need to be calm now, Moss. You need to be calm.'

She is sobbing. 'He-he ... he found me. He-he was going to-to take my-my bloods.' I look at her swollen cheeks, her wide, uncomprehending eyes. She has never looked more like a child.

'What? Tell me exactly what happened, Moss?'

'HE WAS GOING TO TAKE MY BLOODS.'

I look at the bed, the rumpled sheets, the tear in the leg of her trousers. There is a small cut across her brow. I look at the body on the floor and I see the belt, unbuckled.

'Oh...'

Silas rubs his eyes. 'How did he find her...? How could he have known?'

'He was looking everywhere for her,' I say. 'The Folk don't come here but he had a ... special interest in her.'

Moss still holds the knife. I take it out of her hand; the blade is made of bone – animal or human I do not know, but it is old. Older than Moss, older than me. As old as the land. Where did she find it?

I hold her face in my hands. 'Breathe, Moss. You must breathe. You must be calm.' I press my hand firmly to her chest and I lift, and I press, slowly, slowly. 'Follow my hand.'

She nods inside my fingers. There is such a savage sound inside her I wonder if it might break all the tendons in her throat.

'Breathe. You've been breathing all your life. You do it in your sleep; you do it without knowing you're doing it. How many breaths do you think you've ever taken?' I keep speaking, moving aside the trouble in her mind. 'Thousands and thousands, Moss. You breathe through every day. You will do it tomorrow and the next day. Infinite breaths. So what's one more right now?'

She gulps, putting her small hands over mine, as if she wants to reach inside her head and take out the things that trouble it.

'I-I – woke up and he-he was in the bed. He-he was touching my leg. He was trying to get to my-my pocket. My private pocket.'

'Your pocket...' Silas's eyes widen then. 'Oh. Oh...'

'Did he put anything inside your pocket, Moss?' I ask gently.

She shakes her head. 'I found a knife the other day. I took it. I was scared. I'm sorry. I kept it under my bed.'

'What happened next?'

'I screamed. He put his hand over my mouth and undid his belt. He was angry. He said I'd been hiding from him but he'd been looking. He'd looked all over the island. He said he knew I wasn't dead. He said he could smell me. And he'd followed his nose.'

'I thought you were safe here, Moss. I'm sorry.'

'I reached for the knife.' She wraps her arms around her body. 'Is he dead, Silas?'

He nods, looking at the body. 'Yes, Moss. He's really gone.'

'I killed him. I killed him.'

I will not tell her she shouldn't have done it. Hers is the right to defend her body.

'But...'

'It's alright, Moss.'

'But...'

'Everything will be alright.'

Her legs twitch and she falls to the floor. I bring her to the bed and smooth the hair from her cheeks. She is shaking, and I do not think the shaking will stop until there is light in the sky.

'Silas and I are going to move him, okay? We won't be long. I promise. Will you be alright?'

She nods. She is watching the moon intently, her lips parted, pale wax. But she's not really seeing the moon.

I look at Silas, and we move as one muscle once again, gathering arms and ankles. It is a struggle to bring him down the stairs, but we manage, neither of us shivering at the sound of his body knocking on the stairs. Then when we reach the bottom, we look at each other again.

'How did he find her, Silas?'

'I don't know. But we need to protect her.'

I nod. 'What do we do now with the body? My God, does he have any family?'

'No. He has no one. The Folk will think he has gone to Harvest. We could throw him in the sea, but if he washes up, and anyone sees the knife mark, then it will set fires in the village.' He pauses. 'We'll bury him. No one comes to the moors usually. They shouldn't look for him here.'

'He shouldn't have looked for Moss here. But see what's happened.'

Silas sighs. 'Can you think of anything else?'

'I was so frightened when I woke up and heard her. Do you think anyone else did?'

'We'll know soon enough. Give it an hour. If anyone comes, we'll have our answer.'

I press my fingers to the man's cheek. There is some warmth there still. 'I'm not sure she'll ever breathe properly again,' I say, and I think, *Things like this, they sit in your chest, and change the sound of your voice.* 'After this...'

Silas tucks a hair behind my ear. 'She will. We'll help her.'

'Where do we bury the body?'

'Follow me.'

Silas is not shaking. Neither am I. We do not have time for it. We gather the body and carry it out the back door and down the path. Silas brings two shovels, and we sweat and dig, too stunned to speak.

When it is done, Silas and I stand looking at each other. Our cheeks and fingers and eyes are red.

'Can you hear anyone coming?'

'No.' Silas wipes the sweat from his neck. 'I don't think anyone can have heard.'

'Do ... do you think he would have killed her afterwards...?'

Silas nods. 'Yes. Orsan has always had a temper. He's the worst of the Folk. She fought him. He wouldn't have liked that.'

'He deserved it.'

'Maybe he did.'

We have cut our hands ripping heather and gorse to cover the raised soil.

Silas cups my head, then guides me to the door. 'Come on. Leave him. Let's go and be with Moss.'

When we enter the room I see she has not moved. She is still watching the moon, only now she is silent. What is more concerning? This or her crying? I think it is this.

I lift her head and slide into the bed. Silas does the same on the other side. We do not speak.

Then Moss tucks her face into the hollow below my arm and chest. She says quietly, 'I'm sorry.'

Silas and I did not sleep. Moss woke up crying twice in the night and we soothed her together. Now she is so far gone, Silas leaves the room to shower and it does not wake her. I continue holding her little body, and yes, I think there is something different about the way she breathes now.

It is still changed when she wakes and quietly lifts her head, and looks at the space where Orsan fell, as if she is reminding herself that she is the one who made him fall. She does not speak.

Not when Silas brings in food for us. Nor when I change her clothes and bathe her. It is afternoon when I finally encourage her to step out of the room. Silas has gone to open the inn. If he does not, it will raise questions we do not want asked.

I lead her out the door and to the river. I guide her fingers into the water. 'It's taking all the worries from your hands. Can you feel it?'

She shakes her head.

I ponder what to say. Perhaps distracting her is not what will help.

'You ... you went for his neck.' Why did she not go for his chest? Or his stomach? 'Why?'

She looks at her hands, then her legs, all the places he must have been. 'I ... knew it would kill him.'

I thought so. She is smart, even when she is frightened.

'You did what you had to, Moss.'

She is pale, like chalk, I could write my name across the ground with the colour of her.

'I didn't mean it, but I meant it. Does that make sense?'

'Yes. It does.'

'I had a bad dream last night. I had lots of them.'

'I know. You were crying on my chest.'

'I'm sorry. I'm really sorry.'

'You don't need to be. Silas and I don't blame you for anything. We are just glad you are safe.'

She nods. Then she is silent.

A flock of crows tilt above our heads, flawlessly making shapes for us to watch. It is rare to see them. Birds do not come here. That's what the Folk told me when we arrived. But they appear now, as if they're saying *Death! Death!*

We know, I think. We already know.

Moss rests her head on my shoulder. She is too still, after all that has been done. By her father, and by a man who hunted her. She is still now, but there will be unspent storms inside her. A violence, a wildness like these wild birds. She may supress it for a time, but her body will remember. When it has softened at its edges and her skin has loosened across her shape. The memories will come back to her mind, and she will want for nothing more than to take her heart out of its bones.

'I dreamed of so many bad things,' she says quietly, looking up. 'Do you think birds dream too? Do you think birds dream of bad things that have been done to them? When their brothers and sisters are shot down from their trees, do you think the ones left dream of falling themselves? Again and again. Out of the skies?'

'I don't know, Moss.'

She breathes.

'I just don't know.'

'Or do they dream of nothing? It must be quiet, dreaming of nothing. It must be so ... calm.' Then she says, 'I'd quite like to feel like that.'

I stroke her head. Then a shadow falls across our bodies and it does not fall from the birds.

We look up together.

Della.

HER – THEN – Obel

'What are you holding?'

Della tucks it into her pocket. 'Nothing. It's just something Dad made me.'

'Well, what is it?'

She sighs, offers me a coin fashioned from wood. On its face is a portrait of a man, his face wearied, his strong hands guiding a paddle through grim waters.

'What is it?'

'It's an obel.'

'What's an obel?'

We sit outside our home, muddied knees bent to our chests. Our mother and father whisper to each other in the kitchen, snatching glimpses of us when they think we aren't looking. They think we cannot hear them but I know they plan to separate the two of us. Father will take one, Mother will take the other. Father is saying he knows where to go; he's heard of a place a long way away, a place so full of stories, it hurts the ears that listen.

But where does he mean?

The God-Forgotten, he calls it, this strange, rotten place.

Della looks at the dead bodies – hedgehogs, voles, mice, even birds – that have laid themselves down in our garden. They are old deaths, and any animal that comes to enjoy their poisoned meat dies too. Della shakes her head, then puts it into her hands, as if it is too heavy for her to hold up. Her face is pale, too pale.

'Della?' I say, nudge her with my knee. 'What does it mean? Please tell me.'

'Those stories Dad tells us about Charon, the ferryman – the ones you cover your ears at. Well, Charon ferried souls to the Underworld. But for this, he required payment, an obel, a coin laid on the body of the dead. Nothing is free.'

'What if you couldn't pay him?'

'Then you'd become a ghost, and like all ghosts, you would be restless. No ghost can settle.'

'That's sad.'

'It's only sad if you can't pay him.'

I have a hole in my stomach at her words, so I wrap my arms around my middle. I wish I had not asked. 'I don't have any money. If I die, will you pay him for me?'

Della strokes my hair, her careful eyes lingering on mine. 'You have the most perfect face.' She lifts a coil of it and twists it into a rope. 'A perfect voice.' She wraps the rope around my neck. Tighter, tighter. 'You'll break hearts.' Then she says between her teeth, 'But you shouldn't be anywhere near those hearts.'

'Del ... Del!' I claw at her fingers.

She cinches the rope tighter.

Then she releases suddenly, and I suck in breath after breath.

'Why did you do that?'

'Because I hate you, Lil. You know that. And I wouldn't pay the ferryman anything.'

I wipe my nose. 'But ... but you have to! You have to pay him. Or he won't take me with him.'

Della laughs. A bitter noise made in her throat. 'Then pay him with one of your smiles.'

The hole in my stomach grows; I can feel all its ragged edges. 'He won't take it.'

'Then you'll be restless for the rest of your life. But Charon wouldn't take you even if someone did pay.' She strokes my lips, my chin, my eyes. 'He would drown you.'

'Dad would pay. I know he would.'

Della snatches the obel from my hand. 'Then why didn't he give you one of these? Why didn't he make you one too?'

'You say mean things. You're full of mean things.'

'You did that yourself. You made all the things in me mean.'

Tears slip down my cheeks. I wipe them away, hide them in my pocket. My pocket will be soaked through. It will drip with all my tears. I will drown in an ocean I have made.

'I didn't do anything.'

'You were born.'

I look at our parents, still clutching each other's trembling bodies. Mother is crying and Father is biting his fist. He cannot help it. He does it to stop himself crying too. He does it such a lot now. There are teeth marks in his hands that he can never get rid of.

I open my mouth, then close it as Della grabs my chin, shakes it. 'Call for them, Lil. Do it.'

'Let go.'

'They are talking about us again. We won't be together much longer. Mum will take one of us, Dad the other. And Dad will go such a long way. He might never stop driving. He might drive off the edge of the world.'

'I'm scared.'

'You're not scared. You don't know what that feels like.' She wipes sweat from her forehead, looks at the sheen on her fingers, a line of worry appearing between her brows.

'Did you mean what you said yesterday?' I ask. 'That when you are older, you will leave me behind?'

'You know I did.'

'Will you go and have a family? Without me?'

Surprise momentarily clears her face of pain. 'A family...?'

'Yes. Will you get married and have kids?'

'Kids...?'

'What will you name them?'

Della doubles over, her lips so pale, I reach out and pinch them.

'I'm colouring,' I say to make her laugh.

'It hurts! Why does it hurt?'

'Is it your month?'

She groans. 'No, Lily. It isn't my time of the month.'

'You don't look very well. Are you sure you're okay?'

'I'm fine.'

'Really?' I hold her hand. 'You're really pale. Do you want me to get Mum?'

'I'm fine!' Della holds her stomach now, a keening escaping through her lips. 'It hurts!'

I stroke her hair behind her ear. 'Della ...?'

'Oh God. It hurts so much! What's wrong with me?'

'Maybe you ate something off. Or drank something out of date.'

She frowns.. Then her body convulses and she throws herself forward, heaving into the grass. I cover my nose at the smell of sick.

'Della?' I ask, rubbing her back. 'Della?'

She rises, turns to me. Her eyes have emptied, hands clutching at her belly. But I am not looking at any of that. I am looking at the blood running down her chin, making a river of her.

I scream and bring our parents running.

HIM – Folksong

They do not speak of the man they buried.

They do not know how to. It is something they carry inside their eyes, and when they look at each other, they upset each other with the memory of it.

The Folk wonder where he has gone. They look for him but they do not look for long; they say he has gone to Harvest, and Silas thinks they are relieved the Devil has taken him. They sing songs, they are so relieved.

Silas thinks of Lily and Della, how the land has changed since they arrived. Orsan isn't the first dead person Lily has seen.

'Did seeing his body bring back memories of your parents?'

'Yes.'

'It made me think of the pregnant girls. He deserved this.'

'Perhaps he did.'

'But it wasn't just because of him. I saw Della whispering into their ears moments before they killed themselves. She pushed them to the edge.'

'What do we do?' Lily asks.

'I've never seen anything like your sister before. Except perhaps for mine...'

'She'll start on Moss now.'

'She could come and stay with me. You too. I could keep my eye on you both.'

Lily shakes her head. 'No. I can't. I need to be close to Della. Keep my eye on her.'

'So what are you going to do?'

'I don't know.' She rubs her eyes. 'Maybe Moss *should* come and stay with you. You'll look after her, won't you?'

'Of course.'

Lily leans into Silas, and he puts an arm around her shoulder. But his fingers pinch the skin of her, and he enjoys holding another person. He enjoys the feel of her meat between his nails.

HER – Buried Flowers

'Are you alright staying with Silas?'

Moss is digging holes in the earth, fingers sharp and persistent. I do not know what she is digging it for. The river gushes across our feet and it brings memories to me that make my pulse quicken.

'I'm okay. He's quiet. I don't think he knows what to say to me after what happened.' Soil sinks under her nails. 'He likes you. I can tell when he talks about you.'

'Really?'

She nods.

'How are you feeling ... after what happened with Orsan?'

'I-I feel like I want to shake myself. Shake something off, but there isn't anything there. You get me?'

'He's gone, Moss. He's in the earth.'

'But I can still see Orsan's eyes.' She covers her own eyes with the backs of her hands. 'I think he must live inside my head and he watches my mind work while I sleep.'

'He can't see you, cricket.'

She is sobbing now, lines in every part of her face. She looks so young, and I am once more reminded that she is twelve, a child stretching into an adult. 'I want to feel clear. I haven't felt clear in such a long time.'

I guide her hands below the water and tell her that all her hurts are passing into the cold. 'Give them to the river,' I say. 'All those hurts inside your hands, give them to the river, and the river can take them away.'

She nods, and for five furious heartbeats, she is silent, her ribs barely rising. Then a smile plucks at her lips.

She sits back, and I blow on her slim, pale fingers to dry them. 'Better?'

She nods. 'Thanks.'

'What ... what are you doing?' I ask, gesturing to the holes she has made.

She sighs, tears three flowers from the ground, then buries each one with soft hands. 'I'm burying them. People like to take pretty things but if I bury them they can stay in the earth. They can still be themselves.'

'You know, when I was your age, one of my favourite things to do was to run into the trees outside my old home. I would go as fast as I could, barefoot, listening to the ground crackle beneath me. It makes the same sound as a fire.'

Moss's eyes are big and round, her lips parting into such a child's face, for a moment I am undone. 'Did it hurt?'

I smile. 'A little. It made me run faster, and the faster I ran the better I felt.'

'Did you get far enough away? From what was bothering you? Something must have been?'

'For a moment, it felt like I did.'

She turns her fingers in front of her eyes, and I wonder what she is seeing, but then I realise, she is playing with the sunlight, as if she can really hold it, move it. Sliding and spinning it between her fingers like another girl would turn a coin.

'Did your feet have cuts?'

'No. I walked everywhere barefoot when I was a girl. Della did too. Mother despaired of us. Told me I would damage my feet, but I didn't care. I liked the feeling of the earth.'

'I want to feel it.' Moss takes off her shoes and wanders in circles around me, smiling. 'It's nice. I like it.'

I rise, give her elbow a pinch. 'Go! See what it's like to run with fire under your feet.'

She laughs. She is fast, but I am faster. I focus on a smooth, sweet space on the back of her neck and run like I used to. I run to catch this girl who buries flowers and plays with the sunlight between the softness of her fingertips.

HIM – The Height of the Sky

'Why aren't you like the Folk here?'

Moss is watching him. She has not spoken to him since the night they buried Orsan. She is learning how to hold death, how to breathe around it, like a rock in her lung. She is careful never to touch him, to get more than three feet of him, she eats the meals he makes for her but otherwise she is silent.

So when she speaks now, it surprises him.

'I only live here. But this place doesn't live inside me. Does that answer your question?'

'Why are you helping me?'

'Because I want to.'

'What's wrong with all the Folk here?' Her face has reddened, and her fingers tremble round the spoon for her cereal. 'Don't they know they are mad? Can they feel a madness like that?'

'No.'

'Lily is trying to keep Della away from me. She's scared of her sister.'

'Do ... do you know their story?'

'Everyone knows the Pedley sisters: they grew up on the edge of a forest and played strange games within the trees. Girls went missing in the town closest to them but they never found the man who took them. Their county has troubling stories, but none so bad as the two sisters who killed their parents.' He thinks it sounds like she has just recited a newspaper article.

'Has Della come near you?'

Moss frowns. 'She said something to me the other day ... and I don't know what she meant but it was something bad. A warning. That's why I'm here with you, isn't it? Because Lily is trying to protect me from her sister. It must be.'

'You are safe here.'

Moss nods.

Silas recalls seeing Della with Stina in the village the day before, the black under her eyes. All the time he has known her, Della has looked like she is full of ghosts. Now, she looks empty. All of her ghosts have left her. But why?

Moss scans the old photographs on the wall. His family stretching back generations, colour dripping into black and white, all the old faces his face has come from.

'Who's that?' Moss points to a photo of two figures.

'They are my ancestors.'

'Why is she so big?'

Silas smiles. 'She towers over him, doesn't she?'

'He looks like a child.'

'He was actually six foot.'

'Was she eating something to make her grow?' Moss is touching the frame with her finger. 'Can I eat it too?'

'Some people said she had a giant's gene. She made everyone look like children. In fact, children used to be frightened of her ... and adults too. She walked and the earth used to shake.'

'Really?'

'Those are the stories. She was supposedly so tall she could walk through the sea and reach the mainland without the water ever reaching her chin.'

Moss is smiling, so he keeps talking.

'Some of the mainlanders used to say that they could see her body from all that way away. They always thought it was a man though. A tall, tall man.'

'What was her name?'

'Ura. Her arms were so long, she could reach right down a well and bring the bucket up herself. Brave kids would wrap their arms round her legs and cling to her as she walked. She would shake them off like fleas and send them flying. And she was so tall, it was like she was part of the sky – a little like Della. Folk were afraid of her.'

'I would like that.'

'What?'

'For everyone to be just a little afraid of me.'

'Really?'

She scratches her ear. 'Maybe just the men, then.'

'Hm.'

'So ... why are you so short?'

A sigh slides down Silas's throat. 'Long story.'

'Do you have any brothers or sisters?'

'A sister. A long time ago.'

'Was she short too?'

'No. She was tall.'

'What about your mum?'

'Tall.'

'Your dad?'

'Tall.'

'Oh.'

'Yeah.'

'That's a shame for you.'

'I manage.'

'Do you, though?'

'Yes.'

She shrugs. 'If you ever want me to reach something down for you, let me know.'

Silas looks at her, the wide innocence of her eyes, the worry lines she already carries across her forehead. He wonders if she is being purposely hurtful, but he realises that she still has the bluntness of a child because she is a child.

'Thank you. I'll keep it in mind.'

She reaches a small hand across the table and pats his own once, then she kicks out the chair and runs out the door.

HER – THEN – Soul Factory

'The trees look like they are watching us.'

'Perhaps they are. And they pity us,' Mother says.

I try to take her hand but she slips it inside her pocket. There her hand remains. She watches the trees, as if she can see more than I can. She is far away from herself, Mother. She no longer moves with any compulsion. She is untethered and now her body only knows it must breathe and move because it remembers it once did.

I cannot reach her hand so I squeeze her hip to remind her I am close, then I look for Della. Father is away, and Mother needed to escape the house. But it is not the house she needed to escape really.

We have come to Kennall Vale, a woodland that is so quiet I can hear bird wings and little else. This place was an old gunpowder factory, buildings scattered through the trees, now coming slowly to nothing. I clap my hands together and send animals running. The past keeps its fingernails buried into this earth, and I wonder how many bodies must surely be here. How many men must have died their deaths here? How many souls walk through this old factory?

Sunlight freckles the ground, and I find Della standing in a glade, curling her hands around shoots of light. 'Are you cold?' I ask her.

'No.'

I go to one of the nearby buildings and dig holes all around the walls. Mother is sitting on a bench, hands cupped in her lap. Her eyes watch the river but they do not see the river. Della goes and sits with her, whispers into her ear with that lipless mouth.

'Can you feel the men? I wonder if they still walk here.' Della pats Mother's leg and her leg shivers. 'Do ghosts walk? A man died here a long time ago and the explosion ripped apart his body and they found pieces of him miles away. He had ten children. I wonder if any of his ten children found any of his body.'

Mother does not answer. I carry on digging, spearing worms with my fingers. Something sharp cuts the pad of my thumb, and I wipe the blood on my sock where no one will see it. I think it must be a shard of glass or a nail, but as I bring it into the light, I see it is a bone.

Della has roamed away from Mother, and I show her my find. 'It's a femur,' I say.

She snatches it from me and taps my leg. 'Do you think if I take out your bone and put this bone inside your body, you'll walk like they did?'

She runs the sharp point of it down my skin. 'Do you think you'll run like they did? Will this leg take you somewhere else? Will it walk you away from me? Shall we see?'

'Stop it.'

'This leg might be able to dance. You've always wanted to be able to dance, haven't you?'

'Give it back to me, Della.'

'Come here. Let me see your leg. I'll do it now. I'll be free of you then.'

'I told you to give it back.' I swing out my arm and try to wrestle it from her cold hands. 'Della, I mean it.'

She pushes the edge of the bone into my stomach, harder and harder. When blood seeps through my T-shirt, she throws it down and walks away. I wash the cut in the river, enjoying the slow creep of water across the skin. Then, I crouch by Mother and cup my hand round her ankle.

'Mother, do you love me?' I whisper.

Her empty eyes go to Della.

She brings her hands to those eyes and weeps.

HIM – Bad Moon

'What do you think Hell is made of?' Moss asks.

The three of them sit round his table. Lily is distracted, eyes pinned to her own house through the window. Its lights are on. But Della is not inside those rooms. She is outside somewhere, picking through the darkness like a tick on a body. She moves through the wet and the wind, and she will be watching them round this table. He knows. Lily knows. Moss knows. And they all lean a little further into each other's bodies.

'Are you alright?' Lily taps the back of his hand.

He nods. 'I'm fine. To answer your question, Moss, I'm not entirely sure. The Folk think it is like a chamber. A chamber under the earth. This earth. This mountain. They think it is so vast, it could have its own cities, its own rivers, its population spreading out further and further. They have tried to find it. Their ancestors have been driven mad by their search. They've cut holes into the earth. Tried to find a doorway. They've tried to make doorways themselves.'

'But?' Moss is leaning forward, Lily too.

'But everyone thinks something different.'

'Hell is a bad place. Why would anyone want to find it?'

'The Folk believe the Devil will be lenient. If they perform the Tithings. If they have their Devil's Day and their rites, he will be kind. They are frightened. Always so frightened. So they try to appease him, make him love them.'

'The Devil isn't kind. He doesn't love. Everyone knows that.'

'The Devil loves his own.'

'Dad told me Hell was made of fire. That bad kids went there. And they burned. He told me I'd burn.'

Lily wraps an arm round Moss's shoulder, her voice rising firm. 'You are your own fire, Moss. And fires can't burn themselves.'

The girl smiles, some colour lifting her cheeks. 'What happens to bad people, do you think?' she asks Silas, and her eyes are wide and open and unarmed. Silas wonders if he ever looked like that as a boy.

He doesn't think Lily can have. 'If bad people don't burn, what do they do?'

'Maybe they have to live out their own worst imaginings,' Silas says. 'Or experience the sins they commit in their lives. Maybe they suffer, and it's endless.'

Lily shivers, eyes still fastened on the window. 'I always thought Hell would feel like being lost,' she says.

'What do you mean?' Silas asks.

Her eyes come to him, and he counts the threads of red, the threads of worry there.

'Well,' she says. 'Lost is a universal feeling. As a child, you feel lost when you lose your mother in a busy place. As a teenager you can feel lost with your peers. As an adult, you can feel lost when a loved one dies. "Lost" is always there.'

Moss bites her cuff, spittle drying into the knit. 'Did you feel lost as a kid?'

Lily nods. 'I always felt lost. Moonlight, a girl at school once called me, because she thought moonlight was strange.'

'Why were you strange?'

'I used to be quiet, watchful. I kept to myself.'

Moss nods. 'I don't think moonlight is so bad.'

Lily pats her hand. 'Thank you, cricket.'

'What about you, Silas? What were you like as a kid?' the girl asks him.

'Moonlight,' he confirms.

'Then I must be moonlight too,' she says.

HER – THEN – Sage

I open my eyes and smell burning.

'Della? Della, are you awake?'

She does not answer, but her eyes are open. I can see the whites of them shining in the moonlight as it comes through our bedroom window. She is looking over my shoulder, her gaze so intent, I am afraid to turn to see what I will see.

'What is it, Della? What are you looking at?'

The door is open, and the blackness of the hallway frightens me. As if something has come in. It smells of burning, of something earthy that sticks in the throat.

'Della, what is that? Can you smell it? What is it?' My voice is high, flayed. 'What are you looking at?'

She does not answer, only stares sadly behind me. I pull the blanket up to my chin, take sharp breaths. What has come in?

'Della...' I cry, quietly.

Then I hear it. A noise made deep in the chest. Coming from behind me. I gasp, too afraid to move.

'Della... help me...'

The noise rises, changing cadence to something gruff, sad. A whimper...

I sit up suddenly and turn. I know that sound.

Mother stands above me, tears streaming down her pale, pale face. The burning comes from the sage stick she is moving around our bedroom.

'Why was Mother doing that last night?'

'To get the wolf out of the room.'

'There isn't a real wolf, Della. That's just what Pedley means.'

'Hm.'

'Is Mother okay?' I scratch my head. 'She seemed sad.'

'I know.'

We walk through the woods, following the path we have made to the river to the red flowers that grow on its sides. We have stains of green on our bare feet. We have never worn shoes, even to Penzance, or Market Town as we call it. I think now, if we wore them, we would not know how to move.

'Do you want me to tell you a story about why Mother does that in the night?' Della is looking at me from the corner of her eyes.

'No.'

She pulls my hair, pulls at the corner of my mouth. 'You look so perfect. Perfect hair. Perfect lips. Perfect girl.'

'You're jealous!'

She strokes my cheek. 'This pretty face...' she says, as if it is something dangerous she touches. 'I hate this pretty face.'

'Stop it.'

'Do you even know what sageing is? What it means?'

'Yes,' I say, but I don't.

Della looks at me in disgust. 'You are like something from a fairy tale.'

I smile then, dance round her body, through the red flowers. 'That's the nicest thing you have ever said to me.'

'All fairy tales are horror stories, really.'

'I am a story! I am a myth.' I laugh, throwing out my arms. 'Am I mythic?'

'Mythic?' Della grabs my wrist and pulls me close to her mouth. She spits, 'You are damned.'

HER – Chaos We Keep in Our Lungs

Della is waiting for me.

Her wet clothes hang from her body. Anyone else might think she had been crying. But I know she has no tears, and the storm clouds must lend her theirs.

I have just come from Silas's house. I risk a glance over my shoulder and see two faces watching me from the window. Silas and Moss. They asked me to stay with them after our conversation about hell. But I could not. Now my sentinels watch protectively, closing into one another, a fist, so fierce it is like a violence.

Her hands are clenched, and the vein across her forehead is bursting through the pale skin. 'You should be home with me. Not there with them.' Her eyes are like coals, and I take a step back.

'You were watching us. I knew you were. I could feel it. Were you standing out there the whole time?'

She nods. 'I'll get past you. You can't keep her to yourself forever.'

'Moss is safe.'

Della shakes her head. 'Is that what you tell her? Do you take her to the river to tell her this? You and your rivers, Lil.' A smile tears itself into Della's face, and I clutch my arms across my stomach.

'She'll always be safe with me.'

She smiles. And I think her face looks taut. I can see all the bones inside her, and I wonder, do mine match hers? Do the similarities outside our bodies match our insides too? If you bring away our skin and unclip our bones, do our hearts have the same corners, the same cavities, the same chaoses? If we were side by side, with only the veins from our hands and the meat of our lungs, would anyone say, 'Ahh, yes, these are sisters'?

No, they would not. Because we have never been just that. We are different. One of us has always been too much for the world. One of us has broken the world's fingers. And now it cannot hold us, it shakes when it tries to.

'You can try all you want, you won't get to her,' I say. 'Not Moss. I won't allow it.'

'I'll have Moss. You can't be everywhere at once, Lil. If you think you can, you're mad. Mad, mad, mad.' She strokes her finger across my chin. 'You have to sleep, you have to close your eyes. You have to eat and walk and live. And I'll get to her ... while you're living. Mind me, Lil.'

'I have Silas. He won't let you near her.'

She smiles. 'That small man? He's frightened of this place, of the Folk he has known his entire life. Perhaps he is frightened of them because he has known them his entire life?'

'He's safe. He's helping Moss.'

'Lily!'

Our eyes snap to a body that stretches from the darkness. It is Silas. He is reaching for me.

I scramble into his body. He holds me to his chest. I am shivering and so is he. Della's eyes go back and forth between us, then a wearied smile fills her lips.

'Fascinating...' she says.

HER – Murmuration

The next morning I walk through flowers, through nettles, until I come to this wood. It is not like the Hanging Place, there are no ropes, no ghosts through the trees, but I wonder if this place is not itself a ghost, if it is not some creature that breathes, and now I am walking along its body.

The wind tears through the trees, and then there are birds, birds! More than I have seen anywhere. This is where they all come. But why have they all come here?

The murmuration lifts into the air, bending into unfathomable shapes, a language of wings. They beat so loudly, it feels like I have wings inside my ears. I stumble back, try to breathe, but there must be a cut in my throat. I feel so small. Birds cover the sky, they take the light. I have never been frightened of birds before.

I turn back the way I have come. I wanted space from Della, with her eyes and her burning touches, from Silas with his affection and his too-tight fingers. But now I wish I had not walked into these woods.

The birds gather, swells of bodies. Has anyone ever been killed by a murmuration? I shudder, shoulder my way through the branches.

'Hello?'

No answer.

'Hello!'

There are no Folk here. I do not think this place is a good place to walk, even for them.

'Hello!'

I run, throwing a glance over my shoulder, and dear God, are the birds following me? They are. They are!

'Help!'

The trees are too close, I cannot see anything, no openings, no rivers, no life. I throw my eyes up and look at the dark temple of wings. I pray for Silas, for Moss.

A bird sweeps into me. I change direction, run faster, and then I see a divide in the trees. The darkness thickens into a shape. It is a building. An old shepherd's hut. Covered in moss and crumbling at its edges. A candle flickers through the window, and I run towards its light.

Then I hear a voice, old and cut by sharp things. As I turn, I think, *The Devil is no man. He's a woman.*

But this is no woman.

This is nothing like anything living I have seen before.

Her arms hang by her sides, too long, long enough to skim her knees. Her skin is so full of lines, I wonder if she ever could have been young. Or did she come into the world as she is now: an ancient wrong.

'Who are you?' I ask; it comes out as a whisper.

She does not reply, simply lifts her eyes to the wings above us. And she says to the birds: 'Who are we, she asks of us.' Her sudden laugh cuts through the air. 'You are in our forest, girl. Who are you?'

'I'm Lily. I did not know this land belonged to you.'

'This land belongs to Him-under-the-Earth. Why have you come into our trees?'

'I was ... lost. What is your name?'

She stretches a blackened hand, opens my coat to see my body, lifts my hair and pushes back my lip. 'You're fresh skin, aren't you? You are not Folk-on-the-Cobbles. You're across-the-water-people?'

'Yes. I am new to this island. Why have I not seen you in the village?'

'We do not go there.'

'Are you not afraid of the birds?' They circle us, so many eyes I couldn't hope to count them. But I can feel them. All.

'We like it in the trees.'

'How long have you lived in the trees?'

'You should go, girl. Back on your way.'

'What is your name?'

She looks at the birds. 'Our name is Brid.'

'Do they ... they belong to you?'

She shoulders past me. I should go. I should continue back home, to Silas, Moss. But I cannot. Because there is something frightening about this woman, something inside her, like blackness below fingernails. And I want to pick it out.

I follow her bent figure to the door of the shepherd's hut. Inside, there is a billowed chair, covered in lichen and feathers, with stains I refuse to name, and a stove. There is no bed, there is no sink, there are no photographs. There is nothing to tell me she is human. Even animals like softness to sleep on.

'Why do you not live with the rest of the Folk? Do you not have family in the village?'

She shakes her head, lowering herself into the chair. Two birds creep across the threshold and bury themselves under her armpits, fine, silken heads poking out. They watch me, and I want to stick a pin in their eyes.

'The Folk do not like us on their cobbles. They say we are bad for the soil, bad for the land's milk.'

'Why? I don't understand.'

She looks at me, and it is like a cold hand has laid across my chest. An imprecise fear that I cannot fathom. There is something restless to this woman. A thunder that makes all bodies around her shiver. I press my hands under my legs to keep them still.

She does not answer, so I try a different approach. 'How did you train these birds? They are wild, aren't they?'

'Folk-on-the-Cobbles say that we carry messages down to Him-under-the-Earth with our wings. They say we tap our beak on their windows to wake their children. They say we fly across the island between three and four, as the darkness passes into the light, listening with our ears for news.'

'Isn't that the Witching Hour?'

'It's the hour everything comes together ... or apart.'

'Oh.'

'Have you seen our Him-under-the-Earth?'

'No. I don't tend to go looking for devils.'

'Devils come to you. That's how it always has been.'

'How old are you? How long have you lived in these trees?'

'Longer than you have been breathing this world's air.' She takes a bird, small and nut-brown, in her fist and squeezes it. Her knuckles crack and the bird's eyes bulge in its sockets ... but it does not try to free itself. It simply waits for her to finish hurting it.

'Why did you come to this place? Of all the places on this island.'

'We came to these trees when we were a girl. We do not remember much of being a girl though. Our skin was tight.. It smelled of newness, milky and sweet. Our legs did not make noises when we stood and ran and flew. We had eyes that were blue and saw everything everyone didn't want seen. Secrets they wanted secret.'

'You have black eyes.'

And suddenly those eyes snap back to me, and I fidget in my seat.

'We spent too long looking on dark things, so the darkness came into our body.' She releases the bird and it goes to sit between her feet. 'We always loved these trees. It is our safe place. It looked after us when the Folk turned us away from their cobbles.'

'Why did they do that – turn you away?'

'Because we killed our children.'

HIM – Effigy

The day begins with a burning.

Smoke coils between the bodies of the Folk. The sun has not yet risen, so the bonfire is their sun, and it puts violence in the shadows and makes them all look like they have beasts inside their skins.

The children clutch effigies made with sticks and wool and twine. As well as the festival, the Folk do this to appease the Warden. They make the figures at school, fingers sticky with glue, and when their teacher tells them to snap the legs shorter, they do. 'We must appease the Warden, children. Make your creations the best you can.'

Silas remembers when he was a boy, the offering he made from an old shirt. He had been so proud of it, even gave it a face; the only offering to have eyes. But his teacher, the old crone who still teaches now, broke its back and threw it at his feet.

Silas sees Della across the fire. She is watching him, her slim fingers from this distance looking like bare bones, and he shivers. The Folk have gathered to her but she is not listening. She swings out her arm and they stumble out of her path. And then she comes to him.

He is still not used to her voice. It sits inside his ears, and he wants someone to scream just so he can get rid of the sound. Della lifts a finger and runs it down the soft meat of his wrist. To some, this might look tender, a sweetness, but Silas knows there is violence to tenderness, and she is reminding him that he is exactly this: meat.

'She is not yours,' Della says. 'You do not know her so you cannot have her. Lily has never belonged to anyone.'

'Except you?'

'You watch her like an animal.'

'Then we are both animals.'

'Are you lonely here? Have you always been lonely here, Silas?'

'What?'

'I watch you. You're not like these Folk. Everything you do is precise and considered. And watchful. You are a little like me.'

'I am not. We are nothing alike.'

'Aren't we?' She shrugs. 'You have such a small life here. You pour their drinks, you listen to their whining. But what else do you do?'

'I...' This is the most he has ever heard her say.

'Are you frightened to leave? Or frightened to stay? Nothing is simple with you, is it?'

Silas opens his mouth to answer, but Della taps his fingers, one by one, tapping the word back between his lips.

'You find my sister warming and bright.' She is holding his hand to her chest now, eyes bearing into his own. 'But you know nothing of the Pedley women, Silas. You know nothing of where we came from, of fires in the forest and the Red Room. You can't have my sister. She does not belong to you.'

'I ... I've seen what you've done to Lily. Those marks on her arms. All the stories. She's told me.'

'"No girls"? Is that what you mean? We have always had our games, Lil and I. We will always play them.'

'We or you? It's not a game if only one participant wants to play. You killed your parents. What game was that?'

She smiles sadly. 'Not a game of chess, I think.'

'What are you going to do with Lily? Will you just keep her close to you, like some bird in a net, for the rest of her life?' Silas must stretch his neck to even come up to her collar, but he does not care. There are burnings in his fingers now and he wants to take her body and shake it. He would shake the soul from it.

'Lily is frightened of you, so she's followed you here, because she knew if she ran, *you'd* follow her. And you'd punish her for it. I've guessed correctly, haven't I? I won't let you upset her anymore. I'll be with her every moment of every day. I'll *mind* her. I'll protect her from you.'

'Do as you like, Silas.' She smiles, then she is gone, making a seam in the Folk, making the smoke part for her.

Silas takes a breath, then takes another to clear his lungs of the smell of her. He does not want her on this land. He does not want her near Lily. Since her arrival, he has looked on her as a chaos he cannot contain or touch, but she is just a body, and a body only needs a cut to bleed.

'Gather. Gather! Pick up your creations, kids. We will offer them to our Warden. It's time.'

The Folk circle the fire, smiles sharp, arms lifting close enough to the flame so that their fingers sting and they wince. Della does not though. She stands with Moss. Della is whispering something into her ear.

What is she saying?

Silas moves to be closer to them but he cannot hear over the Folk. Della has a hand on the girl's shoulder. Her fingers are turning white. She gestures to the Folk, to the fire, lips moving so quickly the words do not look like words at all. Moss puts her hands to her head, confusion in her eyes. What poison is falling into her mind?

Silas watches it all. As the fire throws out its light and the Folk sing and the children throw their effigies to the burning.

HER – THEN – Witch-Made

'A witch made you. Not Mother.'

Della looks at me from the corner of her eye. That worry line deepens across her forehead. I reach out and stroke it. We sit by the river in the woods by Dyowles House, our legs crossed. This place has not healed from the bad thing that happened here yesterday. The air is contaminated, condemned.

A fire burned here. Then it did not.

'What do you mean?' I ask Della. 'Of course Mother made me.'

'You weren't grown in a belly, you were brewed in a pot.'

I curl my arms around my middle. 'Don't. I don't want to hear it.'

Della smiles, a cruel curve to her lips. Something catches her eyes, and she lifts a hair clip from the ground. It is in the shape of a butterfly, with pink-and-purple wings. It is not ours.

Della's eyes snap back to mine then, a new fury inside them, and yet she holds the butterfly to her chest with more gentleness than I have seen her use before. 'You will listen, Lil.' She knots my legs into hers, to keep me from running. 'This story is about you.'

'Don't, Della.'

'Once upon a time, there lived a witch and a wolf. The witch lived inside a tree—'

'How did she live inside a tree?'

'It was a tree as big as a building. She scraped out the tree's insides and lived away from the world with her wolf. Still the witch was unhappy. She wanted someone wicked to share in her wickedness, so she brought a pot to boil and poured into it all the bad things the world contained, using the seven sins as spices. But she needed one last ingredient to finish the recipe.' Della pauses here, a sadness entering her face. 'She needed something alive.'

I tear Della's fingers from my wrist, baring my teeth. 'Let go of me.'

'So the witch went outside and caught a wolf. She cut off his ears and threw them into the pot. The wolf ran far away and never saw the witch again. He did not understand why she had hurt him or where his ears had gone.'

'Stop telling me this story.'

'The witch stirred the pot and when she was done, she lifted out a baby. Pale-skinned and smiling. This girl was perfect. She looked like a fairy tale. But like all fairy tales, she was a dark story. There was something of a beast about her. Something of a wolf.'

'A wolf?'

'A wolf.'

'What happened?' I am holding my middle so tight now, I cannot feel my insides.

'Years passed and the baby became a girl and the girl became a woman. And the woman did many bad things. She murdered the witch who made her, burning her down in her tree. She blistered through the world with all her wickedness and many faces, and the world cried fat tears.'

'What happened to the wolf?'

'He howled and howled, looking for his ears. He missed the sounds of the world. He looked under every flower, behind every waterfall, inside every tree. He looked for a very long time. But he could not find his missing ears.'

'You tell sad stories.'

Della holds her head in her hands. 'Do you want to know what happened to the woman?'

'No.'

'She tricked innocent people with her pretty face. She upset many people with her wickedness. One day the woman travelled a long way from home and came upon a wolf in a wood. A wolf with missing ears.'

'How is this story about me?'

Della squeezes my knee, fingers biting into the shape of me. 'On seeing this woman, the wolf lifted its nose to the air and smelled all the bad things this woman had done and so the wolf tore her limb from limb.'

'But ... but why? Did he not want his ears back?'

Della shakes her head, her eyes boring into mine. 'He killed her because she had hurt so many people; he could smell it, and he did not want her to do any more bad things.'

'But his ears...?'

'Lily, listen to this story.' Della pulls me close, but her hands hurt. 'Bad things come back.'

'Why is this story about me?'

'Do you know, if you looked closely, the woman had a sharpness to her ears. Like points. Like the living thing she was made from.' Della brings an unkind hand to my head and traces the line of my ear. 'She had something of that wolf about her.'

I shiver. 'I don't like this story.'

'That's because it's about you. And you die, Lil.'

Panic rises in my stomach, to my cheeks, pinching them with colour. I throw off Della's hand. 'I am not a wolf. If I have to be an animal, I'll be a bird!'

'Come with me.' Della drags me to my feet and to the river. She holds my head still so I am forced to look at our reflection. 'Do you see? Your ears ... they are pointed.'

'Let go!'

Her fingers cut into my cheeks. 'You were not born. You were made,' she spits. 'You did not come from our mother.'

'I am not that woman in the story!'

'You are. I have never noticed how closely "woman" sounds like "omen". That's you. An omen come to upset the world.' Della pinches my nose, my lips, my cheeks. 'Even with that pretty little face. So perfect. You don't deserve a perfect face. I hated you as soon as Mother brought you home.'

'You're jealous.'

'I'm not jealous. I just don't think you should have it.'

'Stop it!' I am screaming now, despair spilling into every corner of my body.

Della whispers into my ear, 'I will tell you the story of yourself for as long as we live.'

HER – She-in-the-Trees

The birds are following me again.

If these Pale Bones rise like bodies around me, then the birds are their eyes, far up in the leaves. I did not think I would return. I thought Brid's words would still any desire to do so, but here I am. When she told me about her children, I ran so fast, tripping on my way, that I made her laugh. I fell asleep that night to the sound of her, and I worried she was outside my house. She was not, and now I am outside hers. Once again.

'We knew you would be back. We knew as soon as you left your door; we saw it on our wings.'

She is sat where I left her, tattered and feathered, only holding different birds to keep her hands warm. I did not notice it before: she and her creatures share an alertness, a keenness to their faces. But there is more. It is like they have the same eyes.

'If you and your birds see everything, how did you not know my sister and I had come to this island?'

She smiles. 'You are cleverer than those blue eyes and blonde hairs and peaches cheeks. You know that though, I think.' She nods, pondering. 'Yes. You do. You think and think. More than anyone knows.'

'Are you ... comfortable here?' I gesture to the chair, which has bursts of bright fungi growing from its seams. I am breathing in the husk of the earth and the mouldering of a living body.

'Is this really what you want to ask of us?'

She is small, this woman, even smaller than I am myself, with a body that creaks and so many lines to her skin, they are impossible to count, but there is something feral there, old and wise and sharp. I do not like cut fingers so I keep them inside my pockets.

'I do. I want to ask you about your ... your children.'

'Our sons and daughter were horrors in ribbons.'

'What did they do?'

She smiles. 'Their sweetness made our bellies ache. They never misbehaved. They loved their mother and kissed her every morning like she had jam on her cheeks. We hated them. We hated their smiles and the teeth inside their smiles, which made our nipples bleed. We hated their fat bellies that made ours soft and hang. We hated their fingers that tore at our hair.' Her face is different now, it is dark. Her fingers are tightening round the little brown bird.

'I think ... he needs some ... air.' I point.

She is not looking at me. 'We hated how they ran, but we laughed when they fell. We laughed when they burned their hands on our candles and when their fingers broke when we closed the door on them. We laughed and laughed like our bodies were full of it.'

'But ... w-why did you hate them?' I swallow. 'What happened to them?'

'We walked through the trees and collected bones in our pockets. At night, we would put the bones on the children's chests and the badness of the bones, of the animal's deaths, would give them bad dreams. We cursed them. They would scream for their mother, and we would laugh then too.'

'Why did you hate them?'

'We have always hated children. But we love our winged ones, so we found some cotton and we stitched feathers into our children's arms and snapped their legs so they could be winged ones too.'

'You...?'

'The Folk-on-the-Cobbles hated us. Because we drowned them, dragged them down, down to the water, the two boys and the girl, and they floated with their feathers all wet. Then we reached down, down, and pulled them out. We have long arms – Nelly-Long-Arms, we were called once.' She pauses. 'The boys died first and they cried the most.'

'I know ... I know this story. I've been told about you. You're the woman who killed her children, then brought them to the kitchen and sat their bodies round the table. Cooked their bodies a dinner. That's you. And your husband too.'

She cackles, and the trees outside all seem to lean further away from the hut. 'He died fucking. He was always fucking us or Women-on-the-Cobbles or himself. He was inside of us when we put the knife inside of him.'

'But why not just leave them? Take yourself away from this land?'

'Because we couldn't leave something that is something of us. Those children looked like us. They stole our nose and our eyes and our long arms and the sound of us sneezing. They gave it all back in the end.'

She smiles at me, and I wipe it from my eyes.

'Do you believe in the soul?' I say. 'Where do you think theirs went? Down to your Warden?'

'We made them into birds, girl. They are up in the trees.'

'Where will you go when you die? Will you be in the trees with them?'

'We will come back as an owl, and we will open our long, long wings and fly from window to window and take this land's children down to Him-under-the-Earth.'

'You will anger the Folk.'

'The Folk-on-the-Cobbles are full of madness.'

And you are not? I think. *No, you are not.* Because what she is feeling does not feel like madness to her.

'Does anyone know you are here still?'

'The boy who lives on the edge of the land.'

'You mean Silas?'

'His family is old. Older than ours. His blood has been in this land for so long, if you taste the soil, you'll taste him.'

'Is he really the only one who knows you are here?' I frown. 'He hasn't told me this.'

'He lets us keep to our trees.'

'What do you mean?'

'If he told the Folk-on-the-Cobbles, they would come to rip out our wings. But he is a quiet one, always has been. His sister was a fire and she liked to burn his little-boy fingers. His fingers are still sore now he is a man.'

'You talk in riddles.'

'But do you understand our words?'

'Yes.'

'Then where is the riddle?'

I wrap my arms round my sides. 'Does he visit you?' I ask.

'No. He is not welcome in our trees.'

'But I am?'

She sucks her teeth. 'You are interesting, girl. You with your scars and your mouthful of words you do not say. If you keep back those, what do you keep back in your head? You are careful, so very careful, always.'

I rub my arms. 'Yes.'

'What is keeping you so careful?'

'Nothing.'

'You have more skins than the one lying on your bones. More faces.'

I pinch my wrist, to see if she is right. 'You are mad, Brid.'

She laughs. 'Men call women mad when the women are wise and furious.'

But you are, I think. *You are mad.*

'People say things about me ... everyone thinks something different. Before I came here, people said my sister and I murdered our parents. I have a different skin for every pair of eyes. Sometimes even I am confused.'

I shiver. I am beginning to speak like her.

Brid watches me, keenly. She does not blink. Why would she? She does nothing as everyone else does. Then she says, 'No. Don't pretend with us. We know you know your skins. We see you ... little wolf.'

Only now I realise, her knuckles are white, so tight round the little body I think it must have been a very slow break. I did not hear its death but I watch the nut-brown bird fall, leftover grace dripping into the mossy earth.

HER – THEN – Stories of the Wood

'Do you want a story, Lil?'

We sit with our legs crossed by the river. The water laps at us like a hundred mouths. I always bring us here. To the river in the wood by our house. I have always loved the river.

Della smiles, a worry line in her forehead. She is young, only fifteen, but she looks like Mother and Father: they have that same worry. They've had it for such a long time. Della says it's been there for ten years. It arrived on the day I arrived in the world, slipping from Mother's legs like an omen.

I touch the worry line. Della removes my hands. 'That's yours,' she says. 'Does it feel familiar? Does it feel like something of yours?'

'No.'

'Strange,' she says. 'Because you put it there.'

'How did I?'

'With all of your small fires.'

I smile, take her nose and wiggle it. 'Why don't I tell you a story instead?'

Della brings her knees to her chest. 'What?'

'It's something we learnt about at school. The legend of Romulus and Remus. Two brothers born, then abandoned by their father.' I rise, circling Della, laying flowers onto her shoulders, her head. 'Then the brothers were found by a wolf and raised in the wild. Don't you think that is exciting? To be raised by a wolf?'

'That's something only a child would say,' Della says; then: 'We have finished playing now, Lil.'

I lay down more flowers, across her legs, her feet, her hands. 'But I'm making you pretty, Del.' I continue. 'The brothers grew up and wanted a city to rule over. But they couldn't agree on where to build it. They fought and fought. They had very bad tempers.'

Della looks at me suspiciously from the corner of her eye. 'What happened?'

'What do you think happened?'

Della hums, low, tuneless, in the back of her throat. 'I don't know.'

'One day, Romulus killed his brother, Remus. One had to win, one had to lose, you see.'

'Do you know what the word is when a sibling kills a sibling?' Della asks.

'No.'

The trees lean themselves close to us. The birds, if there are birds, come to silence.

'Fratricide,' she says. Della throws off the flowers and begins to bury me. 'It means to kill your sister...'

HIM – Ghost in Her Eyes

Lily leaves the trees, pinching the space between her thumb and forefinger. Her eyes lift to the sky, and she watches the birds make their strange shapes. She thinks they are following her, but they are not. He knows where she has been. He knows she's visited Brid, who is the island's crone, discarded by society and left to the wild because the wild accepts all.

Silas saw her pass his window this morning and followed her. He sits at his window often now to watch the sisters' house, to check on Lily through the many windows. Moss brought him a sandwich and poked him in the ribs. 'Isn't this a bit ... creepy?'

'I just want to know she is alright. That's all.'

'She's lived with her sister all her life and she's still alive. So she must be alright, huh? Anyway, Della has never upset anyone here, has she? She's not hurt you. Or any of the Folk. Have you ever seen her touch them?'

He shook his head; he hadn't. But he *had* seen her whisper madness into the girls' ears. He had seen her push them to the edge.

'You are very perceptive. Do you know that?'

She wiped her nose with the soft part of her wrist. 'Erm ... thanks.'

'How much do you know about the Pedley sisters, Moss?'

'Everything.'

'Do you know what people say they did?'

'Killed their dad – like I killed Orsan.'

'And their mother.'

'Oh ... yeah. I forgot about her.' She frowned. 'I feel bad for her. But I get it about the dad.' Her eyes slipped down to the sandwich she had made. 'But Lily didn't do it. Do you know how I know that?'

'No, Moss.'

She smiled. 'Because I cut my leg yesterday on barbed wire, and she cleaned it and wrapped it up. And she must have checked it hadn't gotten infected at least five times. Someone who worries so much about a cut couldn't cut another person. You get me?'

'I get you. Strong logic.'

She nodded firmly. 'So listen, do you want this?' She patted the bread with her finger.

'Ah ... no. Not hungry. You help yourself.'

A smile. 'Okay. Thanks.'

'The other night, you and Della were stood talking by the bonfire. What was she saying to you?'

Moss shrugged. 'Loads of stuff. Strange stuff.'

'Hm.'

'She had this look on her face ... It was weird.'

Silas frowned. Moss was the last girl left. Would Moss be her last victim? Did Della know Moss killed Orsan? Did she know he and Lily buried his body? Would she tell the Folk?

She shrugged, then tore away, through with their conversation. He waited until she had left the room, then continued watching the sisters' windows.

When Lily came out of her house, he followed her and now he is glad he did. Brid is not safe; she is not someone Lily should be spending time with.

'Lily!' he shouts as she approaches. And she smiles, opening her arms for him. 'You've met Brid then?' he says.

'Why didn't you tell me about her?'

'It sounds cruel but for the most part, I forget she is there in the Pale Bones.'

Her eyes dart back to the trees. He wraps a hand round the back of her neck, guides her where he wants her to walk. 'Come back to my place. Moss is at the river – don't worry. She's fine.'

'How did you know where I was?'

'I saw the direction you were headed. And I'm the only one who knows who lives in those trees.'

'Do you not tell the Folk out of pity?'

'She doesn't cause any harm. Not now anyway. And I think the worst punishment is to never feel calm. Did she seem calm to you?'

'No.' A pause. 'Your ring is sort of digging into my neck.' She winces.

'Sorry,' he says, but he does not remove his hand.

'Have you ever felt calm, Silas?'

'What does calm feel like to you?'

Lily considers. 'It ... it feels like a balancing, a stillness in the small parts of me. It feels like a breath, but a breath you take with your skin, your fingers, every part of you that you use too much and all of the time. It feels like rest.'

'When do you feel this?'

She smiles; he can see all of her teeth, even the molars. There is something animal about them, and he wants to tap his fingernail along each of them. Make a music of her.

'Oh. When I am by a river.' She shrugs, and the smiles goes. 'What about you – what is calm to you?'

Silas shrugs. 'I've never been calm. I think some people are born restless. Just as some people are born furious and fighting.'

'Do you think you'd feel differently if you left this place?'

'No. It would just be a restlessness I'm unfamiliar with. I would have to learn the world and the world would have to learn me. Where's the calm in that?'

Lily nods. 'You're right.' She gestures to the trees behind them. 'Will she die alone in there?'

'Yes. The forest will pick her apart, probably.'

'She drowned children and put feathers into their joints and now they live in the trees above her head. Did you know all this?' Lily shivers, but there is a flush to her cheeks, a lightness to her eyes, and Silas wants to hold all of it inside his hands. He wants to feel and know all the parts of her as if he lives inside her skin with her.

'Yes, she has a ... troubled past. She tried to bury herself once.'

'She tried to kill herself?'

'No. Not that. She thought if she dug deep enough and covered her body in the soil, she would be close enough to hear him – like someone putting their ear to a door. She thought she would be pulled through. That she would be honoured as a guest, a lady of the under-earth. But no hands came for her.'

'What happened?'

'One of the Folk pulled her out.' He pauses. 'This was before her ... well, her kids drowned. No one would pull her out now.'

'She almost doesn't seem real.'

'What do you mean?' Silas takes Lily's hand and draws it into his pocket, so she can familiarise herself with his warmth. She can have all his warmth if she would like it.

'She's like a ghost. When you turn your head, you can see it, out of the corner of your eye. But when you turn back, look with all of your eyes, she's not there. She's like something in a story: real, but only real because it's something that came from someone's mind and read itself straight into the mind of another.'

'You're very eloquent.'

She laughs. 'I'm delirious. I think she's rattled me.' She strokes her arm with a finger. 'Look,' she says. Goosebumps.

He blows his breath onto her arm. 'There. It's gone.'

She nods. 'Gone.'

Silas sighs. 'You'll go back again, won't you?'

'Yes ... Yes, I think so.'

'Why?'

'I don't know.'

'She killed her children, Lily.'

'Why do you think she chose to drown them?'

'What?' Silas wraps an arm around her shoulders. 'Why are you wondering these things?'

She glances back to the pale trees. 'Drowning, it's one of the slowest ways to kill another human. It's no bullet or bleeding. It's a careful, elegant death. Why did she choose that kind of death for her children?'

'I have no idea. I have not thought about it.'

Lily looks at him, right into the insides of his eyes. 'She hated those kids so why didn't she just stick a knife into them like she did with her husband.'

'Only she knows that.' He pauses. 'How could anyone ever hate their children?'

Lily takes a breath. 'Well, it depends on the children.'

'Are you thinking of your sister?'

'Can you imagine if I were to have a child – what if it was like Della? And it came from me, fighting to be rid of me. I don't think I could ever risk that.'

Silas's chest is string, tight, holding in his breaths. 'Brid has really got under your skin.'

Lily nods. 'She makes you think, cricket.'

Silas shakes his head, turning hers away from the trees. 'You shouldn't go back in there.'

'Why? If she were going to hurt me, wouldn't she have done it just now?'

Silas rests his fingers on her hair, where her skull meets her neck. *She is hurting your thoughts*, he wants to say. 'You love children. I've seen you with children here. You are always wanting to hold them, to be close to them. I've seen you cross the room to sit on the floor with a little girl playing with nothing but her fingers. You lace up their shoes, you sing to them. You dance with them.'

Lily smiles, and again he sees all of her teeth, the flexing of her jaw. 'Yes,' she says. 'I do all of that. But—'

Silas stops her. 'Do not go anywhere near those trees again. Brid is not a ghost you want in your head. She'll rattle around inside your ears and you won't be able to hear anything over the top of it. Understand?' *You won't be able to hear me*, he thinks.

She nods reluctantly. 'Okay...'

Silas gathers her up. She is thinned out. She hangs like he is holding just skin. If he were to raise her up, the wind would take her out of his arms. He cannot allow her to go there again. The witch in the trees will do her harms she might not even feel. His fingers close around the nubs of her spine.

'Don't go into the Pale Bones again, Lily.'

HIM – The Poor Maidens

He wants Lily close enough to smell her.

He wants to breathe the air she has had in her lungs, so he can have it inside his.

He wants a stitch from her body to his, so they are only ever a step from one another.

Silas is drawn from his thoughts when he sees Moss in the distance. She dances round the four standing stones – they are like fingers that have risen through the soil to meet the evening sky.

Since he was a boy, he has always felt a sadness here. His mother walked him through the stones, and when he came out the other side, he felt ill. She asked him why and he told her that he had a badness between his eyes.

He did not know how to tell her that this place made his body feel haunted.

Moss does not seem to notice. He is about to call to her but then he sees Della appear. She moves like poison water, drowning the good land. Her eyes follow Moss. Her thin lips press into a pale seam. He wonders if a body can really be haunted. Can a dead thing live inside a living thing? Can a mind in ruin ever escape its ruins?

He is about to run, drag Moss away from Della, her grim waters, but he finds he cannot move his feet. They have not seen him, and he decides to remain where he is. To watch them.

Della stops outside the circle.

Moss jumps. 'Oh!' She steps back hurriedly, putting one of the stones between her and Della. Her eyes are large in her head. Her blushed cheeks begin to pale. 'I ... I didn't know anyone else was here.'

Della steps into the circle. 'You should be mindful, girl.'

Moss wraps her arms around her stomach. 'Of what?'

'Of this land. The things you don't know about it.'

Silas recalls what Lily told him; how Della uses stories to upset minds, to pursue and unsettle and unskin. He is about to go to Moss to help her, but then Della speaks and he begins to listen to a story he has known since he was a boy.

'What do you mean?' Moss asks.

Della touches the standing stone with a bony finger. 'Do you know the name of these?'

'No. They're just rocks.'

'They're called the Poor Maidens. They have a legend just like everything does. A sad legend.'

'How do you know this? You're not from here.'

'The Folk told me.' Della points out each standing stone. 'One, two, three, four. Four sisters born hundreds of years ago. That one you're hiding behind is the shortest; so she was the youngest. The sisters lived with their grandmother in the village. They lost their parents when they were infants, and their grandmother was frail and old so they entertained themselves by dancing and weaving and singing out here. They loved to sing.'

Moss steps into the circle. 'What were their names?'

'No one knows. They are nameless now.'

'What happened to them?'

Della is moving closer and closer to Moss, and from where Silas stands he can see the muscles flex in the back of her hands. He wonders if he should find Lily. He wonders if he should pick up Moss and run from this beast.

'The legend says one summer's evening the girls danced here, late into the night. The sun left the sky and the moon took its place. Their feet beat the land so hard, like eight drums, and they woke the Devil.' Della crouches and bangs the ground with her hand; Silas feels the rhythm of it in his legs.

Moss moves closer. Her mouth is open, and he thinks she has never looked more like a child. 'Why didn't they stop?' she asks.

Della shrugs. 'What girl would ever think harm could come from her dancing?'

'Did they realise what they had done?'

'No. Not until it was too late. The legend says the Devil was so furious, he came up through the soil to punish them. He cut their throats, one, two, three, four. Four poor sisters dancing, then falling. The youngest, the smallest, she was the last one to go.'

'This is horrible.' Moss lowers herself to the ground, crossing her legs.

'The Devil turned their bodies into these standing stones as a reminder to all his Folk not to wake him, not to anger him.'

'Did it work?'

Della smiles, and the sight of it troubles Silas, more than any smile has ever troubled him before. 'Yes and no,' she says.

'What does that mean?'

'The grandmother loved her granddaughters. They were all she had in the world, and she was sad and furious and full of old fire. She could not bring them back and so she visited the stones every day, sitting before each of them in turn. She worried there was something of her granddaughters still alive in there, still listening. So one day she began to sing. She despaired. She mourned. And she sang. Long songs filled with stories.'

'Could the sisters really hear her?' Moss looks around at the circle she sits in, rubbing her arms. 'Are they still inside the stones now?'

Della nods. 'She believed so. She worried her granddaughters were lonely, and so she would come here every day to keep them company until eventually her voice travelled and it brought her neighbours to the circle. They listened and they sang too. Then more Folk, then more, until all the island's women sang the same song for these poor sisters.'

'Did they hear it?'

'They must have. No song could be louder.'

'Did it help them?'

'I think it must have. Would it help you?'

Moss frowns. 'Yes,' she says. 'Yes.'

'The grandmother passed away two months later. She died singing.'

'That's sad.'

'The girls were forgotten. They became lonely. And it is said that's why this piece of land is so bare. Nothing grows. Because the sisters are still inside, listening, and they are sad.'

Moss shrinks. Her cheeks are red now, tears drip onto her chin. 'I didn't know. I was dancing round them. I ... I didn't know...'

Della nods. 'Only the elderly remember. When they die, no one will know the sisters. These stones will just be stones. They won't even be a story.'

'Why are you telling me this?' Moss wipes her nose. 'What's wrong with you? I ... I know about you. About what you did. Lily says I need to stay away from you. And she's right.' Moss's voice rises, and she pulls her legs to her chest.

'I'm telling you a story within a story. You hear about four sisters dying and you think only of them. But did you forget to hear about the grandmother? She brought the entire island here to sing for them. There is more to the things you hear.'

Moss shakes her head. 'You're strange.'

Della smiles, but it is a smile of sadness. Silas has never seen her face like that before.

'What are you smiling at?' Moss cries. 'No one would come for you. No one. If you were like the sisters, you would have no song.'

'I would not want it.'

'Lily would not come. I know she wouldn't.'

'She would.'

'She is frightened of you.'

'Lily would come. She is my sister. She would come and sing me a bad song.'

Moss frowns. 'And you would have to listen.'

'Yes.' A pause. 'Even without any ears.'

Moss shifts, wiping her eyes. 'Even without any ears.' She looks at the stones. 'How do you hear a song if you don't have any ears?'

Della wraps a hand round her own throat, and it looks violent. 'You'd do this. You'd listen with your skin.'

'Like holding a song in your hand?' Moss's eyes brighten, but only for a moment.

Della nods. 'Yes.'

'What would that feel like?'

'Like music you can hold. Like a breath you need to take.'

Moss smiles. 'That's … nice.' Then the smile leaves her face. 'I don't have anyone who would give a song to me. Even a bad one.'

'I'll sing one for you,' Della says, and there is a softness to her voice. Silas can hear it.

'Even if I don't have any ears?' Moss asks, sweetness in her eyes.

'Yes,' Della responds. 'Even if you don't have any ears.' A pause. 'I'll sing you a song when you die, girl.'

HER — THEN — Fruit, Spider, Sister

We hold small fires in our palms.

At least that is what it feels like.

Pomegranates, still blistering from when we put the lighter to their skins and watched them burn. This game was Della's idea. Setting fire to fruits Mother gives us, blowing them out and holding the burn. This trial of tempers, this test of resolve. We are always playing our games.

We thumb a hole into our pomegranates, pick out beads that shine like something we would have round our necks. Della opens her mouth, and I see the back of her throat. A tear comes into her eye.

We blink three times, and on the third, we pour the beads onto our tongue. The agony of it sings. The juice tips down our chins. A keening sound comes from Della, her eyes opening so wide, I can see every vein in the whites of them.

My body hums, and I cannot differentiate the pain in my mouth from the pain in my palm: it fills my nerves and there is nothing that does not hurt. We are made of fires.

Della watches me. I watch her.

The forest has come to stillness, to silence. If one of us screamed, would Mother and Father hear? Come running from home, through the trees, to see their daughters, burning their palms with fires they have made from their fruits? Would Mother blow on Della's hands and press her lips to the wounds? Would she pick every seed from Della's mouth? Would they cry for our burnt fingers? Would they demand to know why we play this game? Do we know?

We are fourteen and ten, and we have always played.

'I hate you,' Della says. 'Know that, Lil. You are the worst thing in these trees.'

'You don't mean that. There are ghosts in these trees.'

'You're worse than any ghost.'

I spit in my palm, but it does not help the sores. The fruits are on the ground now. A spider dips its body into the juice, retreats, returns, retreats again. Then flies comes to the sweetness, and the spider comes again for meat.

We hold our palms to our chests like we are praying; but our neighbours call us Godless. Or one of us, anyway.

'What do you want to be when you are older, Della?'

Her mouth opens, then closes.

'You could be one of the people who find old bones.' I wipe my mouth with my cuff. 'You could find one of these.' I pinch her wrist. 'Or one of these.' I tap her chest. 'Or this.'

'An archaeologist. No, I don't want to find bodies. I've seen enough bad things already.' She carefully removes my hands.

'Or you could be this?' I lift a violin made of air and imagination, run my fingers along its glossy wood, make its song in my mouth – still raw so I make a raw song.

'A musician. No.'

'What about this?' I rise, pointing my toes, lifting my arms into an arch. I dip and twist and make my body the music this time. A music you see with your eyes.

'A dancer? No.'

'Then what?'

'I'm your sister. Sisters are there to mind their sisters. That is all.'

'I could be a singer. You could be a solider,' I say. 'Oh! Or a linguist and a pilot.'

'A mathematician or musician,' Della says.

'An explorer or an Olympian.'

'An astronaut or a Hollywood actress!' she says. 'That pretty face will take you to Hollywood.' Her voice has darkened.

We pause, watching one another. Like beasts, Dad always says, holding his stomach.

HER – Him-under-the-Earth

Brid opens the door for me this time. The bird she killed in her hand two days ago still lies at the foot of her chair, its legs pointing at her, condemning her. She does not care for its condemnations. She huffs and lowers herself, tearing arrows of dead skin from her bottom lip. She mops up the blood with her cuff.

'Why have you come again, girl?'

'Silas says you are dangerous. He told me to stay away from you. But I think if you wanted to upset me you would have already done so. Am I right?'

'We have no need to upset you, Girl-with-Many-Faces. You have not upset us.'

I nod, I decide to play into her delusion. 'Have your birds told you about the deaths of the travellers – the Americans?'

'Yes.'

'Oh.'

'You *know*.' Brid taps my wrist with a finger, eyes fixed on mine. 'You know why the girls died. So many thoughts inside your head. Has anyone ever known any of them?'

'My sister.'

'Your sister?' Brid takes the dead bird from the floor, begins picking the feathers from its wings. 'She is weary now. We know. We see how she goes door to door, strange things on her lips.'

I smile. 'You are speaking in riddles again.'

Once the bird is bare, its skin stiff and wrinkled, Brid throws it out the window. I hear a small thump as it lands, and I think, *Poor bird*. I imagine Brid's bent fingers twitching over my body, and I run my hands up and down my arms.

'Will you tell me about the mark all the Folk have on their fingers?'

'The tithing.'

'Explain.'

She lifts a feather quill to her mouth and picks out the food; but she leaves the filth under her nails. That can stay.

'When a baby is born, it is taken to the woods and it is cut with a knife that has cut hundreds of babies before it. It cut us, it cut Silas, it will cut all the babies who come after. A mark we all have in our skins.' She lifts her left hand, the three lines in the meat of her third finger. 'See, girl.'

'What does it mean?'

She smiles, taps it twice. 'It means we are one of His Folk. We belong to Him-under-the-Earth.'

'Part of his flock?'

She laughs. 'No. His Folk. We are no sheep.'

I feel Brid's eyes watching me. Fear skims across my back and shoulders like a bug.

'What about Silas's sister ... She left, didn't she? She managed to escape this place.'

Brid's fingers stop. 'Gaia? She did not leave.' The feathers fall from her fingers. But they are no longer simply feathers. They have been twisted and tied with a scrap of cotton pulled from her sleeve. They have a shape. Three figures. She has made a dead bird into her children.

I tell myself to breathe. Brid smiles, and I think there really is madness between those teeth. At the back of her throat and up to her mind.

'Gaia is still here.'

HIM – Poisons

She has gone back. He knew she would.

Brid lures her into her pale trees. She is about as harmless as a storm to storm-watchers. Lily will come away from there with blisters.

Silas opens the door to Lower Tor. He smells Della, the unwashed skin, the dirt of her, and beneath that, the sweetness of Lily. He is slow: he has time. He moves through the rooms, touching the things her skin has touched. But touching the things Della has too – he quickly puts his hands in his pockets.

Right now Della will be roaming through the streets like a ghost the street cannot get rid of. She is paler now than when she arrived. She has shadows. The darkness of those eyes run down to her cheeks. Perhaps it is an illness, but no, an illness would not dare.

Silas cannot remember a time the Folk were so anxious as this. They scare at the sound of their own breath, they walk with their hands out, as if they might fall or something might fall against them. Every word on every lip, every worry on every brow, is about the girls who died.

He follows Lily's smell up the stairs to a door on the left. Her room is simple: a bed, a chest of drawers. She does not have many personal possessions. He lies on the bed, wrapping her duvet across his chest and imagining his warmth is her warmth and his arm is her arm, delicately wrapping round his hip. He loves her right hip, the way it juts out above the waistband.

She has such nice hands.

She has such nice skin on her hands.

She has such nice bones under her skin.

Silas draws a leather bag from beneath the bed. It holds nothing of value: a set of pearl earrings that chip when he scrapes his tooth over them; a ripped page from a play – Shakespeare's musings on the Devil; a pink sock with lace trim. And more things – old and used and possibly second-hand. Silas digs his fingers deeper and withdraws the red ribbon he has seen Lily with. Usually she keeps it knotted round her wrist. He wonders what it means to her. He wonders if it is something she saves for her own child.

A creak on the stairs jolts him from his reverie.

Della watches him from the landing, some grim hum building in her chest.

HER – Girl-with-Many-Faces

'What do you mean?'

Brid cackles with such force, I think her teeth will come loose. 'Gaia never left. She's still here now.'

'I ... I don't understand. Where is she?'

'No one knows. Only Silas.'

'But why didn't he tell me? He ... he told me she left years ago.'

Brid plucks a mushroom from some stitching in the chair, drops it into her mouth. 'That boy with his bruising. All that gone-off blood. Like sour milk.'

'What do you mean?'

'Gaia hurt him. She played him with her fingers.'

'Do you mean...?'

She grins. 'She used every bad thing she could think of. She made a mess of his mind. He has a messy mind, that one – still.'

'So where is she? This island is small.'

'Nowhere you would care to go, I'm sure, Girl-with-Many-Faces.'

'Why do you think she hurt him?' I am leaning forward, my knees nearly touching the floor.

'She was born a girl, and the big man wanted his firstborn to be a boy. A baby knows things, and she knew she was not wanted as soon as the air hit her cheeks. She wasn't born crying like other babies. She was born silent. She was born knowing. And she fought and fought, until she and her brother were all twisted up.'

I want to meet her but I do not say this.

'How do you know all of this?'

'Gaia used to speak to us. She told us many things when she was alive.'

Brid looks out of the window at her birds. They are trying to get in, making so much noise I cover my ears. 'Someone is waiting outside our trees,' she says, and she smiles a grim smile. 'It is Silas. He likes you. A little too much, I think.'

'This land ... all its wretched stories. It's like it's infected. There is so much that is ... wrong with it. Before we came here, a man on the mainland told us that a devil fell to the earth long ago and he never left. This was where he fell.'

'Yes.'

'Do you think he fell like a man falls over his shoe? Or do you think he came here because he looked for it and liked what he found?'

'Clever, clever girl.'

'I've never been anywhere like this before.'

'Over time, we have had travellers come to this place for its beauty. Brides and their grooms. Mothers and their children. For fresh starts, for new beginnings. To run, to run away from old worries. But they always find new ones here. And they always leave with burnt feet.'

'Do you think you will always be safe?'

'What are you saying, girl?'

'One day someone might come and they might burn *your* feet. They might burn up everything living on this land ... and everything living underneath it.'

Brid looks at me, right into my face, and I think she sees everything I do not want her to see.

'We are left alone.'

'But for how long? Fear can run out. The people living on the shore might run out of fear.'

Brid nods. 'This land has scars on top of scars from all the times fear has run out.'

'Huh?'

'Many furious men have tried to ruin this land. One of them sailed his boat round the cliffs and he set fires. So many fires. It chewed up our crops and killed two of the Folk-on-the-Cobbles.'

'Did the man ever come back?'

'No. Then a woman came ashore one night, and she went from house to house and killed five men. Just men. She had filled a sock with crystals from home and she swung, swung.'

'She was angry.'

'Another broke into the school, and she gathered all the children to her and tried to take them away. She killed the teacher with a knife and she loaded the kids on a boat. But kids here are made of sterner stuff; they have grit in their blood. They fought back.'

I nod. Then, 'Why did you have your children, Brid?'

'We did not want them. Every month we would pray for our bloods. But when we felt her kick me with that little fucking foot, we planned and we laughed about our plans for her. And for the two boys who came next.'

'Have you always hated children? What about when you were young yourself?'

She spits. Then she whistles, and two birds fly into the room. They nestle on her shoulders. I wonder if she'll kill these too. If she does not control her temper, she will run out of birds.

Brid has hair down to her stomach. A smell comes from her scalp and the close places of her body. Not of rot. No. It is a badness, nevertheless, a wrongness, as if the world birthed her and realised its mistake. She speaks in riddles, as if she does not know how to use the words, how to carry them in her mouth.

'You're a cast-out,' I say. 'But you like it that way, don't you?'

'Yes.'

'I wouldn't.'

'No,' she says, and she looks right into me, as if she is pinching me. 'You enjoy people too much.'

'Don't you mean "like"?'

'No. I mean "enjoy".'

I nod. 'Can ... can I bring you anything? Any food or clothes or...'

'Give me news. What news of Harvest?'

'An old man died, about a month ago now. I do not know his name and I do not know if he was one of the three.'

'How did he die?'

'I don't know really. He had a mark on the back of his neck.'

She nods. 'Then he was the first of the three.'

'How do you know?'

'Him-under-the-Earth is cunning. Violence is man-made. Violence is human. But he does things with more care and more carefulness than that. He cuts them there because he is the voice in the back of your head, the one on your shoulder whispering into your ear. He is where thoughts come. At the top of your spine. He lives there. The same place you might feel a chill before it goes down your back.'

'How do you know who will be next?'

'You wait. It might be you next, Girl-with-Many-Faces. He might not like your many faces.'

'I don't believe in your devil. A man died, and the rest ... the rest is life. There is no Harvest. There is nothing under the land. There are just people. That's bad enough.'

Brid nods. 'People hide madness inside their bodies. But tumours push through skin to find air. And madness breathes.' She reaches towards me and pinches the soft skin over my spine where my devil lives. 'Who do you think puts it all there?'

HIM – Sore Thoughts

Lily appears through the Pale Bones, pinching the baggy space between her thumb and finger. He blows a feather from her head and wraps an arm around her body. She frowns, puts distance between them, but he eats it up again.

'I told you not to go in there.'

'I wanted to understand her, cricket.'

'And do you?' he asks.

'A little more.'

'Brid doesn't make happy thoughts. She'll make your head sore.'

Lily smiles tiredly. 'That's exactly how I feel right now. Like I have something sore in my head.'

'What did she tell you?'

Lily looks at him. 'She told me your sister is still here, cricket.'

'She's mad. My sister is gone.'

'But she seemed so sure.'

'I know more about my sister than Brid does. Gaia is gone, and this place is better for it.'

'She also told me about some of the people who have come to this island. About the things they did.'

'It's not a pleasant history, as I have told you before.'

'She talks about her dead children like they were monsters.' There is a frown on her face he wants to smooth out. 'Maybe children really are monsters.'

'No,' he says. 'No, no. You don't really think that. If you did, you wouldn't love Moss as you do. She's a child. No monster there.' Panic makes his throat thick; he struggles to swallow. 'You would do anything for her. You would do anything to keep her safe. Lily, don't let Brid turn your mind.'

She nods. 'You're ... you're right. Where is Moss?'

'She's by the river again. I think that's your influence. Why do you go there so much?'

'I can always think better by the river. What about Della?'

'I don't know. She looks very ... gaunt lately,' he says.

Lily sighs. 'That's because she barely sleeps. She's always got her eyes on me and Moss and you. I wonder what our lives would have been like, Silas, if we had not had our sisters. Do you ever think about that?'

He nods. 'Every day, actually.'

'Thanks for waiting for me.'

'You're welcome, hun.'

'Hun?'

He touches her hip. It is sharp and so smooth. If she has a daughter, the daughter will have her perfect skin. They would make such smooth children. But if she continues to see Brid, listen to her poisoned riddles, Lily will lose any desire to have his children.

'Come back to my house. I'll make us something warm to drink.'

'Alright.'

'You know ... you smell like a bird.'

Lily laughs.

'Now you know what you want to know, will you stay out of those trees, like I asked?'

'No, probably not.'

Silas guides her to his door.

HIM – An Unravelling

Della waits for them outside Higher Tor, fingers bent round something inside her pocket; a threat or a warning, he cannot tell.

Lily stops, going so still it is as if her body will never find any movement again. Her eyes travel across her sister, this language they speak, one Silas is still trying to learn. But he cannot learn a language they say with their bodies as much as their words.

'Where have you been, Lil?' Della demands, turning the shape in her pocket.

'Nowhere. I've been nowhere.'

'Tell the truth, Lil. Where have you been going these past days?'

Silas will not have Lily punished, so he speaks for her. 'The Pale Bones. The forest. A woman lives there. An outcast, you might say.'

Della nods. 'Come home. Now.'

'No.'

'Lil...'

'I said no. I will not come with you.'

He turns his gaze to her pocket. What is it she holds?

'Mind me, Lil.'

'I am finished minding you, Del. I won't be coming home tonight.'

Della brings her hand from her pocket, and Silas prepares to leap between them, but what he sees surprises him: a pomegranate. Red and full, and shining like a bruise.

Della tucks a curl of hair behind her sister's ear, drops the fruit into her hand and bites out, 'You'll mind me for as long as I am minding you.'

HER – Fragile Tempers

After Della leaves us outside Higher Tor, the pomegranate still in my hand, Silas draws me into his home. His fingers are gentle, but gentle fingers should not make me feel fragile. I have noticed small things about him, too many things that I have pushed to the back of my thoughts lately.

He tells me a story of a boy lost on the moors, and the worry rises in my chest. I listen, and I am an ocean of it.

'This was many years ago,' he says. 'The boy was young, only tall as my hip, and he was frightened of the dark. He begged his family not to take him out. He thought things lived in the dark, like stories live in a mind. But his family would not listen.'

Silas strokes my third finger, as if he is admiring the smoothness of it, whereas his is scarred. I sit on my hand so he cannot hold it.

'Why did his family not listen?' I ask.

'They hated the boy. The boy could not make them love him.'

'Why did they take him out onto the moors?'

Silas strokes another part of me, then another, as if my body is made for him. But my body is made to live, not to live under his fingers. I put some space between us.

'They took the boy out there to lose him,' he says.

'What do you mean?'

'They told him they were going to play a game. Hunt-a-boy it was called. He would run and they would chase. The boy did not know the moors. But he thought he would be safe, because he was not alone out there. His family would find him.'

There is chaos in Silas. Where did the chaos come from?

'Did he lose the game?' I ask, a coldness at the seams of me.

'He won the game. But only because his family didn't look for him.'

'Why not?'

'They left him on the moors to die.'

'And did he?'

Silas shakes his head. 'No. The boy turned back the way he had come. He walked and walked. He cried for his family. He was afraid of the dark, afraid of the moon. His family did not return for him.'

'How long was he out there for?'

'Too long. He hurt his throat from all his screams. He curled his fingers into fists, like this.' Silas drags my hand into his own. 'And he wept. He was sad. Sad that his family did not love him. That they lost him on purpose.'

'This is horrible.'

'The boy kept walking, so cold he could not feel his feet. Eventually the boy's sadness left him, dripped into the land. And the land gave something back. It put anger in his bones. He ran and ran. He was furious with his family for tricking him.'

A shiver gathers at the bottom of my spine. 'What happened next?'

Silas smiles. 'The boy found his family in the end.'

'What did he do?'

'The boy made them regret playing their game.' Silas lifts my third finger, presses his lips to it. 'His family took him out on the moors to lose him. Well, he made his family lose themselves in the end.'

I dreamed of Silas last night. He stood below my window and sang songs, of the island, of the greedy boy at the bottom of the sea. And of the other boy on the moors. So many stories, this land is ill with them.

The songs made my throat sting, because I wanted to scream at him to stop. I saw the boy in my mind, on the moors, sad, then furious, then murderous. I sweated through my sheets.

But he kept singing. I heard him rip flowers out of the beds and make himself comfortable, lying outside my house, throwing out his voice for me.

When I woke this morning, I rubbed my eyes and walked to the window. I could still hear him singing.

HIM – The Shape of Life

Silas sees Della and Moss by the old well. They are stood apart, Moss keeping distance between their two bodies, her eyes lifting hesitantly to the woman, who moves like she is only pretending at being human, like she is something even gods shiver at.

'Do you know the legend of this well?' Della asks the girl.

'No. Is it bad?' Moss chews her cuff, tucking one arm around her belly. She does not trust the animal in Della.

Della touches the bricks. They are hundreds of years old and crumble under her fingers. She wipes the dust on her trousers and points into the darkness.

'A girl used to live in this well. Her story became legend. Or so I've been told.'

'How can you live in a well?' Moss asks.

'Her name was Aine. She was seventeen years old and she was from the village.'

'Was she daft? She must have been daft if she wanted to live in this thing.'

'The girl was rumoured to be simple, yes. She would find the dark, close spaces across the island and hide in them. She was an adult but she did not feel like an adult. Then she became a mother without ever being asked if she wanted to be one. She did not like the horrors of childbirth, the way her babies upset her body, changed her belly and the shape of her. She did not like knowing herself, then feeling as if she did not. She did not understand her children, who cried and would not take her milk. Her husband was cruel and she did not understand why he did the sad things he did to her.'

'What ... what things?'

'One day Aine left her babies sleeping and walked out of her home, and she kept walking and she found this place.'

'Did no one look for her?'

Della sighs. 'Everyone looked for her. They were not sad or concerned for her. No, because that is the cost of care. They were simply angry because she left when they had not given her permission to.'

'What happened?'

'Aine did not want to be found. Her life frightened her. So she climbed into this well, she hammered nails into the wall and she made steps down to the bottom. The well had been dried out a long time, and she made a home down there in this small, small space. She liked the dark because it was quiet. She liked the close space because there was room only for her body inside it. She wasn't like other people. She needed these things to feel safe.'

'Wasn't she lonely?'

'Everyone has a different kind of lonely, Moss.'

'But ... she didn't have anyone.'

'Not everyone needs anyone.'

'Oh.'

'The years passed, and Aine's children grew. From babies into a girl and boy who looked and laughed like her. She watched her children grow from afar. She did not speak with them or play with them, but she grew to love them. She watched them pick flowers in the woods nearby. She loved it when they danced round her well. She watched it from the trees. She loved their smiles and laughter.'

'Didn't she want to be with her children? How could she love them properly?'

'Everyone has a different kind of love in their chests, Moss.'

'Oh.'

'As time passed, the children grew. They did not know their mother but something inside them missed her. They walked the woods, picked their sweet flowers, sang songs for her. A lament filling the land. And their mother listened and watched. But then Aine fell ill and died. Her body became part of the soil, and the rumour is that with her last breath she made herself into something for her children.'

'What?'

Della smiles. 'She made herself into flowers for them.'

'But ... why?'

'So she could be with them and they could be with her. Aine gave them herself, her life. Which she had never been able to give them when she was alive.'

'That's so sad.'

'No, it's not.'

'She died though.'

'But she lived too. And now, she is everywhere. She covers this land. Her children had children and those children smile at the sweet thing she created. There is no sadness here, Moss.'

Silas watches the girl press her fingers to the well. Della pats her wrist, a brief, light touch – a touch that surprises Silas.

'Why did you tell me this story?' Moss asks.

'To show you that good stories live inside the bad ones. Stories have many tellings. People have many faces.'

Moss frowns. 'You're strange...'

Della lifts a brick free from the well. She pushes her fingers into the space and withdraws something small from the dark. Cupping it in the bowl of her hand, she lowers it for Moss to see, tender fingers round the shape of a tender life.

A flower.

'You see. Still living.'

HIM – Bathwater

He can smell Lily.

He lifts his chin and follows the scent into the sisters' sitting room. The walls have coats of mould on top of coats of mould. There is no television, no radio. But there are books, dozens of them. On flowers and fungi, on gods and goddesses, books on how to save a man and also books on how to poison him. They must be Della's, those, he thinks.

Silas has always had a proclivity for smells. When he was a boy, learning to walk, to know faces, he grabbed people's wrists and brought them to his nose. First he learnt them by their smells. Gaia's was wood and smoke, something that caught in his throat. He used to struggle to breathe near her.

Lily is lavender, and something thick and sweet, like milk. Sometimes when she has her back to him, he will lean close and breathe down the smell of her neck. He'll hold it in his lungs and pat his stomach, working her into every part of him.

She caught him yesterday, her eyes widening. 'What are you doing?'

'You smell good.'

'It's soap.'

'Very nice.'

'Um, thanks.'

'You always smell nice.'

'Thanks.'

'What do I smell like?'

'I'm sorry?' she asked. 'Um … you smell like the earth, or something below the earth. Sickly. Something like pages, and something musky and a little like smoke. You smell like a lot of things.'

He had smiled at that. She liked the smell of him.

Now he sits in the chair he imagines she sits in, drags his nails along the armrests. He passes his hands along her books, opens them, turns their pages, just because she has turned them too.

Lily and Della have gone to the village. Silas watched them leave from his window, Lily following behind her sister, as if that is all her body knows how to do.

He climbs the stairs. Steam fills the air and it is bloated, heavy with her sweetness. He reaches out his hands, brings it to his nose. The bathroom, it comes from the bathroom. He opens the door and breathes in as deeply as his lungs will allow.

The bath is still full, the water cooling, forgotten. Broken lavender floats across the surface. He imagines her small, pale body filling the tub, then he peels his clothes from his own body and lowers himself into the warmth.

He enjoys the touch of the water that has touched her. He rubs it into his hair and between his fingers. Inside his ears, across his eyelashes. He covers himself in her. He wonders what she thought about as she lay here. He wishes he could think about it too.

'The Folk are living on their nerves,' Lily says.

She has returned from the village and now they sit at his table. He wonders if she notices he smells of her.

'They jump at the rain now. They jump at their own footsteps. I dropped my bag, and all the fruit fell onto the cobbles. Do you know what they did?'

'No.'

'They put their fingers to their mouths and told me not to wake the Warden.'

'They are frightened. They don't trust even each other right now. Mothers don't trust their children. Children don't trust their mothers. They have suspicion in their heads now. They think the Devil is punishing them but they don't know why. You could tip them into believing anything. But it would become ... something bigger than you would know what to do with.' Silas takes her hand and squeezes it until it cracks. She winces. He loves her bone music.

'They're all frantic,' she says. 'None of them can sit still. But they are sad too. About the men they have lost to Harvest.'

'Men?'

'Yes. I heard in town. Someone called Tom Willis was found in his kitchen yesterday. A wound in the back of his neck.'

'Two men now then.'

Lily sighs. 'I wasn't sure the Folk here could even feel sadness. That's such a human emotion. I thought all this history here would have cauterised them.'

'Everyone feels sadness,' Silas says. 'Sadness is our minds bleeding.'

'Yes, I suppose it is.'

'Where is Della now?'

'She's home. Probably having another bath.'

'*Another*—?' Silas stops, his chest tightening.

'Yes, another bath. I can't stand them. But Della boils herself. She comes out looking so red, I think she will blister.'

'She ... but...' Silas's tongue is thick, useless. He tries to swallow and finds he cannot.

'What's wrong?' Lily asks.

'I thought that was why you smelled like lavender ... because you had baths in it.'

'No ... no. That's Della. The smell of her just rubs off on me, I think.'

'Oh.'

His body itches. He has Della all over him. She is in his hair, in between his fingers. He is still wrinkled from the water she soaked in.

He wants to set his skin on fire.

Oh, God, he wants to take his skin off.

HER – Apostle

There is something about his eyes.

I thought it was something inside *my* eyes, a hallucination fallen into the corners where tears come from. I was seeing things. But there are alarms in my ears, and when I cover my ears the alarms are still there.

Yesterday, how he sewed a loose button onto my shirt and when he cut the thread, he held up his shirt and mine and said, 'Oh, I've sewn us together.'

How I smell him in my room, the oil of hair, the sharpness of cologne. When I am on the moors, alone, how I think of him and he appears, but it is not as if my thoughts have called him, it is as if he was already there, only hiding from my view. How he drips compliments into my ears.

'Your eyes...'

'Your hair ...'

'Your skin...'

I am more than my skin, I think. Don't you know I just wear this?

'You're so, so smooth,' he said yesterday, rubbing his cheek over my thumb joint. 'And you have such a nice smile. I can see all your teeth.'

'When you say that, you realise you are saying you think I have nice bones? Every day we smile and we speak, and we show each other our skeletons.'

His mouth opened, then it closed as if my insight had wounded him. 'Well, you have the nicest skeleton I've seen.'

I pulled my thumb joint away from him; it was *my* thumb joint after all.

'What?' he said. 'Am I not allowed to enjoy the look of you?'

'I'm going to go home.'

And he came with me. As if it was his home too.

'Why are you following me?'

'It's rough out here today. The wind might pick you up and take you away.' He smiled, lifting his eyes to the sky. 'I'll tie a rope round you and fly you. Then I'll pull you in and wrap you round my wrist.'

My chest hurt, then my wrist did too, as his fingers cinched tighter, tighter.

'That hurts.'

'Well, I'm holding you tight because I don't want the wind to take you away from me.'

'There is no wind...'

'There is. Can't you feel it?'

'There is no wind, Silas.'

'I think I'll hold on tight anyway.'

I picked his fingers away. I locked my door. I rubbed the red skin where his hand had been and wished I could rub my mind too, take the worry out of it.

Moss notices. She listens to our conversations sometimes, and now, when he leaves the room, she asks if I am alright.

I nod. But am I?

How long will I be alright?

I am reminded of our conversation by the river, of a God and his many faces. Of identities taken up, used and worn by a body, then discarded. Was he telling me something? If I looked deep inside the remote corners of his eyes, to the redness of his throat, will I glimpse another man? Or worse?

There is something in his face. I cannot look at him now. He has ghosts inside his eyes. Such hungry ghosts.

HER – Red Wings

The Pale Bones have changed. They have always been pale and bare but they had movement, they made a sad sort of music. They were alive in a way I could not stretch my mind to. Now they feel as if they have lost their flesh. They are silent; their bodies make no sounds, and all of their movement has gone.

I lift my eyes to the sky. Where are the birds? Brid's wardens and carers. Her sky-bound children.

Despite all his ghosts, I almost wish Silas was with me now. Moss. Someone. The trees are too quiet.

'Brid?' I call.

There is no answer. I follow the path I have made through the trees to her hut. My feet disturb the silence and I wish I could walk without them. The wind does not blow; it holds its breath back, as if it mourns.

'Brid? Are you there?'

I enter the glade and then I stop.

I have found the birds.

'Oh...'

Their bodies fill the ground. Red-wings. Eyes turned to a sky they cannot reach. Some of them still twitch, bring their heads round to me. Looking, looking. But most are dead. And I cannot help the living ones or the dead ones.

I step between them, struggle to find room for my feet. Blood coats my toes and I can still feel the warmth of it. Perhaps this one time, I should have worn shoes. There are cuts in their chests, knife wounds, and I wonder why this has happened. Why would she do this? It must be Brid.

I recall the little bird falling from her fingers the first time I met her; she had not even realised she'd killed it. Did she realise this time?

'Brid?'

My heart is throbbing in my chest, and I begin to run. I slip and right myself, then I throw myself through the door.

Brid is on the floor, a crown of birds around her head. Her eyes are on me, as if she expected me to come and she was watching the door, ready. They are empty now. They waited too long.

I kneel, press a finger to her neck. She is dead. I know how to identity death; it's something I have known how to do for a long time. Something about the eyes when they have been left.

'Bri—'

I see movement from the corner of my eye and rise, stumbling backward. A body lifts itself free from the shadows, and a scream curls round the bones of my throat. Della comes to me.

There is blood on her feet too.

HER – Sky-Bound Children

'What ... what have you ... you done?'

The words come out half formed, just shapes from my mouth. Della looks at the bodies on the floor, then she takes a blanket from Brid's chair and wipes her feet.

'Why did you do this? What harm did she ever do to you? And the birds ... the birds!'

Della does not respond, simply runs the material across her heels. She sighs, then she looks at me. 'I warned you, Lil. Didn't I warn you?'

'How dare you do this? HOW DARE YOU?'

'If you play with sharp things, Lil, you'll cut your fingers. Haven't I always told you this? You played with something sharp. Now look what has happened to this woman. This is your doing.'

'What? Why go this far? This is too much.' I look at Brid's body. At the birds. 'She thought they were her children, you know. She was mad but she made a sort of sense too.'

'She killed her children. A long time ago. I know.'

'How do you know?'

'You're not the only one with ears.'

'You didn't need to kill Brid.'

Della's stare is right inside my eyes, round the nerves. It makes them raw. She says, 'You believe the first thing you see, just like everyone else.' She pauses. 'Do you know the story of Icarus, sister?'

'No. I don't want to either.' My hands are shaking. But this is not fear. I am furious. It blinds me.

Della nods, notices my balled fists, then smiles. 'Icarus was the son of a master craftsmen. His father could make wonders. He could even contain monsters with the creations of his mind. Kings lauded him. He prospered. But then he made a mistake and he and his son were imprisoned.' Della picks a bird from the crown Brid is wearing, breaking it. She strokes the bird's head with something that looks like gentleness. 'But our inventor was clever and he fashioned wings for himself and Icarus, made of feathers, beeswax and cotton pulled from blankets. He warned his son to not fly too close to the sun. The sun would melt his wings and he would fall.'

She passes the bird into my hands.

'Do you know what Icarus did next?'

I nod. 'He fell.'

'He fell.' She taps my head. 'Because he did not listen. He did not mind his father.'

I drive the bird into her stomach, and she stumbles backward. 'We are not made to mind others.' I wipe the blood on her shoulder. 'You went too far, Della.'

I close Brid's eyes with my thumbs. Then I turn and I leave Della with her crimes and her wet feet.

HER – THEN – The Map of Death

'Do you think she'll tell us how we die?' I ask.

Della is humming again, deep inside her chest. I see that worry line in the middle of her forehead and stroke it with my little finger. Petting it, this thing I have made.

Della did not want to come to Penzance today. She does not want her palm read; she does not want to know her future. But now we stop outside the shop. Incense ropes round my legs, puts steps in them. Della follows.

'Do you think she will tell us how we die?' I ask again, before I open the door.

Della has stopped humming and the silence of her chest is strange. She pinches my neck. 'I don't care how I die. Or you. I only want to know who dies first.'

We are greeted by crystals, tarot cards, dreamcatchers, air so thick, oily like butter. I stroke a finger through the air and expect a sheen to coat it. There is nothing, but I lick it anyway, just in case. Della rolls her eyes.

The crystals are polished to a shine. I lift one to Della's eyes. 'Black like yours.'

She lifts one to mine. 'Red like yours.'

'I have blue eyes.'

'I know. They are too nice for you.'

A woman appears from the back room. She has lines like tributaries on her face. When she cries, do the tears separate like rivers, meet back at her chin? She wears so many crystals, she makes a rhythm when she walks. She pauses, her eyes going between Della and me, as if she cannot see us properly.

'Hello.'

'Hello.'

'You two are alone? You must be careful – girls such as yourselves have gone missing from this town lately.'

'We will be careful,' I say.

'Are you sisters?'

'Yes,' Della says, and it is as if she is saying *we have something dying inside us, and soon we will be in the soil.*

'Yes. I can see it.'

'No one ever thinks we are sisters. We look so different.'

The woman shrugs. 'I can see it.'

Della takes a step forward. 'How did you know we were sisters?'

'You're both stubborn, proud, curious. I can see it.' She looks at Della. 'But one of you has the Devil inside you. I can feel him.'

'Can you read our palms and tell us our futures?' I say, opening my hands to the woman.

She gestures to the back room. 'Take a seat. I would like to know this myself.'

We sit in velvet seats, surrounded by drapes with bells on. I stick my hand down the chair, find a crystal the size of my little fingernail.

'Open your palms. The little one first.' She looks at me. 'The sweet-faced one.'

I do as instructed.

The woman runs her fingers over mine as if she is touching something that could hurt her. 'The life line, the heart line. The death line. A map of you. I can see your behaviours. I can see your traits. I can see parts of you like I would see fragments of a reflection in a broken mirror.'

'What can you see? Do you know how I will die?'

Della is humming. It is so quiet, almost imperceptible. The worry is back in her.

'I cannot tell you how you will die. It might be of old age, it might be of illness.' The woman traces the lines in my palm, her nose nearly grazing my skin. 'You are a strange creature. You have lots of ... faces.'

'What do you mean?' I touch my cheeks and chin. 'I only have one face.' Then I shake my head, shrug. 'When will I die?'

The woman's expression hardens. She looks at me, into me. 'I don't know that. But you will die a sad death. Painful. You will be with someone close to you. But they will not love you.'

'Oh.' I pull my hands back.

Della sags against me. The worried hum she makes in her chest has stopped. Her eyes are wide, staring at the woman. 'What ... what about me?'

'Give your hands to me.'

Della opens her palms. They are shaking; I have never seen her hands shake before. I curl my fingers, drop them in my lap, as if they are useless now and have no function if they cannot tell me a good future.

'You are a different kind of strange creature. You will grow old. You will finally be able to stop that hum you have in your chest.'

Della looks at her ribs. 'It will stop?'

The woman nods. 'It will stop. Soon.'

'Does that mean I will die soon?'

'No. It means you will no longer need to have a song that takes the worry out of your body because there will be no worry.'

'Okay.'

I look at the lines in Della's palm, compare them to mine. Are they so very different? What does this woman mean by it all?

'Who will die first?' Della asks.

The woman shakes her head. 'Why do you want to know this?'

'I just do.'

The woman nods sadly, sympathetically, as if she understands something else Della has said. But what does she understand? 'You will find this out for yourself.'

We rise, throw back the curtains, head for the door.

The woman snatches at my shoulders, her fingernails cutting into the meat of me. Her eyes are darker now than they seemed to be moments before. The room seems too close, too small, and I snatch up breaths. I try to shake her off but she is strong.

The woman leans in and says to me, so quietly, 'You will die because of your small fires.'

HIM – End of Story

He meets her at the treeline.

He brings tissues from his pockets, begins cleaning her fingers before she has even said a word. Her smooth, smooth skin is stained and ruined.

'She's dead, Silas. Brid is dead.'

At first he thinks she is crying, but she isn't. She is shaking, her face redder than he has ever seen it. He can see her gums, lips pulled back.

'Are you alright?'

'She had to take Brid away. She had to get carried away with it all.'

'What?'

Lily pushes his hands away. 'She took it too far.'

'What?'

Silas tries to touch her face, but she takes his hands and pins them to his hips.

'She knew I was getting close to Brid.'

'Perhaps ... perhaps it is a good thing. Brid was dangerous. Just because she hadn't hurt you yet, didn't mean she wouldn't. She was wild and volatile. I worried for you when you went in there.'

'I was safe. She just wanted someone to talk to. She was like me – she was furious. Every breath she took was furious. She was contained by everyone around her. And she hated her story. We were like each other. She knew me. She actually knew me.'

'I know you.'

Silas tries to bring her into his body. She shivers out of his arms.

'Stop trying to hold me. I don't want you to hold me.'

Silas sighs, kneels, begins to clean her feet. 'Look at the state of you. You're a mess.'

'Did you hear me?' Her voice is high, and Silas sees a thread in his mind, pulled two ways until it is taut.

'Be calm, Lily. Let's get you cleaned up.'

She snatches the tissue and throws it across his shoulder. Then she runs.

And if she is running, he is running.

HIM – Moonlight

She closes her door on him and he tries to get inside but he can't.

'Lily?'

'I need some space. I'll come and find you later, Silas. But now, I need some space, understand?'

He nods, and he turns.

On the way back to Higher Tor, he passes Della. Her feet are clean but she is holding a dead bird in her hands.

She tips her chin at him, 'Poor you.'

'What?'

She continues walking.

'What do you mean, Della?'

Silas returns home. He pulls a chair to his window and watches their door. And he waits.

The sun sets and furnishes the sky with wounds. He closes his eyes, and the light through his lids is bright, matches inside his eyes. He enjoys the warmth. But he does not enjoy waiting.

It is dark when the sisters' door finally opens. Lily has her arms curled round her chest and across her shoulders. She looks so small. Her knock comes a few moments later. He is at the door already.

'How was the space?' he asks.

She breathes. 'I'm sorry. It was a shock. I didn't mean to take it out on you.'

'I saw Della. She said something strange to me: "Poor you." What did she mean?'

'I don't know. She is full of strange things. Best not to listen to them.'

'She was holding a bird.'

'She's put it on the wall. It's a reminder for me.'

'Of what?'

'What do you think?'

Silas guides her into the kitchen, rubbing his fingers up and down her arms. 'What does it mean?' he asks. 'The fruit. The other day, when she upset you. She was holding the pomegranate.'

She sighs. 'It's something we did when we were little. We'd each have half a pomegranate. Mother put them in our lunch boxes. She told us they were good for us. But...' Lily's eyes wander. What is she seeing? Whatever it is he wishes he was seeing it too. 'But ... it became a game. It hurt. We always made it hurt.'

'What did? Eating your fruit?'

'Yes. And the things we did to ourselves and each other.'

'Those games of yours again.'

'There were so many of them. But the worst ones were the stories Della told me.'

'You are the youngest. That sounds like the childhood of every youngest sibling.'

She smiles. 'No.' She says again, 'No.' Then tears come to her cheeks and rinse off the blood. 'No. No. No. No.'

Silas twists his fingers through hers. 'It's alright.'

'She's always going to be there. Always. Even when she's not in the room, she's in the room inside my head. Do you understand? Do you know what that feels like? I can feel her, hurting me with those damn pins. I swear, I can feel them now.' She hits her temple, softly at first and then harder. 'I wish I could shake my head, and she would fall out like something rotten from a box.'

Silas grabs her hand before she can bruise herself. 'Stop, you'll ruin your smooth skin.'

Lily's face is red. He tilts her chin and blows on her cheeks, dries the tears.

'That's ... nice,' she says, as the tension leaves her body.

'Then I'll never stop.'

'Do you know what I'm talking about, Silas?'

'Yes. My sister, Gaia, used to tell me stories, as you know. I think they might be what I think about as I die. What will you think about?'

'Della.'

'We will both think of our sisters. What a shame. What a pity.'

'You've told me about the boy at the bottom of the sea. What other stories are there?' Lily's eyes are large, peering up at him. He wants to brush his nail across the lashes. 'I'd like to know,' she says.

'She would tell me a story about a man who lived on the moon.'

'The moon?'

'She told me he needed no air because he had no lungs; he needed no food because he had no stomach. He had no name, because he was not a person like other people. He was an empty body made for one thing. He was there to watch *me*. To observe. If I did something to amuse him, I'd think the half-moon was him smiling. And if it was full, I'd think I'd angered him and he was filling the sky, hurting my eyes, trying to punish me with his light. You know that feeling of being watched? I've had that all my life.'

'Why did you believe Gaia? The moon is just the moon. No one lives up there.'

'I was a child. I trusted her, and that's a powerful thing. If you trust someone utterly, you'd believe them even if they told you your hand was on fire. You'd be compelled to check.'

'But ... you think someone is watching you, even now?'

'I can't help it. I look up and sometimes I think I can see him. He was put there to observe me, and he'll do it until I expire.'

'There's no one watching you, Silas. There are no gods and devils, no men on the moon.'

He looks out of the window, shivers, and Lily takes his hand. He strokes her fingers, one by one. 'You're so smooth, do you know that?'

She frowns. 'You say that a lot.'

'It's nice.'

'Gaia was cruel to frighten you with those strange stories.'

Silas sighs. 'I close my curtains and I put safety pins in them to close up any gaps. To stop him seeing in.'

She draws him into her arms, and he curls his shoulders inward to fit her better. 'Don't be afraid. You don't need to be.'

'It's funny – the things that you hear as a child, they are lasting. Those things do not expire.'

'Why were you frightened of him if all he did was watch?'

'She told me if I ever angered him, he would come down to the earth and hurt me. So I avoided leaving the house at night, I screamed if my mother tried to take me out. Gaia always liked that.'

'That's so sad.'

'Ghost stories are about more than ghosts.'

'My ghost lives in my house. She eats pomegranates.'

Silas nestles his head into her chest. 'I can help you with yours.' He thinks she might be smiling. 'Can I help you with yours?'

'Yes.'

He tilts his chin and brings her mouth down to his. Her cheeks are wet, and he dries them with his sleeve. She tightens her arms, and he is surprised by how strong she suddenly seems. He takes the kiss down her throat, onto her palms, between her fingers. Then he rises, gathers her up and carries her to his bed.

She is so quiet, he forgets to check on her, to speak to her at all.

HER – Wolf

I wake with a scream coming out my throat.

I am in darkness, something sharp cutting into my hand. My eyes adjust, and at first I think Silas is praying, kneeling in the middle of the bed, chin tilted to some god he has not told me about, but then I see what he is doing with his hands.

Pain slices down my skin.

'What are you doing? What are you doing?!'

Silas lifts his head and smiles at me.

'What are you holding?'

'I wanted you to be like me.' His face softens. 'I just wanted to make you like me. You can understand that, can't you?' He opens his arms, as if I will come to him, as if I will give my body to his. 'I love you.'

'You don't!'

This is not love; this is a sour love, a burnt love. Love turned inside of itself. A love that is dry as tinder before it flames. Something coming to nothing.

He has cut three lines in the meat of my third finger.

'I want a family,' he says. 'You do too. I know you do. You want something outside of Della. Something of your own. You've been stuck for such a long time. You know, before you came, I was going to cross the water, be brave. I was going to look for someone to love, to have children.'

'What ... what are you talking about?' I listen for Moss upstairs, grab my clothes; I will take the stairs two at a time and I will carry her too-big body in my arms if I have to, across the moors away from this beast living inside a beast.

Silas smiles at me as if I am simple. 'What's your name, Lily?'

'I-I ... what are you talking about?! What is wrong with you?'

'What is your name?'

'Pedley. You know this.'

He nods slowly. 'And what does your name mean?'

My breath sticks in my chest. 'It means wolf.'

'Now ask me what mine means?'

I do not speak. I am afraid to open my mouth.

'Silas Mair. Mair – do you know what it means?' He is inching closer.

'No. Why would I?' My chest is tight, and I put out a hand, palm up to stop his progress. I do not want his body anywhere near my body.

'I thought you'd know. I think your sister does. I think she might have guessed some time back now.'

'What? I don't understand.'

His eyes are so still I cannot look at them. There are those ghosts I've seen before. Cold curls between my fingers, down the soft spaces of my spine. I feel it everywhere. What does he mean?

'What does she kno—'

'Lily?'

I swing round and find Moss in the doorway. Her frightened eyes go back and forth between us, and I am reminded again of how young she is.

'What's wrong? Why are you fighting?'

I move quickly, without thought, only muscle. I snatch her hand and I pull her along with me.

She does not fight. She comes, says quietly, 'Why?'

I look at her. 'There are too many men like your father.'

Her hand tightens round my own.

Silas follows us, screaming. He grabs hold of Moss, and pulls her back. 'Lily. Stop this. COME BACK!'

I swing with all of the strength I can muster. My nails make holes in his skin. There. He'll have slivers of me inside him now. He pats the wound, then he looks at me, and it hurts the backs of my eyes. I have never really seen him angry before.

'Moss, MOVE!'

She runs. The lights are still on in Lower Tor. Della stands in the doorway. She is opening her arms for Moss, willing her to be faster. But I will sort my sister later; Silas will not have Moss and nor will Della.

I keep running until I am dragging Moss along after me. She falls, palms bloodied. I pull her up and carry her. She is too big for my body, but I do not care.

When we are inside, Della takes Moss from my arms, and I close the door on the moon and the man it watches over.

HIM – Boy at the Bottom of the Sea

He watches the house. He hums under his breath, an old song this land has always sung. He can hear the tide drag and draw across the rocks.

He imagines Lily older than she is, with hair to her waist, lines around her lips. He imagines the swell of her stomach, a child curled like a nut inside. He imagines putting his hand on her, his creation warmed and growing below. He imagines her when she has calmed from all this madness and comes back to him. He smiles.

He wonders if the boy at the bottom of the sea can hear him and hums too.

HER – Sirens

I hear Della's voice in the next room and stop.

'I need you to come and get us. Please. I'll tell you the truth. All of it. You were wrong. Everyone was wrong.' A pause. 'Don't you see? PLEASE. Get us away.'

Who is she talking to? What has she already told them?

Della's voice rises, in pitch and desperation. 'Did you really wonder?' A sigh, wearied. 'No one ever wonders.'

Who is she talking to? We have no one. No one from home. No one anywhere.

'Will you come and get us? Please. As soon as you can. I need your help. This place is dangerous. It always has been but now it's worse.'

Who is she asking to come and fetch us? Della and I have not spoken about this. I hear a muffled voice on the phone, a woman's voice.

'Where are you? NO. Please! We need you. It has to be straight away.' Della is screaming now. 'Please! Come and get us. Take us away from this place. I don't know who else to ask. We have no one. It has to be you. You said you would help.'

My chest hums. I hold my head. Who is coming?

'Thank you. Thank you! Hurry. You must hurry.'

The call ends. I push back the door. Della looks at me, her pale face older than it should be. Than it ever has been. There is something burning in the sink. I glimpse a number before it is gone.

Della takes a breath. She lets it go. And I feel the warm sadness of it brush my cheek.

Then she turns, putting out our fire.

HER – Harvest

Moss is asleep.

There is only darkness outside, the stillness of night before we tip into dawn. She has her fingers curled together against her chest, as if in prayer. Her forehead is creased, and I wonder what horrors happen behind her eyes.

I pick apart her fingers and break the prayer.

She wakes, tossing her head, wondering where she is.

'It's alright,' I say. 'It's alright. I'm sorry I woke you. You're in my house. Remember?'

Della haunts the corner of the room, eyes never venturing from Moss. It is like she has grown into the wall. Earlier, after she refused to tell me who was on the phone, she said, 'You didn't mind me, Lil.'

But she said so much more with her eyes; we have always been able to communicate like that. A language Mother and Father could never understand. I think they were thankful they couldn't understand it in the end.

'What's wrong with Silas?' Moss asks.

'I don't know. I think maybe I was wrong and he's like everyone else in this place.'

'But he wasn't … He cared about us. He still does. He must.'

'It's when someone cares about you a little too much, it starts to be concerning.' I kiss the back of her hand. 'He's caring too much.'

She nods solemnly, sticking her hand into her pocket, turning something round inside it. 'Why though?'

'Before Della and I came here, someone told us there was something wrong with this land, something under it, like poison in blood. I think he was right. I think everyone who lives here has poison in their blood. And they give it to their children. I think it's a good thing most people don't know about this land.'

'What put the poison there?'

'Perhaps they put it there themselves.'

'Why?'

'Moss, human nature is no simple thing. And Silas obviously isn't what we thought. He's had this inside him the entire time we've known him.'

'And it's coming out?'

'Yes. Some people are born bad – do you understand? They are bad people.'

Della smiles from over Moss's shoulder. There is a humour in her face I want to take out.

'Can we help him?' Moss asks, bringing a piece of paper from her pocket.

'I don't think we can. I'm sorry.'

'If he's poorly, maybe we can make him better.' She has tears on her cheeks. I rub them away with my cuff.

'Cricket, he's not poorly. This isn't an illness. We cannot mend it. He does not need medicine.'

'But ... we could get him proper help. Professional help, right? We could take him away from this land.'

'No, Moss. No.'

'Why?'

'Because we need to leave. And we need to leave quickly and quietly. Silas cannot come with us.'

'Why?'

'Because there's something wrong with him. He hurt me, Moss. Do you want to see what he did?'

I show her the bandage around my finger.

Her eyes widen. 'Okay,' she says. 'He's another one like Dad.'

'We're going to leave.'

'When? Why can't we just take the boat they use to go to the mainland?'

'You think Silas would allow that?'

Her fingers pluck the corners of the paper, harder and harder until it tears.

'What do you have there?' I ask, taking it from her.

'I found it in Silas's house when I was looking round, and I thought it was weird. I was going to ask him what it meant. There's just a bunch of names written on it.'

I unfold the paper, but I can see his writing, I can see the names already. I drop it. I pick it up. I do not know how to hold it.

'I ... I...'

'Lily, what is it? Lily!' Moss is sitting up, shaking my hands.

But I cannot speak. The list of names is on the floor now. Della is moving forward, alert, trying to see. I snatch the paper and drive it into my pocket.

I know the names. The first two have been crossed out.

~~Penn Melling~~

The first man who died for Harvest.

~~Tom Willis~~

The second man who died for Harvest.

I look at my sister and Moss, and then I look at my shaking hands. Because I cannot look at them any longer.

The third name is Della Pedley.

HER – Warding of Men

The moon is full, and I follow its light. I wonder if the man living up there watches me and thinks:

There goes a woman with violence. There goes a wolf.

I am full of it. My bare feet beat so hard on the earth, I will break this strange and nameless land. I will fall through and meet the Devil. Then I will come back up.

My chest works so quickly, I will stir winds; I will gather all of the Folk to me and I will send them into the water. They will all float with that greedy boy at the bottom of the ocean, then. He will not be lonely.

Silas opens the door for me. I look at him, this time I do not look away. I see his ghosts and I know where they have come from.

There is violence in me. And there is violence in him.

'It's you,' I say.

He smiles.

'Moss found the list.'

'She's found a few things she wasn't meant to.'

I close the door behind me; Moss tried to stop me leaving; she curled her body to mine and cried. Della picked her off me, and I said to my sister, right into her ear so she would really hear me, 'Don't go whispering.'

I know they will both be watching this house now.

'It's always been you.' How did I not know? From the moment I saw him.

He strokes a finger down my arm, right to the edge of my palm. 'My family have always looked after this land. Did you figure out what our name means?'

'No.'

He tugs each of my fingers, stretching them until the joints burn. And then he kisses my cheek; and that hurts too.

'It means Warden,' he says.

HIM – Legacy of Devils

'Warden...'

'That's right,' Silas says. He is surprised she does not already know this. Della does. Della has known for some time, he thinks. She watches, and she sees.

'But ... but how? How have you done all of this?'

'My family has always taken care of the Folk. Everyone needs an idol, Lily. My inheritance is this persona. This identity.'

'Did you know when you were a boy?' I ask. 'About what your family did.'

'Yes. Father of mine taught me how to kill. Small things for my small hands. He never showed me how to cut with a knife, how to tie a knot. "Your hands, your hands, son," he would say. And he would pull each of my fingers until they cracked. "These! These are your only tools."'

'He taught you to take a life?'

'Gaia was furious. Because this is a legacy. And Father did not believe a woman had the constitution. That's why he was so disappointed when she was born.'

'He tried to kill her, didn't he?'

'Yes.' Silas pulls on each of his fingers, and he sighs with the pain of each one. 'She bit him and the fury in her as a baby stayed his hand. As she grew, she tried so hard to soften him, but he was bare, hollowed flesh, you understand? She might as well have lived in the walls. Our ghost.'

'What a sad ghost,' I say, and I look at the walls, wonder if I tapped on them, Gaia would tap back. 'If she's still inside this place, I pity her. Because all she has had to watch is you.'

'When she told me the legend about the greedy boy, tried to drown me, Father broke her leg to punish her. She couldn't dance for months – the one thing she loved to do. So I danced around her.'

'How did it begin? This place has all these stories. Where did the Warden come from?'

'Centuries ago, when my ancestor lost his sight. He could not farm, he could not walk the moors, could not see the Folk. So his wife, Ura, took his duties. She was tall – so tall it was like she was part of the sky. Her head brushed across the sun; that's why her hair was so golden. She was like a giant.

'One night, someone saw her dressed in her husband's great coat, and from a distance, they thought it was a devil walking. Fallen from above. That's why Hell's Mouth has its name.'

'Did the Folk not realise it was just one of them?'

'Folk take what they are given. If the moon dressed up as the sun, would you still think it's the moon?'

'So that's where the Warden came from? A woman?'

'Yes. That is the beginning of the story.'

'What did she do?'

'She realised she could influence the Folk, use their fear of a name, wear that name and become a god. She could do anything she liked. She started Harvest to rid the land of anyone she wanted gone. She was the island's first female devil. And last.'

'This place has its own mass hysteria. One shared delusion, spread like poison.'

'It's a poison they've been drinking so long it tastes like milk.'

'No one knows it's you now?'

'No. Because who would ever guess? This place wouldn't be what it is without my family.'

'What about your sister? Brid told me she is still here. Is that true? Did she ever really leave?' There is a heat inside Lily's face and he wants to touch it.

'Yes. Yes, Gaia is still here. But she's gone.'

'What happened? Tell me.'

Silas reaches for her, and she wraps a hand so tightly round his, he winces. He tries again, and again he is surprised at her strength.

'Do you remember the story I told you about the boy on the moor?'

'Yes. The angry boy.'

'He was me.'

'You...? And the Folk know this story but not that it is about you?'

Silas smiles. 'It's funny, the things they don't think about, isn't it?'

'You're the boy.'

Silas nods. He stretches his thoughts back and thinks he can hear something tearing. He remembers his sister's hand, the shape of it, the heat of it. That hand that led him deep onto the moors. He was a boy, he did not know where he was. He did not think he needed to. He thought that same hand would lead him back.

'Gaia said we were going to play a game. Hunt-a-boy it was called. This was no hide, just seek. So I started to run. "Faster, faster," she said. And I remember my feet hurting because she'd taken off my shoes. She liked to make things hurt.'

'What happened?' she asks.

'It was raining, so hard it was like something was trying to punish us, drown us. I couldn't see where I was. I got scared so I turned back, but Gaia had gone. She did not mean to find me. She took me out there to lose me. You understand?'

'She was trying to kill you.'

'She had tried every other way.'

'But you lived, didn't you? You had to just go on living.' She says it with vitriol. And he wipes it off her bottom lip like water.

'How long were you out there for?'

'Five hours.'

'But you did not die, did you? Devil looks after his own.'

'So it seems.'

Lily's hand drifts to her chest, as if she is holding herself together. He puts his hand there too. He'll keep her whole. He will give her stitching.

'Perhaps you should have,' she says. 'Perhaps you really should have just died.'

'I kept walking and in the end I found her, my sister. She was dancing on the cliff. Always so confident. The land would never let her fall. She sang and she danced, and I got more and more angry, I ran out of room for it all.'

'What happened next?'

'I used the bone knife, the one my family has always used. I killed her. She didn't realise until it was too late. I cut and cut until Gaia returned to where she came from. Earth into the earth.' He smiles. 'I buried her at the bottom of the mountain.'

'So you're the boy in the story. The boy his family wanted to lose.'

'Yes,' he says. 'But I made them all lose themselves in the end.'

'And my sister? Della's name is on the list.'

Silas touches the three lines on his third finger. He says, 'She's been your own personal devil for such a long time. I can free you. I can get rid of her.'

'How long has she been on your list?'

'Since the moment I saw her, I knew I would kill her. I don't want her living on my land.' There is something feral inside his eyes, biting.

'How were you going to do it?'

'I was going to take her to the edge and throw her down onto the rocks. The sea can take her. It has taken worse. It will eat anything it is given. Even if that thing is rotten.'

'She would have fought you. She wouldn't have fallen screaming; she would have fallen silently, cutting you with her nails.'

I see them, their bodies tangled, Silas trying to catch himself, to live. But not Della. She would use the time more wisely: planning all the ways she would hurt his ghost.

'She has known for some time who I am.'

'How?'

'She watches. More closely than anyone I have known. She did not tell you?'

'No. She would have enjoyed seeing you play with me.' I will return home and I will make Della mind *me* for this.

'Why did she not tell you?'

I look at the marks Silas has put on my finger. I am one of his Folk now.

I say, 'Hatred.' I squeeze my finger until it bleeds again. My very own tithing. 'And Brid?' I ask. 'Did you ... keep her there? Is that why she never left those woods?'

'We had an understanding,' he says. 'She didn't know about my family but she knew I was not to be trifled with.'

I hold my head. 'It wasn't ... it wasn't Della, was it? She didn't kill Brid?'

'No. It wasn't your sister.'

'The birds ... you even killed her birds.'

'I was angry. You came out of there with doubts. She put thoughts into your head. I could see your mind turning. Rotting. You would give me such beautiful children,' he says, rubbing his thumb down her neck. 'They'd be so soft. I'd be frightened to touch them in case I rumpled them.'

A shiver scales my spine. 'I-I-I don't want children. I don't want your children. She didn't put any thoughts inside my head.'

Silas nods. 'I've seen you with the kids in the village. You love them, you worship them, especially the girls. But Brid was changing your alchemy. Infecting you. I had to kill her. And, I admit, I was jealous. You spent so much time with her.'

I laugh. It is so high and sharp, it cuts my throat as it comes up. 'You poor man. You poor, strange man.'

'Why are you laughing?'

'Because you're mad. You have seen what you want to see. You've put a madness in the soil of this place so it feels like it's alive. This island. It doesn't have a name,' I spit. 'It doesn't deserve one.'

'I am no madder than any man on the mainland. We all have to have someone to listen to, to gather to, Lily. I wear a name. I keep people in line. That is all.'

'You've been inside my house as well, haven't you?' I say. 'I've smelt you in my room, on my sheets. You've been everywhere.'

'Yes.'

The rope is tight across my belly; I feel as if I cannot breathe. There is air in this room, but it is not here for me.

'Do you enjoy it?' I ask. 'The killing?'

He smiles. 'Gaia was my first. I'd like to be my son's first.'

'Do you mean...?'

'When I am old, I want him to do it. It has a poetry to it. I want him to be gentle with me. But yes, when my time as Warden is over.'

'This has always been your hope: to have my children? For your disgusting legacy?'

'We'd make beautiful little devils, Lily.'

'You're ... you're mad.'

'Don't worry. Moss can stay with us. I know you are fond of her. She'll be my daughter too.'

The rope breaks. I take a step towards him. Then another.

'Moss is not yours.'

'She is. You all are.'

I lay an unkind hand on his chest. I will take out its beat. 'You leave her be, Silas.'

He laughs, and I want him to choke on it.

'We'll be a family. Moss will be our daughter, then we will have a son, and Moss will have a brother. She will teach him songs of this land. Tell him stories. Even if they frighten him. Especially if they frighten him. We will make him strong. And he will be Warden.'

I have a violence under my skin. It fills my fingers. It runs to all of my edges, the pieces of me that can take apart all the pieces of him. I look at my hands; they have moons inside them, bloody and red. I am not afraid anymore. I am something else.

'Moss does not belong to you, Silas.'

'Don't be angry, Lily.'

'I said, she does not belong to you.'

'Why are you being like this? You are so protective of her.'

'Moss is not yours. Understand? She will not be a daughter in your story.'

'But she already is. All this time I have been feeding her breakfast, watching her when you have been away. She asks me questions, such funny little questions.'

'She is twelve. All she has are silly questions.'

'You've always stayed so close to her. She is all you talk about some days. Your face changes when you are with her. I've watched it.' Silas holds his hands to his chest. 'It's beautiful. You're her mother. The only mother she has ever had.'

'Stop it.'

'And I'll be a better father than the one she left behind.'

'I do not want to be her mother. You've seen strange things, Silas. Your eyes are wrong.'

'We'll all live together here. When Della is gone, you'll have your freedom. I can give that to you.'

Silas looks at me as if he wants to bathe himself in me. I wipe my palms on my arms. I gather my calm, on the floor now, then I turn and walk out the door.

'Lily?' he shouts. 'Lily!'

I keep walking. I have my violence in my feet and my calm in my hands. I drag it back home, like a bleeding animal.

I will not have it. Moss does not belong to him. He will not possess her. He will not possess *me*. I will take something from him: his name.

I see two curious faces peer at me from the window of Lower Tor. I pause, glance over my shoulder. And in Higher Tor, another face looks at me.

Rage arrives in winds and rivers inside my body. It tips me back, it pulls my hair and lifts my arms. It moves me. I know where it moves me to.

I am watched. By them all. And I open my fingers and give my calm to the wind.

Then I turn and I begin walking, not to Moss, or to Della or to Silas.

I go to the village and to the Folk.

HIM – Living Stories

He watches her walk to the village.

Why is she walking to the village?

Why is she pulling away from him? Does she not feel for him what he feels for her?

He has felt it for her from the moment she stepped onto his land. He was going to cross to the mainland, to find a woman who could continue his line. He planned to spend a week there looking, then bring her back. He did not really mind what she looked like. But he wanted two children from her. He wanted a boy, and he wanted a girl. He would call the girl Gaia. For his sister. If he had any luck, the child would look like her too.

And he would do everything his sister had done to him to his daughter.

When Lily walked through the door of the inn, he lost all the feeling in his hands. He dropped the glass he was holding, and busied himself cleaning up the glass while he calmed his thoughts. She was perfect, small, blonde, blue-eyed. With straight teeth, shiny nails. She was beauty. Cut her open and she would be sweet on the inside too.

Her sister, he wanted to drown. He could feel her standing on his land. She was a haunting, a ghost tethered to her sister's body. The Folk enjoyed her, the strangeness of her. But that is because they are children, interested by new things, things that can make them feel safe.

'How are you so different to your sister?' he asked her once, soon after she arrived on his land. They were watching Lily play with a girl, curling her finger through the child's blonde curls. Della's eyes were not on the child though, they were on her sister.

'We are made of different things,' she said simply.

'What does that mean?'

'When a mother gives birth, all she wants is to hold her baby. She wants it with her bones.' Della looks at him, right into the corners of his eyes. 'When our mother gave birth, she wanted to put her daughter down. She wanted the nurse to take her back. Can you guess which one of us it was?'

Silas looked at Lily, the way she danced with the child. 'You're jealous of her, aren't you?'

Della laughed. There it was, that wildness inside her throat, a desperate and wearied animal. 'Jealous? You fool.'

Silas opens the door and follows Lily's steps. The lights are on in Lower Tor. He can see two shapes pressed against the glass. Della has an arm wrapped around Moss's shoulder. Moss is curled into her. He turns his back and makes his way into the village.

He cannot see her but he knows where she has gone. He can smell her, the sweet milk of her skin in the street. She is inside the Moloch Inn. He watches her through the window. She is standing against the bar, talking to the Folk. Her mouth is moving so quickly, words cease to be words. They all become one shape.

Is she telling them he is the Devil?

They will not believe her. She cannot tell them their god is not a god. Minds cannot be changed in a night when those minds have had the same thoughts their entire lives. The Folk will not be moved. They will laugh, show their teeth, they will clap her on the back and ask her if she was born with that belly full of jokes.

But they are not laughing.

Lily looks between them all. She is asking them something?

Her mouth makes the shape of his name.

What does she want to know? He has told her everything.

The Folk glance at each other, doubt in their eyes, in their brows, in the nervous tap of their fingers against their pints. Lily keeps talking. She has a gale inside her. She will blow all of these people from their seats.

He catches his name again. What is she saying about him?

The Folk gather closer together, untethered. They are nervous, questioning. He thinks he sees sweat on a few foreheads.

He must know what Lily is saying.

He throws open the door, and like the hands of a clock, all bodies turn, eyes coming to rest on him.

HER – Torch

I set fires.

I set them under skins, then I set them in the streets.

The Folk gather and follow me, bringing fires of their own now. I see it in their faces. In the way they walk as if they can't bear to touch the earth.

The moon throws down its light, and I wonder if the man living up there watches and waits. If he is smiling because his eyes are tired and soon he will no longer have to watch. I wonder if that boy at the bottom of the sea sings a lament for someone who was once meant to join him. Does he feel cheated? He won't be cheated tonight.

I walked my bare feet to the inn and I brought all the Folk close to me. I did not tell them that their Devil is not real, that he is simply a man, a family through the generations. I did not tell them everything they have ever known is false. They would not believe it. They would cut me apart to protect their god. Because what is a god without the violence of devotion?

Instead, I flexed my fingers and dropped doubt in their minds. Right at the back where it is most likely to seed. I will not be dominated. I will not give myself to Silas's delusions. I will not give over Moss. I will break his legacy.

'How well do you know Silas Mair?' I asked them. How well do you know one of your own?

Their mouths gaped at me: suspicion, then confusion. 'What are you talking about?' one of them asked. I did not know his name. The Folk all look the same.

'Do you know him well?' I asked. 'Have you ever been inside Higher Tor? How much do you know of his family?'

'The Mairs are one of the land's oldest—'

'Families, yes, I know. But I'm asking you, how well do you know him? Does he ever talk about himself? Or does he just pour drinks down your throats and listen to you talk?'

'Well ... he...'

'Does he participate in your festivals?'

'No ... he ... he...'

'Do you hear him talk about your Warden?'

'Silas is quiet ... He likes his own company... He...'

I stood, looking from face to face. Even the children. They held their breath, doubt in the dumb shape of their mouths. I lifted my voice, a storm gathering in my belly, curling up my spine and out into my fingers.

'Does Silas ever name your Devil? Does he ever give him offerings? Does he pray to him? Does he honour him?' My voice burns.

They shift in their seats, rubbing their arms as if they can feel some heat. 'What are you saying?'

'I am asking you if Silas really believes in your Warden.'

There was more movement then, suspicion tilting their heads, eyes revealing the whites. Their feet brought them closer to me. I spoke and spoke, gave them a story until their minds were full of it.

'Silas does not worship your Devil. He mocks you. I've heard him. He takes your custom and he listens to your conversation. Then he brings the stories back to me and he laughs. Do you see?' I threw out my arms. 'The morning after I arrived, he was going to leave you. He was going to cross the water and go to the mainland. He is bored of you, of all your talk. He was going to abandon this land.'

'But he ... he has lived here all his life. He is one of us Folk.'

I laughed, made the laugh as big as it would go. 'Those American girls, the travellers? Did you notice, he spent a lot of time with them, didn't he? He was always there, whispering in their ears? Then they died, didn't they?' Lies. All lies. Silas did not go near them.

The Folk were like children, dangerous children. I asked them if they saw something, and so of course they thought they did because they didn't want to say no. The Mairs had conditioned them to move and think within small parameters. So small, I thought, *These bodies are just bodies*. There was no life in any of them. They were behind bars they did not know were there.

'That is why your Warden is angry. Silas took something from him.

Do you understand? He is not one of you. He is not loyal. He is a burden on this land.'

They were shivering. Red faces were turning pale. The children were looking at their mothers. The mothers were looking at their husbands. The husbands were looking at me.

'He is madness,' I said. 'He is not one of you.'

The door opened then and a cold wind rubbed against our bodies. Silas stood there, paused between one step and the next. He looked at us all, something like fear dripping onto his face. And I wanted to laugh, because it looked like tears.

It only took a moment to unmake a man.

I had done it in the space of a breath. I would not be owned. I was no possession. I was no vessel. And neither was Moss. I would possess, I would gather.

Silas took a step back, hesitant at first. I looked at the Folk, at my fires, and then I watched their Devil turn and run.

Now we move through the street, with such a fury inside us, even the darkness moves out of our way. The Folk are galvanised, walking as one animal, beating the land so hard, I wonder if those people across the water will feel it in their feet. Someone wraps their shirt round a branch and makes a torch. They do not speak. They say enough with their silences.

They will not leave the Devil to rest.

HIM – Folk-Horror

He will calm them, he will diminish them. He has been doing so since he was a boy.

They are children, weak children. He can mollify children. It only ever takes a few words. He will be alright.

He goes to his window. He can see a light in the distance.

What did she say to them?

What did she say to them?

They are coming. Panic torches his body. Sweat drips down his spine. But he is cold, because he is afraid now.

He looks at Lower Tor, sees the faces of Della and Moss in the window, and he puts his hand up. He wishes they would help him.

The Folk are coming.

His Folk are coming.

THEM – THEN – The Story of the Pedleys

We were never just two sisters.

We were three.

My little sister cannot speak but she brings us flowers, a different shade to show us every emotion she holds in her body. She cannot speak but she can laugh. She runs through the halls, and Mother, Father and I find ourselves following, just to hear it longer, to keep the sound of it close, as if it can keep us safe from all harms.

She cannot speak; some would say she is simple, but we do not care. Her name is Tab and she draws people as a candle does a moth. How can you look away when something is so bright?

She curls into my lap, small for her four years but so vast in soul, it pours out of my fingers.

'Tab-Tab,' I say. 'Bedtime.'

She refuses to go to her own bed, simply curls up between my legs, the smell of her smooth and sweet like milk. I let her fall asleep like this, then I carry her across our room and tuck her into her covers. But always, she will come back. When I wake up in the night, she is there, once more fitting herself to the shape of my legs. She is Mother and Father's favourite. I do not mind. She is my favourite too.

She is protected by us all. But she has never been safe.

When Mother brought her home and put her in my arms, I made my arms wire. To keep all the harms away from her body. I looked at my other sister, our animal in the corner of the room, our ghost, and I held Tab to my chest, so close it was as if I was trying to put her inside my heart. At least then my bones could keep her safe.

Our ghost had found someone new to haunt.

I wake in the night and stretch my fingers for Tab.

'Tab?' I say, throwing out my arms to gather her up. My arms are empty. 'Tab? Have you gone to your own bed?'

I throw back her duvet but she is not there. I listen for movement inside the house. The rooms are small, and I can hear my mother and father breathing in the next room, the turn of their bodies, the life of them. I can hear the drip of a tap downstairs. I can hear the forest outside, the night music.

I hurry downstairs, check the kitchen, where I have found her before, spoon dripping honey onto her tongue. I check the bathroom. I check above and below. I check the garden. She is nowhere.

Outside, the moon makes everything look as if it is in mourning. Shadows gather, and if I were to lose reason, I would think they are gathering to me. They sit in my joints and hang at the back of my throat. I feel too heavy, as if they might pull me through the earth, all the way down to hell and the Devil.

Where are my sisters?

I stand in the garden, see two sets of footprints. I follow them, closer, closer to the forest. I have a drum in my chest and it bangs so loudly.

Where has she taken her?

I consider waking Mother and Father, but that would take time I do not want to lose. I keep moving. I call their names. The names echo back to me. But my sisters do not come.

We used to play in these trees; we used to dance in them. Mother and Father made games, sent us on hunts. We returned home with aching chests, weary from all the laughter we had made. Tab was given her spoon of honey, and we laughed again at the sweetness of her, at the stick of her fingers when she touched our cheeks. The only one who did not laugh was our ghost. Perhaps ghosts cannot laugh, I thought at the time. Perhaps they do not have the space inside themselves.

'Tab?' I shout.

I throw out my arms, follow the footprints. Even with only slivers of light, I know where I am. I am walking into the Red Room.

I cannot remember which of us called it that first. It was before Tab was born, and we would sit with our bodies close together, a knot of legs and arms that always hurt more than it should. The ground is filled with flowers, their red heads soft as wool. They look like faces, one of us said, smiling. They make the ground look like it is bleeding, said the other.

I look at the space around my feet. It does, I think; it looks like the earth has a wound, and we are walking across it.

I kneel on the ground, brush my fingers across the velvet of the flowers, then I rise, and I continue through the Red Room. A voice fills the air, breaking apart the silence. The birds leave me, frightened. Don't they know I am frightened too? I wish they had stayed.

I know her voice. Even ghosts have voices.

But then there is another voice, a sweeter one. I begin to run. I hear a splash, the sound of laughter coming undone, tearing itself into screams.

'Tab!' I shout. 'Don't go in the river.'

I run faster, the shadows inside me coming together, filling my chest, and I realise they are not shadows. They are a warning, my bones telling me something bad.

'Don't go in the water! Stay away from the water.'

Why did she take Tab to the river? She is too small. It is dangerous. My lungs ache and blood sits between my toes. I have hurt myself but I do not feel the wounds. I push through the branches, and I see them. I see them!

'Tabitha!'

But no. I do not see them. I only see one sister.

I stop. And something inside me stills. Perhaps it is my heart, or my breath, perhaps it is all of it, everything that makes me live.

Tab is under the water, her small, sweet body. Her mouth is open, she is trying to scream, but the water will not let her.

And my sister, she is holding her down.

'Stop! STOP!' I scramble through the blood flowers. 'LET HER GO!'

Tab opens her hands for me. She looks for me. She is afraid and she is confused. She does not understand what is happening and why it is being done to her.

I try to tear my sister from Tab's body, but she is strong, with a steel in her no man, no woman, no god or devil could win against. 'STOP IT STOP IT STOP IT STOP IT.'

Tears are on my cheeks, in my mouth. I take a fistful of my sister's hair and tear it away. But still, she keeps Tab under.

'*LET HER GO.*'

'*No. No!*'

'*You'll kill her!* I fall back and take a rock from the riverbed. I bring it down on her forehead. Blood gushes down her neck. Still she does not let go. She will not let go. I know that face. I've seen that face when she poisons the animals. The violence she came into this world with. I cry, bringing the rock down again and again on my sister's back.*

'*Let her go. Let her go. Let her go.*'

I am chanting, a strange song to stop her. Tab's fists dip below the water, her legs kicking out. Then they are still.

I scream, and the sound of it empties the trees. It empties me. I throw myself under the water and I hold my mouth to hers, I push my breath into her small lungs. She looks at me, a drip of honey still on her chin. The water has not taken it away.

But she does not move.

Tab does not move.

I fall back and I hold my stomach.

She is gone.

She is gone.

Finally, my sister strokes Tab's cheek and she leans back with a clear smile and says, '*Sleep well, cricket.*'

Then my younger sister looks at me. And everything living in me, stops.

'*Lily,*' I say, '*what have you done?*'

HER – Witch Words

We do not leave the Devil to rest.

Higher Tor rises like a beast from the land. It is frightening, but it does not frighten me. Beasts never have. Mother and Father said there was something of the Devil about me. They said I had a wolf in my throat. When I was young I stood in front of the glass, opened my mouth wide until the small bones in my neck cracked, and looked for this animal. The children passing the window at the time screamed, ran from me. I smiled and patted my throat.

The Folk move around me, more than flesh now. They have become gods. Their feet hammer the earth; they will leave holes. Nothing will grow here now; nothing will dare. Their eyes are wide with fires. I can feel the heat of them. The children come – they are angry too. If we are a muscle, our bodies moving together, we are a fist.

I dance between the Folk, whispering in their ears. Mother called them my 'witch words', the bad things I would say. She gave me a glass of salt water once. 'I hope it cleans you out,' she said. I held it in my mouth for a beat, then I spat it at her, laughed when some of it went down her throat. I said, 'Do you feel clean now, Mother?'

The Folk look at me, like pale, sweet lambs. 'He lied to us,' I say. 'He's been laughing at all of us.'

I move to the next one. 'He's false.'

And to the next. 'He has no Warden.'

And to the next. 'He is not one of you Folk.'

They shiver, and the shiver moves down the whole of their bodies.

I did not guess his strange story. Not even when I saw the bone knife Moss found. I stroked the handle when they were not looking. Now I wonder how many skins it has seen the inside of, what it would feel like, sliding it into that of Silas.

I did not guess his story, and he did not guess mine. The beast was never inside Della; it was inside me.

I will not be possessed. And nor will Moss. She belongs to me. She always has. She reminds me of Tab, with her sweetness and questions. I wonder if she will drown like her, too, when the time comes.

I will possess. I will gather.

I look at the moon and smile. I do not care if the Folk see. I look forward to having this land, to taking a name and becoming Warden. As soon as Silas told me, I wanted it. I will step into his legacy, this legend. I will become Her-under-the-Earth.

I lift a box of matches from my pocket. I'll start the fire. And we will keep this man inside his walls. They may not know it, but the Folk are going to burn their saint. They are going to bring down their Devil.

HER – THEN – Salt, Soil, Sorrow

Della and I sit in the Red Room.

I sit with my back to Della as she plaits my hair with red flowers. Her legs are wrapped around my waist, and parts of me are going dead from the weight of her. She does it to keep me still. To keep me close to her. Tabitha is not here. She is home with Mother, licking honey from her fingers.

'Do I look pretty, Della?' I ask, skimming my fingers along the red petals.

'You only ever think about your face.' Della sniffs. 'All your frightening faces.'

I wipe my nose. 'Are you making me into a queen?'

'I would never give you a crown.'

'Why not?'

'I couldn't do that to the world.'

'You always say such mean things to me. You don't say mean things to Tabitha. Dad says I look like a princess. And a dancer.'

'Dad is full of words he thinks will settle you. You're none of those pretty things. You're like an architect. But you don't build with glass and paint. You build houses in my mind with doors leading to bad things. They only ever lead to bad things, because that is how you made them.'

'That's not a nice thing to say ... And I don't want to be an architect.'

'What do you want to be?'

'I want to be bigger than that.'

'What?'

'Bigger than a girl.'

'What does that mean?'

'I want to be powerful.'

'You're a girl. Girls aren't gods.'

'I could be.'

'No ... You'd be a devil.'

'Aright, I'll be a devil. So I'll go down into the earth and I'll watch you all from below. Even while you're sleeping.'

'It's hot down there. You'll burn yourself.'

'I don't mind that.'

'There'll be no rivers down there. Your favourite place to be. What will you do then?'

'Maybe it's like in the stories. Maybe there is a river of souls. I'll cool down in that.'

'They'll drag you down and drown you.'

'Then I'll empty the river.'

'There's a word for it, you know. Katabasis. It means the descent to hell.'

'That's a nice word.'

'Is it?'

'Yes. My new favourite word.'

Silence. Then: 'You'd be an actress, Lil. A strange little actress. And me, Mother and Father, we are the people in your theatre.'

'People love actresses.'

'They won't love you. We don't love you.'

I pinch the back of her hand. 'I don't want you to love me. I want you to worship me.'

Her eyes widen. '...No.'

'Hm.' I lift a flower to Della's nose. 'Imagine words are like flowers. How many flowers do you think you could fit on your tongue?'

'Lots of them.'

'But how many?'

'Lots, Lil. Lots.'

'How many, though?'

Della has stiffened. Then, 'What are you thinking? You have bad thoughts between your ears. I know it. What are your bad thoughts, Lil?'

I smile. 'I'm thinking about flowers.'

Della releases me from the knot she has made, throwing me from her arms. A line of worry sits between her brows. I pat it with my little finger. She is humming. A song to calm herself. To settle fears of her little sister.

'What do you mean?' she asks.

'I'm wondering how many flowers I could fit on your tongue.'

Her eyes boil into my mine, then she looks up to the trees and takes a breath. Such a sad breath. 'Are we about to play a game, Lil?'

'Open your mouth, Della.'

She does not move.

'Lay down on your back, Della.'

She does not move.

'Close your eyes, Della.'

Eventually, she does as I ask, the red flowers framing her face. I cross her arms above her chest. 'You look dead,' I whisper into her ear. 'You look nice dead.'

The worry line deepens in her forehead. I fill my hands with flowers, then one by one, press them into her mouth.

'What do they taste like?' I ask, and smile.

Della opens her eyes and watches me. A weariness in her face.

Her mouth is full now, but I keep pressing the flowers deeper, to the back of her throat.

Her body spasms, and she chokes, fighting against me. I hold her down, strike her head with a rock. She screams.

'You'll be sweeter with more flowers, Del.'

Blood drips from her hairline. Della wriggles, her eyes pleading. My fingers are stained red now. The red of our Red Room. 'You won't need me to bring flowers to your funeral,' I say. 'You'll bring them yourself.'

'Girls...'

Della and I look up, and we see Mother standing above us. Her face is so pale, the moon would turn its own in shame.

'Girls ... what ... what are you doing?'

Her eyes go from me to my poor sister. Her fingers tremble.

'Dear God, what ... what are you doing to Della?'

'We're playing,' I say.

And she screams.

She empties her belly, and empties the trees of their birds. I let Della up, and she reaches inside her mouth, throwing out so many flowers, it is like her body is made of them.

We walk home, the three of us, in silence. Mother is holding Della's hand protectively. She does not hold mine. So I reach out and take my sister's. A daisy chain of women.

Father calls to Mother. 'Darling, are you okay? What's happened?'
He cups her pale, moon face. 'Darling ... what is it?'
   'The girls were playing,' she says.
   'But you ... you look like you've seen a ghost. What did you see?'
   'The girls playing,' she says again.

HIM – Matches

He sees Lily.

She moves through the Folk, and he thinks she moves like smoke, something that is there but cannot be felt, unless it is felt by your lungs as it poisons them. She is smiling. It is not a smile he has seen before. A new face. A girl with many faces.

She has done this to him.

That smile.

That smile.

He wonders if she always planned to do this to him. He wonders if there is some honesty in her name and if there really is a wolf living inside Lily Pedley's skin.

The Folk are furious but they are harmless. He will be alright. He is their Warden, after all.

Lily is dancing between them, whispering. Her words carry, blistering through the Folk's ears and chests, making their spines grow, their hands rise. They have never seemed so alive. So real.

There is an itch inside his scalp. He wants to go out there and calm them, but he has never seen them like this. He does not know what to do. What should he do?

Lily has taken herself away from the gathering now. She is circling his walls. What is she holding? He cannot see. Round and round she goes, like she is hunting him. Is this what it feels like? He's never wondered what it felt like before.

Lily appears again.

She looks up at him.

He looks down at her.

Then Lily lifts her hand and softly strokes the three lines on her third finger

Oh.

Oh.

He knows. He knows it with his chest what she is here for.

Warden.

She knocks her delicate fingers across the wall. He looks at her, and she looks at him.

'You're going to take the Folk.'

'I was made for this, Silas. You know, when Della and I were girls, we would talk about gods and devils. Della would say I'd go down into the earth and make hell my home. And I wonder if there wasn't some truth in it. Some prophecy. If maybe, this was always going to happen. If I was always meant to come here.' She laughs. A girlish laugh that makes his ears hurt. 'I'll look after your legacy.'

'Was any of it true?' he asks, reminded of their time by the river, the story of his many-faced god. Lily has more faces than that god ever did.

'No. The only person who came close to guessing was Brid. She knew. Something in her knew. She could *see* me.'

'It was always you, wasn't it? Della was innocent.'

'Yes.'

'Did Kit know?'

Lily laughs. 'No. Of course not.' She pauses. 'I'm curious: why did you befriend her? Why was she safe?'

Silas remembers the day Kit arrived. He'd thought she might be the woman he needed. His future, the womb to continue his legacy. Her family wouldn't have mattered. She could have more children. *His.* But then Lily arrived.

'I ... I...'

'It doesn't matter now.'

'What about Moss?'

'I like to play with girls. I always have done.'

Silas recalls the warnings he has seen, warnings he has heard. Della, holding her hand to his chest by the bonfire, the sadness in her eyes that only Stina could see, words he did not understand coming from her lips. Because how can a wolf be a wolf when she smiles? How can harm come from such small hands? How can someone have so many faces, when they are human? *Are* they human?

'None of it was real, was it? You killed your parents,' he says. 'Della is innocent. *Della is innocent.*'

Lily smiles at him. So many teeth. 'Poor Silas.'

'I should have known. Della ... everything she has said. She tried to keep the travellers away from you. She tried to protect them. The pomegranate. The words she cut into your arm – no girls. Her warnings. All her quiet warnings.'

'People see what they want to see. We all wear stories. And mine was this.' Lily touches her eyes, her nose, her lips, her hair. So sweet, so clear. So human. 'They see little me. My sister once told me she pitied the world because the world trusts its pretty faces. My sister was right.'

Before he can bring a scream to his mouth, she comes forward and drops something small at his door.

The burning begins.

DELLA – Beasts in Skins

My sister tells people I arrived in the world ready for the world. That I was all teeth, and I came biting. Even as a baby, I had a violence inside my skin, and as I grew, the violence did too.

But don't they know it was her?

Mother brought her home when she was born and put her into my arms. My arms ached. 'Mummy?' I said, lifting the baby away from my body. 'Hurts.'

'What hurts, Della, my darling?'

'Hurts.'

Mother thought I struggled with the weight of her. I did not know how to tell her it was something else.

I knew I was going to have to mind her, mind that violence. What a little beast, everyone said when they looked on me, but beasts come in many skins. And I was never the beast they needed to worry about.

As girls, Lily put smiles on strangers' lips. No smiles came for me. She was small and blonde and sweet-skinned. She kept nice words in her mouth. She was innocence and guile. She realised young that she could shape herself into something the world would adore. But Lily is faster than she will allow people to see. She is stronger than she will show. She is more than her many faces.

Mother and Father saw her violence early, in the animals she left dead in the garden, in the bigger animals they found in the forest outside our home. Mother tried to soothe her, smooth those edges. Mother thought her mother's love might be the medicine.

Mother was wrong.

Father used a different approach: he was cold, strict. He thought he could rid her of this 'famine of humanity'.

Father was wrong.

I tried too, to show her the chaos she stirred like too many winds. I hoped in the beginning, it would still her hands, and the winds would calm.

We were all wrong.

When I was older, I asked Mother: 'Did she feel like a baby when she turned inside you? Are you sure? Did she not feel strange in your hands?'

My sister has always hated stories. I used to beg Mother for them at night-time, and Lily would wrestle from her arms, run outside and stand in the dark until Mother had finished telling them. Because she didn't like stories if she couldn't control the narrative.

So, of course, I told her all the stories I could think of as we grew. Stories from myth, legend – the oldest stories we have. Then I made up my own. This was my resilience, my revenge too. We all have our own ways to survive.

I told her once about the stars. I told her that when she died, she would live in the night, but everyone who knew her would cover their eyes. They would turn their heads from the sky and never look up. It frightened her. Only for a moment.

'I won't look,' I said.

'You will,' Lily smiled, stroking my cheek, lumpen and red next to hers. 'You won't be able to help it.'

'Then I'll bring it down. I'll send fire into the sky and I'll burn you out of it.'

'Not if I burn you first.'

Father found us then, looked at us with the worry he always had in his face. Worry for the world, worry for me. 'Girls. What are you talking about?'

Lily rose, grabbed his chin and wiggled it in her slim fingers. 'We're talking about killing each other.'

DELLA – The Red Room

She called them small fires.

The girls in the market. She called them small fires because she knew they were fires she could put out.

It became a language, words within words.

'Oh, Della. Look at her,' she would say, wolves inside her eyes. 'She looks like me, doesn't she?'

'No,' I would say. 'No, she looks nothing like you.'

'Can't you see it?' She would tap her finger against her lip, as if she wanted to taste the girl. 'She's a small fire.'

And so my sister would begin burning this girl down.

In the town closest to our home, crime was rife, and when little girls started going missing no one ever thought to look closely at the Pedley sisters, who lived by a forest. Their eyes were on the drug-addled men, at the criminals. My sister visited the market to find girls to take to the Red Room. The market was her hunting ground. She was careful of cameras and watching eyes. She used something sweet as flowers to persuade them to follow her, then she drowned them in the river, like Tab.

But when her head was turned, I moved through the crowd, whispering things to any child who was by herself.

'Do you know, children go missing here? Stay close to your mother. There's a man who lives somewhere in this street who likes pretty little things. Don't wander too far.' I always said a man because no one would ever look at Lily and think she could hurt them.

'Why girls?' I asked her once.

Lily shrugged. 'They have my pretty,' she said.

I did not know what she meant. I thought perhaps she had a taste for it after Tab. Now I wonder if my sister thought she was living inside a story, and she could be the only sweet thing, even though, on the inside, she was death dressed up.

'Can't you let them keep it?' I asked, tears between my lips. *Couldn't you let Tab keep it?*

She looked at me. 'It's mine,' she said. 'It belongs to me.'

I could not save Tab. I saved two girls from the market, before they truly realised what was happening. They ran, and I wished I could go with them. But I could not save the five girls who were first drowned in the river, then burned amongst the red flowers. Becoming their namesake: fires.

When Lily was distracted, lighting the match, I put coins in their hands. Payment to the ferryman to take them somewhere good. I hoped there would be better stories for them there.

Lily found me once, untying a girl, and she brought a knife down my back. The wound was the length of my spine so it looked like I had two of them.

Then once, when I threatened to leave her, she put poison in my water. She enjoyed playing with poisons, measuring the quantities and practising on animals in the garden. I was sick into the grass and blood dripped from my lip. The blood stopped, but I never did find my *obel*. Lily screamed to bring Mother and Father running, then she laughed when they began screaming themselves.

I lived with fear in my belly and after that, I knew I always would.

I am something I put between her and the world.

Lily did more harm. Not just to me, and Tab and the girls. Lily played our mother and father like toys taken from a box.

Theirs was a slow dissolution.

'Lily, please go and stand somewhere else,' Mother would say.

'Why?'

'Because you're standing too close and you are watching me.'

'What's wrong with being close to you, Mother?' she asked, so sweet it was bitter.

'You're making me uncomfortable.'

'Why, Mother? Why am I making you uncomfortable?'

A sigh, so many wounds in it. 'Because you've got an animal in you, Lilith.'

'Why don't you call me darling, like you do Della?'

'Because you are no darling.'

'Don't you love me, Mother?'

'I love you. You came from me. But we all have things we don't like about ourselves. Things we wish we could take out of ourselves.'

'Do you ever think about dying?'

Mother nodded, closed her eyes. 'More than I should.'

Lily stroked her head, the back of it where the bones were weakest. She said so softy it could have been a kindness, if Lily had any sort of kindness inside her, 'Then why don't you?'

They went to their room, Mother and Father, after that, and there they stayed. Thinning and pale. I could have picked them up and carried them from the house to somewhere better. But it was only their bodies I could lift. Their minds I could not.

'I'm here,' I would say, sat outside the door. 'I'm here, Mum. I'm here, Dad.'

No response.

They did not come back to themselves. It takes the mind a year to die, I discovered.

The morning I found them, my foot slipped in its shoe and I fell into my mother's body. Her chest, its stilled heart, caught the screams that fell out of me. Lily sat with her legs tucked under her, like a girl. Harmless unless you looked under the many faces of her.

When the ambulance arrived, I had migrated to the kitchen to rinse dishes, water plants. It was a living I knew how to do without thought. My thoughts hurt. It felt like I no longer quite knew how to breathe even though I had been doing it all my life.

Of course, when we were found, they believed I was the cold one. They saw no tears. But didn't they know, you could cry tears inside your body? They drip into your belly and you become an ocean. And on the ocean, you drift.

'Wake her up. Wake her up!' Lily screamed, as if she hadn't been the one to put our mother to her last sleep.

'Are you alright?' the paramedic asked her, looking sidelong at me. 'Have you been hurt?'

By me?

I turned away, kept breathing and living.

They never found any evidence. It looked like a suicide. They did not convict us. And for a time, Lily became the face everyone knew in Cornwall. The face everyone knew in England. With a face like hers, how could it not?

Oh, she had always loved her face. She loved it even more after that. She needed no thick creams; the strength of her will kept it smooth.

Then she tired of Cornwall. We travelled. We followed the stories she heard. We came here. And here I am still, between Lily and the world.

DELLA – Violence of Women

I am a small fire too.

My sister ruined so many parts of me. I pressed my body like I had buttons and thought, here should be my calm, here should be my happy, here should be … well, I can't remember what went here. But I know there was something.

She made such games, Lily. We would sit with our legs crunched into our chests, make cuts in each other's arms. Lily said who could bear the pain longest would win the game. There was no option not to play.

Some cuts I put there myself; I could not bear to have something of her in my body. So I would take a knife and bleed my sister out of me.

Once I told her, 'I haven't had a good breath since you were born.'

'What are you talking about?'

'I haven't been able to breathe. Not properly.'

'You say such silly things.'

'I wonder if I'll be able to breathe when you die,' I said, and I looked at her smile and felt a sickness in every part of me.

'What a mean thing to say.'

'I hope you die before me. Even if it is only by a minute,' I said, recalling the palmist who saw our truths. Then, 'How many breaths can I fit into a minute?'

I am so full and so empty.

We are all made up of parts. Two arms, two legs, a heart, its beat. What happens when these parts decide not to move? I used to look at myself, a beast in the glass. I wondered if I would be minding my sister until I was old.

She told me who we were going to be before we arrived on the God-Forgotten.

I was to be a monster, because a monster is what I have always looked like, with my black hair, my thick neck, my deep eyes. I look like something that will hurt you.

Lily would polish herself, a soft shell for curious fingers. She would cast a pretty net to catch pretty things.

Two sisters: one bitter, one sweet.

We have always been good at playing games. So Lily became me, and I became her. We passed across our identities. I took the way she cracks her knuckles, the way she stretches before she goes to sleep, arching her back until it looks like her spine is about to become two pieces.

I played so I could keep myself between her and whoever came close. She told me to chase her into the Hanging Trees because she knew Silas was watching. A trick to get his sympathy. She told me to hunt her, to hurt her, to not hold back. And I did it all. I enjoyed it too. So perhaps there *is* something of the monster about me.

But she did not realise that Silas was more than a plaything. She did not realise that this bite would break her teeth. They were each other's devils.

I have known for some time there is nothing under this land. Only its stories and superstitions moving like poison in a vein. I knew what Silas was. Everyone has tells: they tell you with their bodies, the things their mouths cannot make the sounds for.

'You've got this land inside you,' I said to him when I found him in Lily's room. 'I'd feel sorry for you, but I think you like it.' I touched his hand, rubbed my fingers together. 'You know what this reminds me of? Symbiosis. Do you know what that is? It means one thing living off another.'

'What are you talking about, Della?'

I smiled. 'You've got something of the devil about you, you know that?'

'No. I'm afraid I don't.'

'You do. But even devils have their own devils, and yours is going to enjoy you.' He thought I meant myself.

I did not mean myself.

When we were girls, Mother and Father took us apart. Father had charge of Lily because he was the strongest of us, and he drove for hours and hours to give Mother and I some peace from our wolf. He took her to the village on the mainland, so she could see this island in the distance and there she first heard the stories of this place called the God-Forgotten. The only story my sister has ever liked.

Years on, we followed the stories to this place. We did not know what we would find.

I have never killed anything. I think, to kill, you must have something in you when you are born. Some violence in the joints, in the veins.

My body doesn't have it.

I did not harm the travelling girls. I tried to help them. I pointed out the lights of the mainland and I told them to leave, leave! I whispered warnings, but they did no good. This land and its stories had polluted their minds. Silas thought the Folk were drawn to me because I reminded them of Ura, the first Warden. But it was more than that: they were reminded of themselves. The Folk and I, we all have our tormentors. We always have. They with their Devil, me with mine. It is something we share.

In the beginning, Lily wanted the travellers gone – she did not want to share the Folk's attention, so she tried to persuade them to take their boat back to the mainland. But then she found Moss Gulliver.

I am surprised Lily thought I had killed Brid. She had been warned to leave Brid to her forest. But no one warned Brid about Lily, a cruelty walking into her trees.

I put two fingers to her old throat. She had been dead some time. I told her I was sorry, and told her birds the same. When Lily found us, I think it is the first time in our lives she has ever been unnerved by me, ever wondered if she should be frightened. It was a good feeling.

I make apologies for my sister. So many my mouth aches.

I saw her play with the Folk's children, dancing with the girls, play-fighting with the boys, touching them, finding their weakest parts, and I wanted to take a needle and stitch her hands to her sides.

And I would not cut her out.

I would bind her inside a tree, then I would burn it. I would put her in the sky, then I would not look up.

I would make her a ghost, and she would haunt herself.

I would make her a story, and I would not tell it.

DELLA – These Spent Bodies

They know now.

Silas knows, as he burns. Moss knows, as she watches Lily burn him. We were called godless women, pariahs, witches. The world had such names for us. But only one of us ever deserved them.

Moss's arms wrap around my middle, slowly, disbelieving, a look on her face that I don't think she will ever get rid of. It will linger just inside her eyes, a resistant tear.

Once you see death, you never really stop seeing it. Lily is something different from a murderer. There is a neatness to murder, to the simple taking of human function. Lily takes more – the innocence, the calm of an unaddled mind. She is a life-thief. She has taken more than I could save.

Moss is holding me so tightly, her fingers pinch my belly. Her small chest is panting, her eyes are red. I lift a hand, hide her from the sight of it all. Her lashes beat against my fingers.

She is shaking. I used to do that too.

'Look away.'

'But...'

'Look away.'

'What is she doing?'

'Nothing you need to see with those eyes.'

The Folk are in a fury, burning their Devil down. Lily is dancing. Then Silas screams, and it sends the birds into the air and a shiver flying down my spine. He wanted her to be his queen. But Lily would take nothing less than king.

I wonder if the people across the water will hear it. If they will send out their boats. No, they are not coming. I burned the number before Lily could see who it belonged to. But we are not alone. *She* is coming.

'What's happening?' Moss holds me tight, taking the breath out of my body.

'Nothing. Nothing.'

'Is that Silas?'

'It's the birds. Just the birds,' I say. 'They are frightened of the fire.'

Lily is singing a song. A lament, about a boy ... a boy at the bottom of the sea. I cannot hear all the words but I know by the shapes her body makes, it is something meant to upset Silas. She is singing it for him.

What happens next? She will take Silas's name and step into the boots of the Devil. The Folk will celebrate her every year. They will dance and sing for her. It will suit her. She will drink it all in like ambrosia. But the Folk have never met someone like her.

She will not stop at three. Her Harvests will clear the land. She has a bigger appetite than the Wardens before her. She will take the little girls to the river, where she took Silas and where she took Moss. There will be no little girls left.

Children first, with all their freshness, their fat bellies and sticky lips. Until, one day, it will just be her. I see her standing on this land that she has emptied. Then I see her, older, stepping into a boat, moving on to the next place.

Poison runs through this land like blood in a vein. But Lily will take all the blood from this body. And Moss and I?

I hug the young girl to my chest. She will be first. Lily will take her to the river; she will hold her below the water. Like Tab. Moss is so like Tab. But playthings are only playthings until they are put down. Fires only burn until they burn out.

Moss is crying – it shivers through both of our bodies.

I stroke her head. 'It's going to be alright. I'm going to make it alright.'

'Why is this happening?'

'I need you to do something for me.'

'Wh-what?'

'Go upstairs to my room and pack everything you can into a bag. Do all of this quickly, calmly. Do it without looking out of the window. Understand?'

'You're leaving me?'

'I'm coming back.'

'What if you don't?'

'I will. Then we are leaving this land.'

Moss nods. I lift my hand and I take her tears right off her cheeks. Lily is in them.

'Don't watch the window,' I say again, then I close the door behind me. I lock Moss inside and the outside out. I do not want anything to try and get in. I do not want her trying to help me.

The voices at Higher Tor fill my ears. They are louder than thunder, louder than anything the world can make.

Silas is screaming. The fire moves. I look for Lily.

She is dancing, making such shapes in the dark. My worrying little sister. I think Mother knew she came into the world ready for the world. I think Father knew too, because he saw Mother open her arms for their baby, then drop them, hands more comfortable with nothing inside them. We all knew. We all know monsters when we meet them.

The screaming has stopped.

I look around for Silas. He finds me as I find him. He is crying now, reaching for me. Despite it all, I pity him. I pity the boy he was before he became this man. He looks up, hands rising to the moon, as if he is praying to it. As if he is asking for mercy. Doesn't he know there is no one up there to pray to?

I take a step to his house just as the ceiling falls, and Silas, the Warden of this land, perishes in the burn.

He is gone.

Lily is still singing. Only now she is singing for his wandering soul.

She turns and smiles at me, that smile a little too full of teeth. I take her hand, drag her away from the Folk, behind the house, to the edge of the land.

'What are you doing, Della? The game is over. He's dead. The Devil is dead!' She spins, throwing out her arms. The world seems to quieten, just to hear her speak. Don't we all?

'I'm leaving, Lil.'

'What are you talking about?'

'I'm leaving.'

She stops and laughs. 'You're not leaving, Della. I've told you this before. If you leave, I follow.'

'You've killed Silas. He's gone. Did you need to kill him?'

'Yes,' she says, tapping the bridge of my nose. 'You found out about him and never told me, didn't you?' She pinches my nose until I must open my mouth to breathe. 'You were next. That piece of paper Moss found was a list. Yours was the third name to be Harvested. Did you know that?'

'No,' I say.

She splits the bones of me.

'Silas was going to kill you. And he was going to make me his wife. I was to give him children, continue his legacy.' She smiles.

'You have what you want, Lil. Why can you not just let me leave?'

She wraps her arms around my spine, and I know she could break it if she wanted. She is small, sweet like honey and milk. But she has teeth people are always surprised to find. Women are something to fear, behind their perfect faces.

'Della, when you came downstairs and found Mother and Father, what did you think?'

'I thought I could help them.' There is a rock in my throat, it cuts as it goes down.

Lily nods. 'You would not have been able to save them. They didn't die by hanging. They died because I put something in their water.' She picks at all of my soft, unprotected places. 'They were dead before I put them up there. But that doesn't mean I didn't have some fun with them.'

'What?'

She smiles. 'Before you came down, I jumped as hiiiiiigh as I could jump and I swung from Mother's pretty little neck. The body makes strange noises when it is dead but still moving like it is alive.' She pinches my spine, giving me my red roses. She pinched herself some nights so Silas thought I did it to her.

'You ... you...' I am too much emotion for this body to contain.

'That's right. I was like a bird on a swing.'

I want the stars to collapse, to fall from their velvet skies and burn her. I want the girls from all of her nightmares, the ones she killed in the river, to come and haunt her while she is waking too. I want to unmake her like she has unmade me.

'Why didn't you do the same to me?' There are tears on my face. The difference between us: she cries pretty, I cry messy, so soft hands never came to comfort me. The difference a face can make. 'Why didn't you put me in the river?'

She strokes my cheek with her thumb. 'Because one of us is bitter and one of us is sweet. Without the bitter, can the sweet taste as good?'

I nod. 'So we're heaven and hell.'

Lily smiles. 'You have it. You make me look like heaven.'

There are tears on my cheeks, inside my mouth. My hands are shaking. I thought they had given that up when Mother and Father died. I thought my body was temperate. I thought it was empty.

But it is not. I am full of knives. I feel like there is a skin on my skin. A second set of bones inside my bones. Another life, a life that has no right to live. I want to pare it all back. But pieces of her have caught now to pieces of me, like death to life. If I remove her, will I take away all of myself?

I can feel her heart through her clothes. But perhaps she does not have a heart like the rest of us, something so human. Perhaps behind that throb of muscle, there is a cavity filled with silence. A red room.

'If you leave, Della, I leave with you.' Lily winds a finger through my hair. She used to put flowers into the hair of her girls, red crowns for pale queens. 'I go wherever you go. You take a step, I take it with you. Understand?'

I nod. 'I'll be minding you for the rest of our lives, won't I?'

'And I'll be minding you.'

'Do you know, I've been holding my breath since the moment they put you into my arms. I used to hope you'd die first, even if it was only by a minute, just so I could breathe.'

Lily laughs. 'Oh, you'll die first, Della. And then I'll follow you. I'll follow you anywhere you go.'

I notice that when two hands meet, skin meeting skin, it sounds like something tearing. We are a tearing, my sister and I. When she came into the world and she was put into my hands, she tore me through.

'We will always be together, Della.'

I pull my sister into my body, these arms that are sore from holding her, bring Silas's bone knife from my pocket.

'Lil, I can't wait that long,' I say, with my chest. 'I want to breathe.'

I push the blade through cloth and skin until it meets the middle of her. Lily looks at me, eyes widening. It is the most innocent she has ever looked.

'Wherever you go to after this,' I say, 'Leave Tabitha alone.'

She fights because it is what she has always done. She came with violence and she leaves with it too. But I keep on holding her. I hold her until she is a ghost and her violence is spent.

I hold her until all I am left holding is a body: two arms, two legs, a heart.

But the heart won't beat.

DELLA – Small Fires

The Folk are quiet now.

A silence has risen from the earth, as if this land cannot fathom what has been done to it. The birds are quiet, the ghosts are quiet. The wind does not move, it does not dare to. I think even time must have been frightened into being still.

I leave my sister's body, throw the knife into the water ... for the boy at the bottom to cut the words off his skin. Some freedom for him. Then I run to Lower Tor, as fast as my feet will move. The Folk watch the house collapse, even the children do not speak. They have removed their Devil. How they would mourn if they knew what they had done. How could a man live if he knew he had killed his god?

Moss is at the door, waiting for me. A bag is strung across her shoulder. She has stopped crying. 'I found this,' she says, and holds up the red ribbon. 'Lily was always playing with this. Do you want it?'

It belonged to Tab. I turn and throw it into the air; it smells of Lily.

Moss looks at me with wide, wide eyes. 'It was never you, was it? It was always her.' Her hands are shaking so violently, I think her fingers might come loose.

'Yes,' I say. 'But I was never going to let her hurt you.'

'She ... seemed kind. She helped me.'

'My sister could be anything. She could look caring if she wanted, kind too. But she was a toxin. And she would have hurt you in the end.'

'Was she always like that?'

'Everything you were told about me is true of her. When we came here, she made me a monster. But it was always her. Understand?'

'Yes.'

'Do you remember those stories I told you? About the girl in the well and the four sisters?'

'I thought you were trying to upset me. They were so sad.'

'I was trying to show you that stories exist within stories. I was teaching you to listen past the first thing you hear.'

'I ... I understand it now.'

'Good. People have lots of faces, Moss. Don't trust the first one you see. Come on. We need to move. Now!'

The street is empty, there are no lights on in the houses. The Folk are all watching the beast fall into the sea. Even the children. Not one of them has been left behind. It reminds me of when Lily and I arrived here. The streets were empty then too. We knew what we were looking for, at least one of us did. A new game, a new fire. She couldn't have known what she would find. A man with his flock. A Folk with their god.

They have been conditioned by years of Wardens. Will they be again? Will someone discover the truth of it, take up the name? Will this cruel land always be this: cruel? Will they find a new Devil? Devils are everywhere in the world.

For what I am about to do, perhaps I am one too.

I pause. Tell Moss to go, go! I wait for her to reach the dock, then I push open the door of the inn, grab two bottles from the bar. I drip it down the streets, splash doorways, windows, the Bleeding Tree. I flood the cobbles of this place. Then I light a match and I run as it burns.

The Folk will live. But by the time they realise, their homes will be gone, the land will be on fire and they will jump into the water. Perhaps they will come to the mainland, perhaps they will not. But I want to stop this land living as it has done.

'What did you do?' Moss asks me as I untether the boat.

'This is a bad place. I don't think the Folk are, not really. They're just afraid. But I didn't want to leave it as I found it.'

She leans into my shoulder, sniffs my hands. 'Do you think it will help them, in the end?'

I do not answer her, simply push us away from the pier and begin rowing. My hands ache, they have done too much tonight, too many bad things. I never wanted to kill anyone. I had to learn to.

'I couldn't leave it as I found it,' I whisper. 'I want to help them. I want to make this place better.'

In the distance, a light, a boat, coming towards us. Kit. She gave me her number on a scrap of paper before she left; and I wondered then if she had suspicions about my sweet sister. Our mother called Lily our wolf.

And what a little wolf she was.

Kit is coming, just as she promised she would. I will tell her the truth of all the games Lily played, all the faces she wore to make people soft. I will tell her our story, this strange story I am weary of that sits in my body and makes it so hard to move.

The smoke smarts my eyes. It rises, creeping, black and rotten, from the village. The burn spreads, slowly at first, but soon it will pass to the Hanging Place, to the Pale Bones to the Maidens. The God-Forgotten will be gone.

Yet there is still only silence over this place. So heavy I feel it with my chest. I pause for a moment, and we sit and we listen and listen and listen to nothing but the water.

We wait.

Then their screams splinter the air, threaten to knock the moon and stars from their beds. They run down the pier, so many bodies thrown into the water. Young and old and frightened. The fire is spreading, and it will keep spreading. Swim, I think, swim!

I hope they are unhurt. I hope they who know nothing of the world meet the world and forget this place. That their Devil becomes a memory, a story whispered into palms before it is forgotten because a different story waits to be told.

Moss holds me. I stroke her head with soft hands; perhaps the softest hands she has ever known. I do not know where we are going but I remind her that she is safe. That where we go, there will be no devils.

Most of all, I remind her that she is a fire which will not burn out.

Cornwall

AUTHOR'S NOTE

Dear Reader,

The story you hold is a story I have been writing for five years.

I wrote it in a fever: six weeks of unwashed hair, crumbs on my keyboard and madness. That story was about a father and son and a crime that ran through three generations. This is a story about two sisters. Now all that is left of the original manuscript from 2019 are the names Lily and Della Pedley.

Small Fires examines generational trauma, female rage and possession. It is about identity, the facades we adopt, the 'faces' we wear to survive the world. How we all turn ourselves into fictions, which we are perpetually writing.

But most importantly, it is about stories and the power a storyteller has in telling them.

The first stories we are given as children are often fairy tales. And the books we read as children become part of our identity, part of our life's narrative. These stories raise us, walk us into adulthood and wait patiently for us to pass them on to our own children. As a writer and a bookseller, I believe in the authority of storytelling, the goodness of it, the power of it, so wholeheartedly, I knew I had to pay tribute to its many mediums in *Small Fires*:

I have written my own fairy tales, such as the 'Boy at the Bottom of the Sea', 'Artillery', 'The Forest of Eyes', 'Áine's Well', 'Witch-Made' and 'The Poor Maidens' in a bid to flesh out the sisters' backstory and enrich the lore of the God-Forgotten. It has given me the most pleasure I've ever had from writing a book.

I have tipped my hat to stories from the Bible, folklore, legends, mythologies and superstitions – the oldest stories we have. You might recognise Gaia, Charon the Ferryman, the Dryads, the Pleiades. I've played with themes, subjects and tropes that might seem familiar from the stories we were introduced to as children. With Brid, for example, I held close to the 'old crone/witch in the trees' character archetype we find so often in fairy tales. She was my joy to write.

I live in Cornwall, a county full legends. With that in mind, I knew I had to bring my beloved home into the book. You might have noticed that Lil and Del lived close to Penzance and spent much of their childhood in local areas such as Tehidy Woods, Kennel Vale, St Michael's Mount. Not only this, I have used the legend of Agnes and the Giant Bolster as inspiration for the chapter 'A Woman, Burning'. If you look up this Cornish legend, you might recognise Silas and Gaia.

Also, filtered through the plot are allusions (Easter eggs) in the place names, which allude to themes in the book.

'Dyowles' from Dyowles House means 'She-Devil' in the Cornish Language.

'Pedley' in Anglo-French ('*pie de leu*') translates to 'wolf foot'.

'Moloch' in the Moloch Inn refers to a Canaanite deity whose worshippers sacrificed children.

'Aine' in Aine's Well is the Celtic goddess of Summer, love, abundance and blossoms.

Small Fires is my tribute to the history of storytelling, and all its many mediums. It has changed many times in five years. Hundreds of thousands of words written, then rewritten. It has had many faces. Now, finally, I've sent it out into the world and I hope the world enjoys it.

Thank you for reading my strange creation.

Keep the fires burning,

—Ronnie Turner

ACKNOWLEDGEMENTS

A true, heartfelt thanks to my agent extraordinaire Emily Glenister at DHH, who has represented me since I was eighteen. You have been a powerhouse and a huge support since day one of our long journey.

Thank you to Karen Sullivan for taking a chance on this book, for your unparalleled passion and for guiding it into the hands of readers.

Thanks also to West Camel for his wisdom, support and meticulous eye. This would not be the book it is without the help, advice and work you have given it. It was a long road editing this book, and I'm genuinely very grateful to have had your support. I owe you a box of chocolates.

To my colleagues and pals at Waterstones. Thank you for your endless support, kindness and humour. You are some of the loveliest people I have had the pleasure, not only to work alongside, but to know. It's a joy every day. You deserve a box of chocolates also.

And finally to my friends and family. You know all that I thank you for.